THE NOVEL OF THE FUTURE

OTHER BOOKS BY ANAÏS NIN

FICTION

House of Incest, prose poem	The Swallow Press
Winter of Artifice, collected novelettes	The Swallow Press
Under a Glass Bell, short stories	The Swallow Press
Ladders to Fire, novel	The Swallow Press
Children of the Albatross, novel	The Swallow Press
The Four-Chambered Heart, novel	The Swallow Press
A Spy in the House of Love, novel	The Swallow Press
Seduction of the Minotaur, novel	The Swallow Press
Collages, novel	The Swallow Press

NONFICTION

D. H. Lawrence: An Unprofessional Study	The Swallow Press
The Diary of Anaïs Nin: Volume One *(1931–1934)*	The Swallow Press and Harcourt, Brace & World, Inc.
The Diary of Anaïs Nin: Volume Two *(1934–1939)*	The Swallow Press and Harcourt, Brace & World, Inc.
The Diary of Anaïs Nin: Volume Three	Harcourt, Brace & World, Inc.

Note to the Reader: All references to works by Anaïs Nin made in this book apply to the above editions.

ANAÏS NIN

THE NOVEL
OF THE
FUTURE

SWALLOW PRESS/
OHIO UNIVERSITY PRESS
ATHENS

Library of Congress Cataloging-in-Publication Data

Nin, Anaïs, 1903-1977.
The novel of the future.

Bibliography: p.
1. Fiction—20th century—History and criticism—Addresses, essays, lectures.   2. Literature—Psychology—Addresses, essays, lectures.   I. Title.
PN3503.N5   1986   808.3   86-1895
ISBN 0-8040-0879-5

ACKNOWLEDGMENTS

THE AUTHOR WISHES to acknowledge the following publishers and copyright holders for permission to quote copyrighted material:

New Directions Publishing Corporation for selections from Djuna Barnes, *Nightwood*, Copyright 1937 by Djuna Barnes; selections from John Hawkes, *The Cannibal*, and from the Introduction to *The Cannibal* by Albert Guérard, Copyright 1949, © 1962 by New Directions Publishing Corporation; selections from *Diary of Love*, Copyright 1950 by Maude Phelps McVeigh Hutchins; selections from Leslie Fiedler's Introduction to John Hawkes, *The Lime Twig*, © 1961 by John Hawkes, © 1961 by New Directions Publishing Corporation.

Dr. Margaret Mead and *Redbook Magazine* for selections from the January 1968 issue of *Redbook Magazine*. Copyright © 1967 by McCall Corporation.

The Swallow Press, Inc., Chicago, for selections from the following works of Anaïs Nin: *Winter of Artifice, Children of the Albatross, Ladders to Fire, The Four-Chambered Heart, A Spy in the House of Love, D. H. Lawrence: An Unprofessional Study, Under a Glass Bell*, and *Collages;* and for selections from Wallace Fowlie, *The Age of Surrealism*.

Bantam Books, Inc. for selections from *The Medium Is the Massage* by Marshall McLuhan and Quentin Fiore. Copyright © 1967 by Marshall McLuhan, Quentin Fiore, and Jerome Agel. By permission of Bantam Books, Inc.

McGraw-Hill Book Company for selections from *The Suicide Academy* by Daniel Stern. Copyright © 1968 by Daniel Stern. Used by permission of McGraw-Hill Book Company.

The Nation for excerpts from a review of *The Diaries of Anaïs Nin* by Daniel Stern in *The Nation*, March 3, 1968.

Houghton Mifflin Company for selections from Jerzy Kosinski, *The Painted Bird.*

The Viking Press, Inc., for selections from D. H. Lawrence, *Twilight in Italy.*

Charles Scribner's Sons for selections from Marguerite Young, *Miss MacIntosh, My Darling.*

The New York Times Company for selections from William Goyen's article on Marguerite Young in *The New York Times*, September 12, 1965. Copyright © 1965 by The New York Times Company. Reprinted by permission of The New York Times Company, William Goyen, and Ashley Famous Agency, Inc.

For selection from *The House of Breath* by William Goyen. Reprinted by permission of William Goyen and Ashley Famous Agency, Inc. Copyright © 1950 by William Goyen.

For selection from *Faces of Blood Kindred* by William Goyen. Reprinted by permission of William Goyen and Ashley Famous Agency, Inc. Copyright © 1960 by William Goyen.

This book is dedicated to sensitive Americans. May they create a sensitive America.

Contents

Realism is a bad word. In a sense everything is realistic. I see no line between the imaginary and the real. I see much reality in the imagination.—FEDERICO FELLINI from *Interviews with Film Directors*

Introduction

WHEN I FIRST began to write fiction I had no intention of explaining or theorizing about writing. I was not involved with teaching and considered myself an independent writer. In Paris, in the thirties, many writers around me were breaking the molds of the conventional novel and experimentation was encouraged. More than that, French literature at that time was dedicated to war against the cliché, the obvious, the traditional, and the conventional—all energies were engaged in innovation. Even those who were not dogmatic surrealists were influenced by its spirit. Chapters of *House of Incest* were included in the last number of *Transition*. I did not realize that with war and emigration to America would come a totally different kind of struggle. In France we felt a part of a pioneering group, but in America we found ourselves isolated and in the minority. Literature was for the masses, it was in the hands of the social realists, dominated by the social critics, all more concerned with politics than psychology or human beings in particular. In America the aim was not to be original, individualistic, an innovator, but to please the majority, to standardize, to submit to the major trends.

The climate of the forties was insular, provincial, antipoetic, and anti-European. Only a very small group were interested in surrealism. The majority associated it only with Dali's pranks.

When I submitted *Winter of Artifice* and the stories from

Under a Glass Bell, I was told that no one would be interested in books dealing with life in Paris, and that the style was too esoteric and subjective. Today, of course, such statements sound humorous. But they were humorless in 1940. My answer was to buy a printing press and handset and print three hundred copies of the two books which were sold by the Gotham Book Mart. *Under a Glass Bell* attracted the attention of Edmund Wilson, and because of his review a publisher cautiously published *Ladders to Fire.*

The book was received with direct attacks on surrealism. The label stuck for years as an expression of ostracism. Very few in America then had read the surrealists. André Breton's *Nadja* had not yet been published in English.

But my difficulties with publishers and critics were slight compared to my difficulties with close friends and people whose opinion I respected. When I wrote *Stella* (which was to be the beginning of a long novel, but which turned out to be a novelette), it was my first attempt to extend the poem, to carry into prose the poetic condensations and abstractions of the poem. I found myself with a group of friends who questioned the "reality" of *Stella* because I had left out so much of the realistic trappings and concentrated only on those having a direct relation to the emotional drama: Stella's clothes, her spiral stairway, a telephone. The questions were sharp and demanded lucid answers. It was at this moment that I began what seemed at first a purely defensive interpretation of abstraction, of deleting the unessential, the upholstery, the commonplace, and the obvious.

I wrote a pamphlet called *Realism and Reality.*[1]

Stella was reprinted in full in *Harper's Bazaar.* I was invited to lecture at universities. I found myself answering more questions and probings. I found it necessary to solidify my attitude, to formulate a theory.

The theory was not an innovation in terms of French literature, but it was to an America which was almost completely Anglo-Saxon in matters of writing in spite of its many expatriates (Annette Baxter wrote an interesting study on the fact that after ten years in France Henry Miller remained a thoroughly American writer). Surrealism was an unpopular term in the 1940s. Even recently it was confused by academic critics with baroque horror stories.

My main theme was that one could only find reality by discarding realism. I was speaking of psychological reality to an audience conditioned to representational social realism. With time the nature of psychological reality became a subject of controversy.

It seemed then as if no one in America intended to follow the direction indicated by D. H. Lawrence, James Joyce, Djuna Barnes, or André Breton.

Each lecture expanded my definitions, and I found myself recommending Wallace Fowlie's book on surrealism, pleading for experiment and individualism in a completely conventionalized world of literature. I seemed to be addressing deaf ears. As late as 1965 a professor admitted he had carried *Under a Glass Bell* in his knapsack but returned from war to write another book about Henry James.

"Why not living writers?" I asked.

The answer was: "Because we have no way of evaluating contemporary writers."

The paradox was that this was happening at a time when people accepted abstract painting in their homes and studied the abstractions of science, but in the jet age read novels which corresponded to the horse and buggy. But in the last few years works of imagination and psychological reality asserted themselves in films, in the theater, and in a few scattered novels. The same lectures now touch off strong responses. I have lived to see what writers dream of, a moment of synchronization with the present, harmony with other writers, so that now I can begin a study of the kind of writing young writers are engaging in today. We are all reading works with roots in the unconscious, and I can now highlight some fine American writers who have written poetic prose.

The purpose of this book is to study the development and techniques of the poetic novel. I will try to evaluate some of the writers who have integrated poetry and prose. It is not a general study of writers, nor even of the writers I mention. It is a grouping, a relating of such writers to trends now acceptable and recognized under other names, "expanded consciousness," or if you prefer, "psychedelic" with emphasis on *psyche*.

To analyze and observe the process of creation I have had to use my own work simply because here I know the steps, the gradual evolution, and by putting it under the microscope, can more clearly indicate the way to achieve such an integration.

CHAPTER ONE

Proceed from the Dream Outward

JUNG SAID: "Proceed from the dream outward . . ."

It is interesting to return to the original definition of a word we use too often and too carelessly. The definition of a dream is: ideas and images in the mind *not under the command of reason*. It is not necessarily an image or an idea that we have during sleep. It is merely an idea or image which escapes the control of reasoning or logical or rational mind. So that dream may include reverie, imagination, daydreaming, the visions and hallucinations under the influence of drugs—any experience which emerges from the realm of the subconscious. These various classifications are merely ways to describe different states or levels of consciousness. The important thing to learn, from art and from literature in particular, is the easy passageway and relationship between them. Neurosis makes a division and sets up defensive boundaries. But the writer can learn to walk easily between one realm and the other without fear, interrelate them, and ultimately fuse them.

Psychoanalysis proved that dreams were the only key to our subconscious life. What the psychoanalysts stress, the relation between dream and our conscious acts, is what the poets already know. The poets walk this bridge with ease, from conscious to unconscious, physical reality to psychological reality. Their profession is to fuse them so that they may function harmoniously. The function of the symbol is to unite and synthesize various forms of reality. Most fiction writers use dreams decoratively, without relating them to daily life, but the contemporary writer is becoming more expert at detecting the influence of one upon the other.

When I was eleven years old I wrote a play which prefigured my life philosophy. It was a melodrama with an unexpected climax. A blind father and his devoted daughter live in extreme poverty in a shack. But the daughter always describes their life, their home, their garden, their friends in terms of beauty and comfort, creating an illusion for her blind father to lull him. Then a doctor comes to the village and operates on the father's eyes. He can now see again. Tragedy? No, when he opens his eyes to the shabby reality, he does not collapse or feel betrayed. He tells his daughter: "It is true you described something which was not there, but you described it so vividly that now I can set about to construct our life as you had dreamed it." The dream has to be translated into reality.

The dream, scrutinized by scientists in various experiments, has been found to be an absolute necessity to man. It keeps our psychic life alive, in its own proper climate. It sustains a life not corruptible and not susceptible to the pressures of society. When we ceased to believe in this spiritual underground, to nourish ourselves on feelings, our lives became empty shells, automatic, mechanical. We only believed in it when it showed symptoms of neurosis. Literature and the poets continued to assert its presence as the source of creation.

Neurosis was caused by our attempt to separate physical and metaphysical levels, to set them up in opposition to each other, thus engaging in an internecine war. If it is true that we do live on several levels simultaneously—drama and action, past and present, personal and collective—we were given ways to unify them: one by religion, the other by art. Separating such levels is only necessary when they conflict, and separation is a result of conflict.

Seeing how these levels can work together in harmony is the task of our contemporary writers.

For this the writer has to learn the passageways. Those passageways are like the locks of canals, feeding each other while controlling levels to prevent flooding. The discipline and form of an artist's work are set in the same system to prevent flooding. The amateur drowns. The writer has to remain open, fluid, pursue and obey images which his conscious structure tends to break or erase. The same writing which is employed by science or the intellect will not carry these images back and forth through the channels of the senses, where they are effective. We categorize and catalogue and file, not so much out of a sense of organization but out of fear. The psychologist, while using dreams as a kind of electronic echo sounder to chart the depths of the unconscious, is often, according to Dr. R. D. Laing, too anxious to draw boundary lines according to definitions of normalcy which really do not exist as finite truths but fluctuate and vary and are altered by new researches.

For the neurotic, the merging of the subconscious and the conscious may be risky, just as it is for the users of drugs. But for the writer who is aware of the way in which this connection exists in reality and nourishes creativity, the sooner he can achieve a synthesis among intellect, intuition, emotion, and instinct, the sooner his work will be integrated.

When one learns the passageways, one discovers a rigorous form and pattern to the unconscious, but one which is not apparent until all the elements are gathered together. One learns the plots of the unconscious from psychoanalysis. It is a detective story of the emotions. This concept was popularized in Eric Berne's *Games People Play*. Any artificial imitation of the unconscious can be easily detected. It is absurd and meaningless, it is chaotic and grotesque. The images are unrelated. They do not lead anywhere.

What the psychoanalyst does is what the novelist also has to do—probe deep enough until he finds where the chain broke.

Traumatic experiences cause such breaks. The psychoanalyst repairs the broken links and allows the unconscious, which has its inception in the personal experience, to merge into a life beyond the personal.

The important thing is to learn from the writer the ways and byways of such passageways between conscious and unconscious. The unconscious can become destructive if it is disregarded and thwarted. Neurosis, based on fear, creates solitary cells to protect itself from invasion. Many of today's writers have assimilated the findings of psychoanalysis and are more expert in linking the subconscious with the conscious. We are beginning to see the influence of dream upon reality and reality upon dream. Art is revealing to us the variety of levels on which we live. This may be what we seek to express in what we now call "multimedia."

Almost all of Kafka's work takes place in a waking dream region, and Proust wrote a classical description of the state between sleep and waking reverie in *Remembrance of Things Past.*

In *Winter of Artifice* (p. 170–75) I sought to examine the different layers of the dream:

When I entered the dream I stepped on a stage. The lights cast on it changed hue and intensity like stage lights. The violent scenes happened in the spotlight and were enveloped by a thick curtain of blackness. The scenes were cut, interrupted, or broken with entr'actes. The mise en scene was stylized, and only what has meaning was represented. And very often I was at once the victim and the observer.

The dream was composed like a tower of layers without end, rising upward and losing itself in the infinite, or layers coiling downward, losing themselves in the bowels of the earth. When it swooped me into its undulations, the spiraling began, and this spiral was a labyrinth. There was no vault and no bottom, no walls and no return. But there were themes repeating themselves with exactitude. If the walls of the dream seemed lined with moist silk, and the contours of the labyrinth lined with silence, still the steps of the dream were a series of explosions in which all the condemned fragments of myself burst into a mysterious and violent life, with the heavy maternal solicitude of the night ever attentive to their flowering.

On the first layer of the spiral there was awareness. I could still see the daylight between the fringes of eyelashes. I could still see the interstices of the world. This was the penumbra, where the thoughts were inlaid in filaments of lightning. It was the place where the images were delicately filtered and separated, and their silhouettes thrown against space. It was the place where footsteps left no trace, where laughter had no echo, but where hunger and fear were immense. It was the place where the sails of reverie could swell while no wind was felt. . . . *The dream was a filter.* The entire world was never admitted. . . . *But with the night came openness.* . . . *With the night came space.* . . . The dream was never crowded. It was *filtered through the prism of creation.* . . . *Time was ordained by feeling.* . . . *By day I followed the dream step by step. I felt lost and bewildered if the day did not bring its replica.* . . . *The dream was always running ahead of one. To catch up, to live for a moment in unison with it, that was the miracle. The life on the stage, the life of the legend dovetailed with the daylight, and out of this marriage sparked the great birds of divinity, the eternal moments.*

As a prose poet becoming fascinated with a rich source of images, I concentrated on describing the dream world, perhaps tempted by the difficulties involved. Obviously the physical world is easier to describe. The first misunderstanding about my work which arose and has continued to the present was that I was writing dreamlike and unreal stories.

My emphasis was on the relation between dream and reality, their interdependence.

The novelist today works parallel to the psychologist, recognizes the duality and multiplicity of the human personality. It should not be any more difficult to orient, to navigate, to chart all these different elements than to guide a missile. Dream, waking dream, reverie, fantasy, all interlock and interrelate simultaneously but on different levels. These two ways of describing the unconscious through the symbol and surrealism paralleled exactly the development of the psychological study of dreams. Symbolism was unfortunately associated with romanticism, but we are obliged to reinstate it as the *most important form of expression* of the unconscious.

A student once asked me, if we dream in terms of symbols and if it is so intricate to understand, why the writer does not translate it for us into a direct message. If the writer translated it for us we would never learn the language. Symbolism is a language we must learn for ourselves, because even if we do not care to interpret our dreams, it remains a fact that we continue to act in symbolic terms. Witness today's headlines: "Students Soak Their Draft Cards in Blood."

John Hawkes, in this passage from his novel *The Cannibal*, focuses on one of these symbolic obsessions: [2]

At the far end of the acre was a small house, the roof curling under a foot of snow, its rear window gazing outward twenty miles and downwards to the depth of a thousand feet. Stella and Ernst, holding hands, silent in wondrous amazement, turning and clapping each other in excitement, walked over this very acre every afternoon and passed the house. A few scrubby trees leaned dangerously over the cliffs. And every afternoon they passed the old man on the doorstep, brittle shavings heaped over his shoes and like yellow flakes blown on the snow. He grinned while he carved, looked up at them, seemed to laugh, and hunching his shoulder, pointed backwards, behind the hut, out into the emptiness. The crosses he carved were both small and large, rough and delicate, some of simple majesty, others speaking minutely of martyrdom. They too fell across his feet, mingled with the sticks of uncarved wood—sometimes a bit of green bark was left to make a loincloth for Christ. Those that were not sold hung inside from a knotted wire, and slowly turned black with the grease and smoke; but the hair was always blacker than the bodies, the eyes always shone whereas the flesh was dull. Tourists paid well for these figures that were usually more human than holy, more pained than miraculous. Up went the shoulder, the knife rested, and he was pointing to the nearness of the cliffs. After the first week, Ernie bought one of the crucifixes, a terrible little demon with bitter pain curling about the mouth no larger than a bead, drawing tight the small outward-turning hands. Then he began to collect them, and every afternoon a new Christ would peer from his pocket through the tufts of fur.

By now his prayers at mealtime were quite audible. The setting sun stained the imperfect windows. . . . She touched his hand, but it was stiff and cold, smooth and pious. She thought at first that she could feel something of his Bishop's creed and was part of this furtive ritual that exerted itself more and more, even when the evenings were rich with color.

The crucifixes began to fill the hotel [pp. 86, 87, 88].

The unconscious cannot express itself directly because it is a composite of past, present, future, a timeless alchemy of many dimensions. A direct statement, as for an act, would deprive it of its effectiveness. It is an image which bypasses the censor of the mind, affects our emotions and our senses. An act has to be interpreted on two levels—one as action, the other as meaning. The *now* has its roots elsewhere, in the past. This fascinating under-world of symbolic act has always been known to the poets. It was Freud who complained that every time he made a discovery he found some poet who had been there before him.

In science we use symbols. Why not in poetry then? Why should the psychoanalyst be the only one able to interpret our dreams and our symbolic acts? Just as mathematical symbols have proved an essential tool in the development of modern science, so poetic symbols are today more than ever necessary in writing novels, not because they are poetic, or mysterious, but because they alone are capable of dealing with the relativity of truth about character.

The mood I fall into when I am truly possessed by my work is one which resembles the trances of the mystics. I shut out the outer world to concentrate on what I see and feel. There is no doubt that the act of creation is very similar to the act of dreaming. The difference is that it includes an activity which has been difficult to analyze. It is not only the power to summon an image, but the power to compose with this image. The second faculty, the faculty of active creation, is what is missing from the use of drugs. Drugs induce passivity. Passivity, like the passivity of India induced by religion, is destructive both to human life and to art.

A SPADE IS A SPADE IS A SPADE IS A SPADE

By a process which I am not equipped to analyze, American literature became the most literal, the most one-dimensional in the world. Academics still interpret the symbolism of *Moby Dick*, but modern students in the fifties could not understand the symbolism of D. H. Lawrence. Symbolism was simply the emotional, spiritual meaning of our acts! There is symbolism in everything we do—sending flowers to the dead, having Thanksgiving dinners, celebrating Passover, religious rites, shaking hands, even in delinquents' spitting at passengers in the subway.

Many American poets, according to Karl Shapiro, wrote prose, not poetry. Prose is literal. Poetry is dimensional. Why should we want to penetrate this realm of the dream? *Because it contains the key to a knowledge of ourselves.* Adventuring into the irrational is frightening to some writers. The realm into which the writer may take us may cause us to *lose the self we are familiar with.* We fear to be changed, influenced, to be immersed in experience, beyond control of the intellect. For it is true that poetry has a subliminal influence. It influences by contagion, empathy, as music does.

Some of the excesses of the young in this explosion of imagination and originality are due to the long repression of these faculties, the standardization achieved by commercial interests, the regimentation which had reached a point of absolute monotony. Art establishes its own controls. Form is a selection, not repression. We cannot disregard the irrational, for we cannot reach a profound order without first exploring and organizing these irrational forces which continue to motivate human beings blindly, compulsively. We are forced to admit that what we considered a suppression of the irrational self by the mind was a delusion. It cannot be suppressed because it is also the source of feeling, life, creation, and religion, but it can be controlled by understanding.

Beginning with Freud, continuing with Otto Rank, and following more recently the pioneering R. D. Laing, we are uncovering charades and masquerades. Our personal responsibility lies in our ability to control each wave of anger, distortion, hatred, which we send out into the world like homemade bombs.

Dreaming is indispensable to man. Man has to learn to live *outside* and *beyond* history as well as in it, or he will be swept like hysterical sheep into its errors (such as the horrors of Nazism). He needs a spiritual island where he can renew his strength, his shattered values, his traumatized emotions, his disintegrated faiths. It is the lack of such laboratories of the psyche which brings despair, pessimism, hysteria. An inner life, cultivated, nourished, is a well of strength. To confuse this with the much persecuted ivory tower is to lack understanding of the inner structure we need to resist outer catastrophes and errors and injustices. If we insist on living inside of history as if we were nonexistent ciphers, we add nothing to history.

Our culture's past denial of art locked out the nocturnal worlds so tightly that many had to resort to dynamite, to the drugs which Huxley described as opening the doors of perception. The dream is indispensable to psychic health. Studies of dreamers were made and it was observed that interruption of dreaming caused nervousness and instability. ("Dreams are a time to be safely crazy, so that we can stay sane during the day."—Mrs. R. Cartwright, Director, Sleep Laboratory, University of Illinois.) The negative aspect of dreaming only takes place when it is disconnected from reality.

With the use of drugs people became passive, uncreative tourists in the world of images. The need to integrate our dream messages with our life cannot be achieved by flooding the unconscious with more images than it can absorb, interpret, amalgamate, and correlate with its other self. The artist pours his dreams into his work; they are contained by the form of the work, the painting, the musical composition, the dance or poem. The hallucinatory drugs only reveal the world of images we contain but do not teach us interpretation, illumination, or enlightenment. By shutting out the outside world, drugs place one not only in confrontation with the dreaming self, but also with one's nightmares. The poets who have poured their nightmares into literature (such as Lautréamont in *Les chants de Maldoror*, Rimbaud in *Les illuminations*, Anna Kavan in *Asylum Pieces*, or Genêt in any of his works) give them to us in a form which differs as widely as the drawings of the insane differ from the drawings of great painters.

The artist, then, summons and induces his own imagery; he is self-propelled. What this self-propelling accomplishes is a strengthening of his abilities to build and create. Images and sensations have to become a work of art, or else we cannot share them with others or create our world according to our own plans and desires. The secret of fertility lies in the geological depths of the dream symbol. Intellect has a dehydrating effect upon experience. To analyze is to dissect; to dissect means to work upon dead matter. The artist works with living matter.

Dr. Robert Haas told me of a painter who went to Freud and said: "You interpret dreams, and I teach people how to dream." A good definition of literature. Jung defined the self as a virtual point between conscious and unconscious which gives equal recognition to both.

There is also a certain point for the mind from which life and death, the real and the imaginary, the past and the future, the communicable and the incommunicable, the high and the low, cease being perceived as contradictions.

Novalis said the world was a generalized form of the spirit, its symbolic picture.

Pierre Mabille in *Miroir du merveilleux:* [3]

He who wishes to attain the profoundly marvelous must free images from their conventional associations, associations always dominated by utilitarian judgment: must learn to see the man behind the social function, break the scale of so-called normal values, replacing it by that of sensitive values, surmount taboos, the weight of ancestral prohibitions, cease to connect the object with the profit one can get out of it, with the price it has in society, with the action it commands. This liberation begins when by some means the voluntary censorship of the bad conscience is lifted, when the mechanism of the dream is no longer *impeded.* Magic ceremonies, psychic exercises leading to concentration and ecstasy, the liberation of psychic automatism, are so many means capable of refining vision through the tensions they induce. *It is a means to enlarge faculties:* they are ways of approach to the realm of the marvelous.

This was written in the forties.

Gaston Bachelard, the French philosopher, wrote: [4] "The dynamic youthfulness of some old artists would seem to prove that imagination is the principle of eternal youth."

Wallace Fowlie in *The Age of Surrealism* [5] reminds us of Freud's teaching the surrealists that man is primarily a sleeper. The surrealist must therefore learn to follow his conscious states as when asleep he observes his dreams. The surrealist must learn to go down into his dreams as Orpheus descended into the underworld in order to discover his treasures.

Fowlie says of *Ulysses:* "In the last episode of Joyce's *Ulysses* the long soliloquy of Molly Bloom the character has ceased being real in any usual sense. She is lying down in bed and the words which pass through her in her half dream, half conscious state convert her into the mythical figure of woman, into the figure of the earth itself."

André Breton was one of the first literary writers to accept Freud as one of the great forces in helping man rediscover the meaning and vitality of words and in giving importance to dreams and the subconscious of man. Breton felt that there is a certain point in the mind where life and death, the real and the imaginary, the past and the future, the communicable and the incommunicable, the high and the low cease being perceived as contradictions. The rationalists defined this as madness, but they failed to see that it was in balancing the dualities and interrelating them that unity became possible. One has to break with the things that *are* in order to unite with the things that *may be.*

Drugs, by shutting out the external world, revived the faculty to dream, but this faculty is not a mere filmstrip to be looked at passively. It has two creative functions: one keeps the psyche alive in its proper language (images and feelings); the other nourishes creation. Alienation comes from a denial of the *meaning* of life. The day we cease to take nourishment from the underground rivers of the psyche, we feel life is *empty.* We only become aware of alienation when neurosis sets in as the symptom of its existence.

As we toughened our young to face "reality," we defined a

"reality" that was inacceptable to them. We desensitized them to psychological realities. We downgraded and denigrated the artist who would have expanded their imagination and consciousness without side effects. Consequently, the young, trained in passivity and acceptance, have become, through drugs, voyeurs in the world of images—not creators.

The young would have no need of drugs if they had been educated in the life of the senses and emotions through art. Art has through the ages given people their heightened sense of life, given them the key to its meaning. The heightened sense of life was denied to the young by the taboo on aesthetics, on the senses, and on the imagination. Proust, whom young Americans refused to read, could "get high" on the contemplation of a bathroom rug illumined by a ray of the sun. The doors of our culture have been shut tight against how *we feel*. The dream has been regarded as a symptom of neurosis; aesthetics belonged to other cultures; art was an obscene word, and surrealism was only associated with Dali's pranks. It was not even recognized as such when it appeared in Nathanael West's work or in Henry Miller's novels.

THE DREAM AS ESCAPE

For a long time in our utilitarian culture the dream was considered an escape, literature of imagination and experiment an escape. The young could only find a way out of such *rigidities* by extreme and dangerous methods. Semantically curious is the use of *way out* as derogatory, when it means *the way out* (or "the leading [or drawing] out," from *educare*) and was once a definition of education. We brainwashed the young as to what constitutes reality. The young are not seeking escape but expansion.

All the while certain poets, painters, and musicians were opening doors to such an expansion of consciousness. The surrealists taught a search for the marvelous, a way of filling life and creation with surprises, a way of heightening life and infusing it with meaning. It was not necessary to reach such expansion by way of drugs. In America we favored the one-dimensional writers who pictured a one-dimensional world. We treated all lyrical flights as disorders rather than flights of imagination. Imagination is permitted only in science and in science fiction. Every flight of fantasy has been condemned as a departure from reality. It was only logical that the young should turn to a synthetic way of reaching the world of the unconscious which was sealed off to them.

Undeniably we carry within us this vast, rich subconscious life as the ocean carries its marine life, and when we do become aware of it and direct it, it may, under stress, manifest its presence in a destructive way. If one's conscious life is too rigid, too regimented, then the surface may crack at times, and we are unprepared for the strange emotions or sensations we experience. These emotions become negative and destructive. In the old collective culture there was always room for the dreamer, the one who dreamed for the villagers, the one who interpreted dreams, omens, and myths, told tales, and preserved the history, ballads, and myths of the clan.

The French doctor Desoillé developed a technique to direct dreams away from what he termed the "descending fearful experience" (now called a bad trip) to the ascending one which is an exercise in freedom. In our culture we talked a great deal about freedom, but we did not *feel* free. The imagination was not free.

The dream was considered as escape, refuge, as a delusion, a way of inaction. Its positive qualities as revelation, as indication of a man's potential, as a blueprint for invention and creation were ignored by all except the artists. The surrealists spoke of the conquest of the dream for the enrichment of the mind, not the surrender to it. By some it was regarded as antithetical to action, but the surrealists and the psychologists knew that it was the source of action. Surrealist flights of imagination, invention, and wit are proofs of the existence of deep subterranean worlds. The one who can interpret his dreams does not need to fear being trapped in them. He is an explorer. In *House of Incest* I describe what it is to be trapped in the dream, unable to relate it to life, unable to reach "daylight." It was never my intention to remain within those realms but to explore them.

A study of the illness of the heart taught us about the normal heart. A study of neurosis taught the relation between dream and life. An increasing number of writers are taking their inspiration from dreams.

Djuna Barnes, in *Nightwood*, has a chapter called "Watchman, What of the Night?" [6]

"Have you ever thought of the night?" the doctor inquired . . .

"Yes," said Nora, . . . "I used to think, . . . that people just went to sleep, or if they did not go to sleep that they were themselves, but now— . . . I see that the night does something to a person's identity, even when asleep. . . . I never thought of the night as a life at all . . ."

"The night and the day are two travels, . . . we tear up one for the sake of the other; . . . To think of the acorn it is necessary to become the tree. And the tree of night is the hardest tree to mount, the dourest tree to scale, the most difficult of branch, the most febrile to the touch, and sweats a resin and drips a pitch against the palm that computation has not gambled. Gurus, who, I trust you know, are Indian teachers, expect you to contemplate the acorn ten years at a stretch, and if, in that time, you are no wiser about the nut, you are not very bright, and that may be the only certainty with which you will come away, which is a post-graduate melancholy— for no man can find a greater truth than his kidney will allow. So I, Dr. Matthew Mighty O'Connor, ask you to think of the night the day long, and of the day the night through, or at some reprieve of the brain it will come upon you heavily—an engine stalling itself upon your chest, halting its wheels against your heart; unless you have made a roadway for it. . . . Take history . . . Was it at night that Sodom became Gomorrah? It was at night, I swear! A city given over to the shades, and that's why it has never been countenanced or understood to this day. . . . For dreams have only the pigmentation of fact. . . . For what is not the sleeper responsible? What converse does he hold, and with whom? He lies down with his Nelly and drops off into the arms of his Gretchen. Thousands unbidden come to his bed. . . . So used is he to sleep that the dream that eats away its boundaries finds even what is dreamed an easier custom with the years, and at that banquet the voices blend and battle without pitch. The sleeper is the proprietor of an unknown land. . . . We look to the East for a wisdom that we shall not use—and to the sleeper for the secret that we shall not find. So, I say, what of the night, the terrible night? [pp. 80, 81, 82, 83, 84, 86, 88, 89]"

Some people, like Cousteau, are only interested in what lies at the bottom of the ocean. Some people are more interested in the past, in geology and anthropology. I was bored with the deceptive surface and drawn to the subterranean rivers which contained not the mystery of our physical birth but of our psychic birth and the secret of its behavior above the ground. The present, *now*, is an action but it has its roots either in the past or in an invisible psychodrama. This fascinating world has been revealed only to the psychoanalyst or the artist. The psychoanalyst explored it; the artist experienced and recorded it.

When Rousseau was asked why he painted a couch in the middle of the jungle, he answered: "We have a right to paint our dreams." When the French postman so dear to the surrealists was questioned about his building of a miniature castle over a period of thirty years with stones he carried in his pocket during his mail delivery, he answered: "When a man has to travel for thirty years along the same road, there is no way for him to be saved from monotony except by the creation of something he dreamed." The same could be said of the Watts Towers by Simon Rhodia in Los Angeles, built patiently for thirty years out of discards from his mason's work. The ultimate symbol of transformation can be seen in the way that Franz Kafka begins his story *Metamorphosis:* "As Gregor Samsa awoke one morning from uneasy dreams, he found himself transformed in his bed into a gigantic insect."

Rilke rejected psychoanalysis. He feared to awaken cured, and therefore cured of poetry. Kafka rejected it, and remained caged in a narrow world of nightmares. Hermann Hesse accepted it, and his imagination was expanded. Fear alone keeps us from the depths. Strindberg was far ahead of his time. He explored the workings of the subconscious during his sleep and saw how the personality of the single dreamer sometimes split into many seemingly different characters. He therefore wrote *The Dream Play*, which, if it had been written today, would be called surrealist, as surrealist as *Waiting for Godot*. Hermann Hesse combined an interest in the philosophy of the East with psychoanalysis to which he submitted, and it may have given him the confidence to break with chronological order in the long dream passage of *Steppenwolf* in which the dissociation of personality lives out its plurality with intense clarity.

Jack London had a recurrent dream of being in a bird's nest, perched upon a tree, in which he believed he experienced the feelings of the primitive man who lived in trees: "I am very small and I was sheltered within a kind of nest made of branches and twigs." On this collective memory he based his book *Adam* in which he described a prehistoric existence when our ancestors lived in trees and the risk of falling was a constant menace. I do not know the scientific facts of this matter, but all children love tree houses and it is possible to draw an inference from this. D. H. Lawrence wrote about watching a tree intently and feeling himself becoming one. "I would like to become a tree for a few moments. It watches there like a powerful tower and I sitting under it feel protected. *I am becoming that tree.* I have its strength in my limbs, its solidity, its untearable roots."

THE INFLUENCE OF DREAM UPON REALITY

Dreams, if allowed to, may act as guides to action, providing, of course, that the conscious mind approves and the emotions respond favorably. I want to give an example of the influence of the dream upon reality. My experience began with a visit to the house in Brittany once occupied by De Maupassant. He wrote most of his stories there. During storms, fishing boats are sometimes carried far inland and deposited in gardens. When the floods withdraw they are stranded, anchored. People turn them into tool houses or guest houses. I spent a weekend in that house. I had asked to be allowed to sleep in the boat but the hosts would not let me. I had a dream that I did sleep in the boat and that it traveled during the night, that is, floated down the river for twenty years while husband and friends called out to me to stop. The next day I wrote the story of the dream. The story set me thinking about how much I would like such a life. Back in Paris I started to look for a houseboat, and found one. I lived on one, and wrote a story and a novel about life on the houseboat. In this case the dream led me to carry out specific actions, enjoyable ones, in my waking life.

For the writer the conscious mind may be the great inhibitor, the great censor. This conscious mind is created by social mores, education, environment, family pressures, and conventions. For creativity it is necessary to work with the unconscious which accumulates pure experience, reactions, impressions, intuitions, images, memories—an unconscious freed from the negative effect of societal evaluations. The conscious mind can only act later as critic, selector, discarder.

In my books I have chosen to write about artists not only because I knew them better than other kinds of people but because the artist usually lives with a greater sincerity and independence, with greater spontaneity than the nonartists. In the art of others as well as in my own, I discovered that the images from real dreams and imaginings are similar. The image of the burning bush which came in a dream, the image of the bird of paradise in color, or the black King, could be easily invented by a poet. But often their relation to a life experience is only clarified later by analysis. Just before publication of the first volume of the *Diary* I had a dream that I opened the front door and was faced with radiation from an atom bomb. It was a terribly intense light. As I closed the door I thought: this will damage me forever. I unraveled its meaning. Publication meant opening the front door to the world, to publicity, television lights, the public eye, reviews. Too intense exposure to publicity might damage me. It was the expression of a fear. I always felt a public life damaged one's intimate and personal life.

Writing itself is often a waking dream. I may reconstruct in my memory a real scene which made a deep impression on me, such as the reconstruction of my impression of San Miguel de Allende in Mexico which appears in *A Spy in the House of Love* (p. 64): "Streets which had been ravaged by an earthquake. Nothing was left but façades, as in a Chirico painting, the façade of granite had remained, with doors and windows half unhinged, opening unexpectedly not upon a household nestled around the hearth but whole families camping under the sky, protected from strangers only by one wall and door, but otherwise completely free of walls or roofs from three sides."

In *A Spy in the House of Love* (p. 68) I used this memory image to express Sabina's desire for: ". . . the illimitable space she had expected to find in every lover's room, the sea, the mountains visible all around, the world shut off on one side. A hearth without roofs or walls, growing between trees, a floor through which wild flowers pushed to show smiling faces, a column housing stray birds, temples and pyramids and a baroque church in the distance."

This is the opposite of a complete, whole, enclosing home—a transient home for the night, easily abandoned, and this image, suggested by Sabina herself, expressed, as a painter would, her restlessness, her wanderings, her unsettled quality, her mobile temperament.

Why should we want to communicate with our unconscious if this has to be achieved by such indirect language, the language of symbolism? Wallace Fowlie answers this in *The Age of Surrealism*: [7]

The conscious states of man's being are not sufficient to explain him to himself or to others. His unconscious contains a *larger* and specially a more authentic or accurate part of his being. It was found that our conscious speech and our daily actions are usually in contradiction with our true selves and our deepest desires. The neat pattern of human behaviour set forth by the realists and which our lives seem to follow were found to be patterns formed by social forces rather than by our desires or temperaments or inner psychological forces themselves. The intellect alone, or a life regulated by the fixed standards of society, or our own conscious states of being, are *three barriers to sincerity*.

The dream then, instead of being something apart from reality, a private world of fantasy or imagination, is actually an essential part of our reality which can be shared and communicated by means of imagery.

CHAPTER TWO

Abstraction

By ABSTRACTION I do not mean dehumanization. I mean abstraction in the sense the Japanese have used it, and some Western painters, in the selection of important details. The new novels in France, especially those of Nathalie Sarraute, carried abstraction to such an extreme that she named one novel *Tropisms*. The meaning of "tropism" is turning, or protoplastic life before all consciousness, vegetable life, life below the level of the unconscious. This extreme dehumanization does not appeal to me. The other extreme, which demands the inclusion of all the familiar, we mistake for realism because it is familiar, so we say it is real. But the familiar may be a façade, not reality. I select parts of the external world which reveal the internal, the parts which are necessary to the inner drama. That is what lies behind my seemingly incomplete characters or descriptions of places. The whole house or the whole body or the entire environment may not be there, but we know from modern painting that a column can signify more than a whole house, and as in Brancusi's sculpture, the expression of the flight of a bird was achieved by eliminating the wings.

In my delineation of character what I leave out is what I consider too obvious, or cliché. I include certain elements because I wish to stress an aspect other than the obvious one, and this aspect gains in strength by being isolated.

I do not hesitate to describe Stella's clothes because they are significant for an understanding of her inner state and eloquent in her case, though not all women's clothes are, and if they do not signify anything, I do not dwell on them. If a stage is too cluttered, a description too heavy, too opaque, then certain elusive elements will be obscured. The process of distillation, of reduction to the barest essential is voluntary on my part because in dealing with the chaotic contents of the unconscious it is necessary to filter, to eliminate the upholstery.

I have dealt with my characters as some modern painters have, leaving out much that we are accustomed to recognize.

The original definition of "novel" was new, not experienced before. I felt one function of the novel should be to exclude clichés, to seek new crystal formations, the never-seen-before.

When I remove a familiar landmark, it is because, once given a familiar character, people seize on resemblances and do not see the new aspect you wish them to see. They only see the familiar aspect. For example, if Uncle Philip in *Children of the Albatross* (p. 153) reminds you of your own uncle, you will complete the picture and make him entirely your uncle, and I wanted to show you a novel aspect of Uncle Philip, one not described before, the dutiful uncle who went to all the family tribal ceremonies but never was a real part of the tribe, forgotten again after each appearance. If I abstract Uncle Philip so he will not awaken familiarity, it is to place a sharp focus on his isolation, his loneliness, in spite of his polite participation. A familiar story line prevents us from capturing a different element.

INTENSIFYING MEANING

It is the function of art to renew our perception. What we are familiar with we cease to see. The writer shakes up the familiar scene, and as if by magic, we *see a new meaning in it.*

In the same way when I leave out doors opening and closing, cars arriving and leaving, refrigerators being opened and drinks served, chairs creaking and curtains parting, it is to pursue and focus on something else, some new facet of relationship, some new angle or point of view. The extreme opposite of this is one of Dahlberg's novels which began: "She was sitting under a 40 watt mazda lamp."

Abstraction (using one thing as representative of many) has a function which is distinct from symbolism (giving outward things an inner meaning). The image is freed of its old associations, a character is separated from its mechanical trappings the better to sharpen our insight.

A concentrated lighting thrown on a few critical or intense moments will illumine and reveal more than a hundred details which dull our keenness, weary our vision. To reveal the elusive inner structure one has to travel light and fast. For example, we are not always aware of the entire content of a room; certain objects speak to our emotional memory and acquire special significance when in some way they play a part in the drama (the glass of water in Pinter's *The Homecoming*, the chairs in Ionesco's play *The Chairs*.)

We accepted abstraction both in painting and on the stage. When Joan Miró wished to depict the gaiety of a circus, he did so with one joyous curved line in space and a red ball. He suggested a playfulness and sense of levitation which no ponderous circus, complete with twelve elephants, fourteen horses, and fifteen trapezists, would have suggested.

I became impatient with the opaque quality of our external world which is used in most novels as a defense against a disturbing deeper world, as an obstacle to reaching it, as an obstruction created by fear. I have an even greater impatience with emphasis on meaningless acts, with all the evasions of the essential drama as practiced by the so-called realistic novel in which we are constantly cheated of reality and experience. Properties for a story in which they have a part to play. No mere furniture placed there for gravitational security.

I do believe that emotionally, as well as scientifically, our words are going to travel more lightly and swiftly, and for this we have to rid ourselves of excess baggage.

The more accelerated our life becomes, the more we have to learn to select only the essential, to create our own repose and meditation islands within an uncluttered mental space.

The world of the dream can reveal to us the mythical way in which we reexperience life, and the way our emotion, our inner-motivated drama, acts like a spotlight choosing only what concerns it. In the dream there are no walls, no contours, and if that is the way our emotions live out their dramas or comedies in the unconscious, it must serve a purpose.

Whatever seems elusive in my novels is due to this shift in emphasis, in focus. It may be an incomplete image for the sake of highly significant moments. Poets are granted the privilege of mystery and are praised for what they do not reveal, because the poet is content with re-creating a flow of images without interpretation. I have only discarded the novel's explicit and direct statement in order to match the way we truly see and feel, in images resembling film sequences.

Some writers have brought the nocturnal life into visibility but, unable to extract any significance from their findings, have emptied at our feet their vast nets filled with chaos and debris. This is what they had found in their unconscious!

This realm, with distilled, sifted, selected matter lies almost in opposition to our surface world. It is first of all ruled by flow, as life itself. It has, like life, a capricious lifeline and a different way of arranging its patterns. It might be compared with jazz. It is unwritten music in the sense that it is constantly improvising. It is ruled by free association. Most of it has a subliminal influence (not clear to the intellect) but extremely perceptible and audible to the emotions. The proof of its authenticity is that it involves us. Only by the seismograph of feeling could one distinguish the authentic unconscious from the artificial one.

The counterfeits can also be distinguished by their lack of meaning. Every authentic dream, reverie, interior monologue has a clear meaning.

In *Children of the Albatross* (p. 99) the adolescent Paul clings to his white scarf even at inappropriate places:

He wore a white scarf through the grey streets of the city, a white scarf of immunity. His head resting on the folds was the head of the dreamer walking through the city selecting by a white magic to see and hear and gather only according to his inner needs, slowly and gradually building as each one does ultimately, his own world out of the material at hand from which he was allowed at least freedom of selection. The white scarf asserted the innumerable things which did not touch him: choked trees, broken windows, cripples, obscenities on the walls, the lascivious speeches of the drunk, the miasmas and corrosion of the city. He did not see or hear them. The white scarf did not lie. It was the appropriate flag of his voyages. His head resting fittingly on its white folds was immune to stains. He could traverse sewers, hospitals, prisons, and none left their odor upon him. His coat, his breath, his hair, when he returned, still exhaled the odor of his dream. When Paul returned with his white scarf gleaming it was all that he rejected which shone in its folds.

Jazz is an improvisation upon a theme until by way of variations the theme yields all its richness. It does not end on that booming climax so underlined and capitalized in some classical music. *This is the end.* Crescendo. *Boom.* No pat conclusion but a trail left in the sky which continues to echo in our ears. No *finale*.

This no-end I first used in the short stories. It prevented them from being published for years. No definite, accented O'Henry end.

AS VARIED AS CRYSTAL FORMATIONS

By obeying the improvisations born of emotions, by abandoning myself to digressions and variations, I found an indigenous structure, a form born of organic growth, like crystal formations. In this world of the unconscious there is an inevitability as logical, as coherent as any found in classical drama. There is a different plot from the one we are familiar with. A plot in which it is our originality, our individuality which give surprising end-ings which never resemble each other. What an exciting vision of the future, to escape the uniformity we seemed to be condemned to only a few years ago. Form created organically by meaning and born of an individual character will be endlessly varied and fecundating as each crystal varies from the next. An organic development is fecundating. It is when we use *will* and *force* to impose an artificial structure that we become sterile.

It is a curious anomaly that we listen to jazz, we look at modern paintings, we live in modern houses of modern design, we travel in jet planes, yet we continue to read novels written in a tempo and style which is not of our time and not related to any of these influences. The new swift novel could match our modern life in speed, rhythms, condensation, abstraction, miniaturization, X rays of our secrets, a subjective gauge of external events. It could be born of Freud, Einstein, jazz, and science.

It is paradoxical, too, that in an age willing to look inside of the human body with all kinds of newly discovered prying instruments, we are fearful of looking inside of our feelings. It is only in emergencies we allow the psychiatrist to do this. We carefully observe and watch the happenings of the entire world without realizing they are projections of our inner selves. What we are watching outside is a representation, a projection of our inner world into the universal. There is no distinction. When I seek to interpret the behavior of a nation, I interpret it with the same means I would use to interpret a human being. Nations have neuroses. Nations have egos. Nations have pride. They have traumas from humiliations and revengefulness for defeat. This understanding is applicable to all phenomena, to the venom of *Time* magazine, the hostility of one camp, one group against the other, one set of writers against another. It seems to me that such a view is far more reassuring than that of considering the world as completely insane, absurd, or else ourselves insane or meaningless. Nations have neuroses as do individuals. I derive the optimism of my work from the understanding of events and people whom I would otherwise see as monsters from prehistoric nightmares.

You can only dispel the nightmare by awareness that it is our personal nightmare, projected on a multiscreen cinerama.

D. H. Lawrence spoke of our need for the symbol by which to express truths which are unbearable or inacceptable. But the symbol has another function. It also expresses, as the poets do, an experience which is not physical, not acted out, not literal. It expresses a feeling, a more complex psychological reality. For example in *Winter of Artifice* I wanted to express the daughter's desire to be very close to her father, as close and as intimate as a daughter and father might be without sexual union. Emotional harmony and intimacy which are not literal incest. There was no way to express such a feeling but by way of the orchestra image. This was at first suggested by the fact that he was a musician. She wants to live in harmony with her father. She wants to fuse their resemblances into a lasting, deep bond. She seeks harmonizations. A separation of ten years has made them strangers, and they must reconstruct the exact nature of the relationship. Such a close scrutiny of a relationship between father and daughter risks being misunderstood, as so many unconscious drives are, except by the analyst. Unconsciously, certainly, the daughter seeks a form of union while respecting taboos. I used the orchestra to follow all the nuances of this risky venture. *Winter of Artifice*, p. 84:

"They looked at each other as if they were listening to music, not as if he were saying words."

Pp. 88–89:

"Inside both their heads, as they sat there, there was a concert going on. Two boxes filled with the resonance of an orchestra. A hundred instruments playing all at once. Two long spools of flutethreads interweaving between his past and hers, the strings of the violin constantly trembling like the strings inside their bodies, the nerves never still. . . . Music spilling out from the eyes in place of tears, music spilling from the throat in place of words, *music falling from his fingertips in place of caresses, music exchanged between them instead of love.* . . ."

In spite of this effort at communion outside of physical union, the critics decided this was incest. And even the final phrase, "the *mystical* bride of her father," did not seem clear enough.

The poet certainly takes risks when he ventures into uncharted areas of human relationships. Yet what could be clearer than the last lines: "Can we live in rhythm, my father? Can we feel in rhythm, my father. Can we think in rhythm, my father?"

Circumventing taboos is not the same thing as breaking them. Intimacy which borders on the forbidden is described through the orchestra's various instruments because it could not be expressed literally without changing its meaning.

In *The Four-Chambered Heart* I used a very plain simile. Houseboats were prone to sink when not pumped daily, and when Djuna feels the relationship with Zora and Rango has become a hopeless prison, she dreams of sinking the houseboat.

The poetic concept of the houseboat as a place of refuge, as Noah's Ark, sailing away from the flood of war, misery, despair, or illness, changes with Djuna's discouragement, and she contemplates in a half-dream sinking their lives which cannot go anywhere. They are moored, enslaved by Zora's hypochondria.

There is nothing mysterious about a symbolic image. In *A Spy in the House of Love* (p. 7), when I had written all I could about Sabina, her voice, her eyes, her walk, her way of talking, I still felt I had not described the feeling she created in others. I tried to convey this through the following violent image: "Dressed in red and silver, she evoked the sounds and imagery of fire engines as they tore through the streets of New York, alarming the heart with the violent gong of catastrophe; all dressed in red and silver cutting a pathway through the flesh. The first time he looked at her he felt: everything will burn."

I used Duchamp's painting "Nude Descending a Staircase" to express dissociation of the personality.

The phrase repetitions give the book the flow of water, the sea breaking and flowing, and the sea symbol is a good one for the background music of the book, pervasively if not actually insistent, the long and short rhythms of failure and success as the incidents come and go. No transitions, but events flowing into each other without apparent break.

BOTH REALIST AND DREAMER

Yet man is both a realist by day and a dreamer by night. His nocturnal life is a mythological replica of and a key to his actions by day. They cannot be separated. Action without meaning becomes animal. The dream without action is equally destructive.

We kept them apart hoping symbolism would disappear with romanticism and remain among a minority of poets, the new untouchables. But Freud revealed that in our dreams we paint like Dali, or Rousseau, we monologue like Joyce, we have fabulous visions, and that this inner space which we thought the familiar abode of artists was now shown to exist in every man.

The act of writing resembles putting one's self in a dreamlike state. Improvisation in the novel may begin either with a theme, or one first line, as in a poem. The writing of a novel is, in a sense, a directed dream, embroidered upon a certain theme or thought or sensation. In maintaining the passageways between various states of consciousness, I became aware of the pull of the conscious casting its nets into the unconscious to lift up its treasures to the light. I am aware of that fragile passageway which becomes the vital conduit.

How the writer arrives at certain descriptions by dwelling on one sensation is interesting. There was an image in *Seduction of the Minotaur* (p. 5) which came from my reaction to the Mexican sun: ". . . where the sun painted everything with gold, the lining of her thoughts, the worn valise, the plain beetles, Golconda of the golden age, the golden aster, the golden eagle, the golden goose, the golden fleece, the golden robin, the goldenrod, the golden seal, the golden warbler, the golden wattles, the golden wedding, and the gold fish, and the gold of pleasure, the goldstone, the gold thread, the fool's gold . . ."

Improvisation on gold.

Later, in my single experiment with LSD, I also had visions of gold: "The smoke of my cigarette became gold. The curtain of the window became gold. Then I felt my whole body becoming gold, liquid gold, scintillating warm gold. I WAS GOLD."

Something could be deduced from the fact that the writer had experienced consciousness of gold before its manifestation under LSD. Such images come from the same source: memory which retains what attracts it and fascinates it (architecture of Bangkok, Bali, which I had not yet seen when I took LSD but which I had seen in films and photographs and books) and observation which imprints the image on the memory.

It may be a farfetched theory, but I have not yet found a disproval of it. The East lives by belief in the spirit, the West by material and practical denial of the spirit. The East, in dress as well as architecture, manifests the presence of light; the West manifests its faith in concrete, and now too late, in a desperate effort to reach the beauty of light, the young have turned to the magic of electric effects. It comes from a machine, not from within, but expresses a need for magic and freedom from steel and concrete.

Combining facts with symbolism is endlessly fascinating. In the description of Djuna's eyes which belong to a real character, I combine paintings of Hebrew wise men by a Jewish painter, Tschacbasov, along with the symbols of Hebrew-Russian culture, to create an atmosphere around what I considered Djuna's inherited, racial, collective wisdom. I saw in Tschacbasov's painting an image of Djuna's unconscious landscapes and so described the painting as if I had read her childhood and entire life through the mirror of her eyes.

Relating one thing to another is almost what I would call a form of spontaneous life. The fusion of them is the alchemist's brew. You can go into any number of sources. I draw from paintings, mobiles, scientific journals, dictionaries, films, plays, cities. I prefer my knowledge animated—that is, represented by a human being: a great doctor, an architect, or a painter.

The living arts and humanities, caught in the moment of creating, talking, living.

The psychological study of myths is enriching. I once read a paper on the myth of the phantom lover. A Jungian made a study of the *imaginary* lover whose continuous presence in a woman's life impedes her from mating with her human lover. The myth came to my mind when I was writing the story of the *Houseboat* in *Under a Glass Bell:* "I await the phantom lover—the one who haunts all women, the one I dream of, who stands behind every man, with a finger and head shaking: 'Not him, he is not the one.' Forbidding me each time to love."

In this case the dream is the obstacle to human fulfillment. The same theme, that of ability to respond to other human beings, is handled in the party scene of *Ladders to Fire.*

But that is merely another way of saying that to achieve fulfillment we have to know first what the dream is, and seek to approximate it, or exorcise it if it is unattainable.

The sharp difference between fantasy, which is passive, and imagination which is active, applies to the use and misuse of drugs. Imagination is creative.

And now what of the bad trips? The nightmares?

Those are housed mostly in *House of Incest.* There I describe the traps rather than the fertile influence of dreams (p. 38): "I hear the passing of mysteries and the breathing of monsters."

Distance and alienation (p. 39): "Distance. I never walked over the carpet into the ceremonies, into the fulness of the crowd life, into the authentic music and odor of men."

"There is a fissure in my vision and madness will always rush through. . . . I am an insane woman for whom houses wink and open their bellies."

I often described *House of Incest* as a woman's *Season in Hell.* I may have been under the influence of Rimbaud. As the book was based on actual dreams and nightmares, I may have selected the nightmares as more dramatic.

The Japanese speak of achieving balance between serenity and intensity. It is very essential in their art and in their life. I sought such serenity and balance in my life and in my work equally, and I often felt that the emphasis on cruelty so prevalent in films and novels, the taste for horror and humor, two extremes, without the middle state of serenity, may be an expression of schizophrenic insensitivity, a need to feel things violently because the sensitivity is atrophied. Violence instead of aliveness, and violence instead of strength.

In *House of Incest*, too, I pursued the experience of original birth in water, corroborated by the scientists. I sought to imagine prebirth sensations. There is also the wish to regress into a place of peace: nonlife. The only peace a neurotic can conceive of is nonlife, absence of conflict by submerging into the womb.

For me neurosis is the contemporary expression of romanticism, where the ideal wish was unfulfillable and ended in withdrawal.

To some, the unconscious is frightening because it endlessly surprises us, drives us in directions which society's rules and rigidly organized conscious mind fear and define as wrong or dangerous. When experiencing such fears, the conscious mind seeks first of all to repress the unconscious, and this gives many the illusion that the conscious mind is strongest.

Suppression requires much energy. It also simultaneously suppresses naturalness and spontaneity and imagination. To examine, analyze, and tame these forces requires less energy and is more fruitful.

Dogmas always die of dogmatism, which is a kind of hardening of the arteries. But the fecund ideas do not die. Surrealism is not a school or a dogma anymore; it is a way of expressing the subconscious. So it will endure. There is no purely surrealist writer, but there are writers who use surrealism to convey a flight from naturalism: Nathanael West, John Hawkes, Henry Miller.

In 1944, in *The New Yorker*, Edmund Wilson, reviewing *Under a Glass Bell*, conceded: "There are passages in her prose which may perhaps suffer a little from an hallucinatory vein of writing which the surrealists have overdone. . . . In Miss Nin's case, however, the imagery does convey something and is always appropriate."

A surrealistic way of approaching a multilevel, multifaced,

multidimensional state will endure, whether word-coiners seek to create their own manifestos or not. At twenty we all created our own manifestos. We were very eager to be innovators. But the more culture we have, the more we know everything has roots in the past, and we owe something to our ancestors. The psychedelic world denies its debt to surrealism, but it is there nevertheless.

The truth is that neurosis came from our unwillingness to balance and relate our outer and inner realities. In a confused world the novelist has a great responsibility not to add to the confusions. Depicting chaos without any illumination of its meaning is adding to chaos.

The only objectivity we can reach is achieved, first of all, by an examination of our *self* as lens, as camera, as recorder, as mirror. Once we know its idiosyncrasies, its areas of prejudice or blindness we can proceed to relate with others. We cannot relate to others without a self. One's insight into others can be distorted by ignorance of one's complexes. One's antennae and receptors should be kept clear to receive impressions and images of others. With this kind of honesty one can adjust the lens, rectify errors. But if one knows nothing at all about oneself and if one doesn't exist as a person, as an entity, as an identity, this causes the loss of contact of which we have complained so much, the origin of alienation, which begins in alienation from one's own self. The theme of alienation has been obsessive in the American novel, but no one connected this symptom with the original taboo on self-development and individuality. The word "ego" was distorted. The self is a conductor of emotion by which we make contact with others. The false, hypocritical selflessness we have admired and fostered resulted in loss of identity.

RESULTS OF COLLECTIVE LIFE

America made an admirable effort to live collectively, a collective life, to live for the benefit of the majority, but it was a deep error to believe that to live collectively meant to level the growth of human beings, level qualities, and create anonymity and emptiness. This sacrifice of self-interest was confused with the destruction of the self, the core. Collective cooperation has its positive side, when a community unites to solve a problem, and results disastrously when a magazine insists all writers write in the style of the magazine, making for a deadly uniformity. The destruction of the core is at the origin of dehumanization and crime. An individual who achieves his full maturity, growth, integration can then contribute to the community. The artist is aware of his self. He is aware that it is more than *his* self, that it is at once his guinea pig for experiments, his potential tool, his instrument, his camera, his computer to be nourished, his medium. When Proust says "I," it is far more than the "I" of Proust. It is an "I" which contains many men, and far beyond that, it is a *symbol* of man. In this lies his objectivity. A new concept of human reality is rising. The absolute became a fiction with Einstein. With Proust we learned the relativity of emotion, the fluidity of time. We are living through the difficult period of fission to obtain new forms of energy (this energy appears in the young).

Marya Mannes commented on the absence of women commentators. She was told it was because women had no objectivity. Miss Mannes responded that the events of the world showed no sign of rationality or logic and could not be discussed objectively. I interpreted this to mean that we need to know who is speaking, who is leading us, whom we are following, a knowledge which requires an understanding of nonrational motivations.

Marshall McLuhan says in *The Medium Is the Massage:* [8]

"The poet, the artist, the sleuth—whoever sharpens our perception tends to be antisocial; rarely 'well-adjusted' he cannot go along with currents and trends. A strange bond often exists among antisocial types in their power to see environments as they really are. This need to interface, to confront environment with a certain antisocial power, is manifest in the famous story the 'Emperor's New Clothes.' 'Well-adjusted' courtiers, having vested interests, saw the Emperor as beautifully appointed. The 'anti-social' brat, unaccustomed to the old environment, clearly saw that the Emperor 'ain't got nothing on.' The new environment was clearly visible to *him*."

There is a curious contradiction between those who complain that we have too many novels obsessed with the incapacity to achieve relationships and those who constantly upbraid the writers who deal exclusively with personal relationship. Men write about alienation and women about relationships. Feminine writing is often attacked as small, subjective, personal. The impotence to relate to another is the impotence to love others, and from this impotence to crime is a natural step.

Paul Bowles ended one of his novels (*The Sheltering Sky*) with: "he could not relate to anyone except by an act of murder." Edward Albee makes the same statement in *The Zoo Story*. A frustrated need for intimacy may explode into crime. It is curious that two of the masculine nocturnal writers I mention are concerned with sadism, cruelty, murder. The women writers I mention are not. Some of the novels written today remind me of Eugen Minkowski's description of the schizophrenic woman who set fire to her clothes to *feel* something.

Nobody has made a connection between alienation and the pressures of collective life. We tried our best to annihilate the individual life, but it is only a well-integrated individual who has something to offer to collective life. To achieve this he must first be related to himself, then intimately to a few, before he can enter collective life. What we have seen is not a participation in collective life but passive submission to it, a blind adhesion which creates nothing and is even dangerous because it can be manipulated by unscrupulous leaders.

Man developed his intellect to gain control of nature. He conquered the sea, the jungle, the desert, disease. But in the exertion of this power of the mind he lost, at times, his contact with nature. Nature is irrational. It creates earthquakes, floods, disasters over which we have no control. Woman did not design ships, cannons, planes, buildings, bridges. It is rather interesting that it was a woman, Rachel Carson, who most effectively pointed out the destructive quality of chemicals used in pesticides. Psychoanalysis is leveling this contrast, because it is showing woman how to corroborate her "intuitions" and where they stem from, and it is demonstrating to man the fallacy of his objectivity. It should bring them much closer.

The man who has made the definitive conquest of nature, the American man, is the one most afraid of *woman as nature*, of the feminine in himself. The American created a monolithic image of maleness which is a caricature of maleness, an exaggeration of maleness (no sensitivity, only toughness, logic, factualness). The European did not achieve such a domination of nature but did not feel totally estranged from it and thus he lives more comfortably in a state of friendship with woman and feminine nature.

Quite recently in a group of Freudian analysts it was the women who understood "intuition," that is an awareness arrived at without conscious knowledge of the steps by which it is reached. The women understood that you could arrive at a feeling about something without being able to describe the sequence of inductions, deductions, experience, memory which fused to make an intuitive opinion. The man says: "number one, number two, number three." The man who proceeds like a woman, in leaps, is the artist, the creative scientist, and the inventor. It was also a man who invented psychology, the science of dealing with the irrational.

The value of the personal relationship to all things is that it creates intimacy, and intimacy creates understanding, understanding creates love, love conquers loneliness.

The writing of fiction has alternated between the hypocritical glamorized and placebo novels which soothe, lull, and disguise life, which do not prepare anyone for the traumatic shocks of reality (in the forties) and the novels which became in themselves acts of vengeance and character assassination, causing more traumatic shocks than life itself.

Academic studies have confined themselves to dead writers, have given little indication or evaluation of new, contemporary novels, have continued to dissect rather than interpret. Fiction which was intended to capture *living* moments finds itself either embalmed or placed in a deep freeze.

THE LANGUAGE OF THE STREET

We have no balance between the idealized images of ourselves, or their extremes: the cults of ugliness presented as reality. In Europe most writers came from educated classes, upper or middle class, but not from the uneducated. So they wrote in the language of literature, not of the streets. With the advent of the uneducated writer who merely transposed the language of the street to paper, we had another distortion. For this language, graphic and (for some people) natural and strong as it may seem, does not say anything in itself. It only expresses the background from which it stems. Someday a study will be made by semanticists of the words which shrink our dimensions and the words which expand them.

It is sometimes difficult to re-create the creative process because it is so complex. Just as it is difficult to re-create the development of a psychoanalytical experience. We are not as familiar with the process of free association as we are with rational patterns of thinking: 1, 2, 3; A, B, C. We obey automatically when asked what follows 2. We say 3 as easily as we say C follows B. But in the correlation of images or of images and the sensations they arouse the pattern is not learned. *It is new for each person.* It is the link which leads from one to another which is difficult to trace. That is why the film of such images seems to jump. If you examine a series of slides, they follow one another. If you accelerate this upon film, say, the link may be missing.

Since creation is an *alchemy*, it is composed of various elements as in the story of the seals in *Collages*. I have observed seals in aquariums. I have seen seals in films. I have read about seals in the dictionary. The link between the old man, who lived on the beach and did not feel related to his human family, and the seals was a correlation made by my own association. I cannot trace why they became associated in my mind. I related a man who was inarticulate and did not care about words to seals who could communicate with man, be trained, and whose playfulness was almost human. So we have one part observation, factual study, one part correlation, and one part imagination (because the friendship between the old man and the seals was invention.) Such correlation is usually born of the interpretation of symbolic acts.

If the drama lies in the cleavage between conscious and unconscious, then there is great excitement in pursuing how the cleavage came to be, how it could be detected. The mystery of people's friendships could be solved by analyzing one's friends as representations of something hidden in one's self: the potential alcoholic, who will not allow himself to become one, becomes the rescuer of an alcoholic spouse. The unpoetic temperament will ally itself to a poet, the bound to a free person, the free to a stable one, breathing through the others the part of the self which is denied.

Correlation of images for me lies principally in the magnetism of interpretation. Dr. Desoillé, who practices the directed waking dream, asks first what do you see when you close your eyes. The first image which comes to mind is the one he will pursue and develop.

"I see a stairway going down, into a cellar . . ."

"Take it. Go down into it."

"I am afraid. It is dark."

"What are you afraid of?"

"Someone will pull me into the darkness."

Any humble occupation can become a symbol. A woman sewing. Mending. Repairing. Torn clothes. A restless, wandering man. Torn feelings. Destructiveness. Vehement gestures. A tear.

In *Ladders to Fire* (p. 57), Lillian is sewing:

When she sewed on buttons for him, she was sewing not only buttons but also sewing together the sparse, disconnected fragments of his ideas, of his inventions, of his unfinished dreams. She was weaving and sewing and mending because he carried in himself no thread of connection, no knowledge of mending, no thread of continuity or repair. If he allowed a word to pass that was poisoned like a primitive arrow, he never sought the counter-poison, he never measured its fatal consequences. She was sewing on a button and the broken pieces of his waywardness; sewing a button and his words too loosely strung; sewing their days together to make a tapestry; their words together, their moods together, which he dispersed and tore. As he tore his clothes with his precipitation towards his wishes, his wanderings, his rambles, his peripheral journeys. She was sewing together the little proofs of his devotion out of which to make a garment for her tattered love and faith. He cut into the faith with negligent scissors and she mended and sewed and rewove and patched. He wasted, and threw away, and could not evaluate or preserve, or contain, or keep his treasures. Like his ever torn pockets, everything slipped through and was lost, as he lost gifts, mementos—all the objects from the past. She sewed his pockets that he might keep some of their days together, hold together the key to the house, to their room, to their bed. She sewed the sleeve so he could reach out his arm and hold her, when loneliness dissolved her. She sewed the lining so that the warmth would not seep out of their days together, the soft inner skin of their relationship.

Sometimes one must pursue one's attractions. The concept of the labyrinth attracted me. It represented, first of all, mystery. One was lost in a maze. The unconscious is a maze. One does not know with the conscious mind, clearly, where one is going. There are many detours. When I saw the city of Fez, I saw in its design a huge, life-sized labyrinth. The whole city was a labyrinth. Later on, this fascination found not only confirmation in myths and legends, but in scientific images of the brain. The mind is a labyrinth. I saw at the Museum of Natural History models a million times enlarged of both the brain, and the cells of our blood. Later the image of cellular growth came to me in wanting to explain the organic growth of Proust's novels. There is also a magnificent example of organic growth in Marguerite Young's *Miss MacIntosh, My Darling*.

Comparison with the labyrinth of the unconscious, in which, as in dreams, the true objective, the true wish is not known, not stated explicitly, followed inevitably. It became one of my favorite images. I wrote *Through the Streets of My Own Labyrinth*. Then I wrote *The Labyrinth*. "I was eleven years old when I walked into the labyrinth of my diary." I combined all the mysteries of the Oriental city with the mysteries of human nature, the human mind, with dreams, timelessness, memory. Memory makes a tremendous voyage. *But we never lose the child in us*.

The self-deception of the conscious mind has become a major characteristic of Western society. It has produced a kind of self-expression that spills over with a great mass of literal descriptions of physical details to divert one from touching upon the truly significant experience. The result is overdensity, and a prestidigitation which eliminates the deeper meaning. This in turn leads to a theory that life has no meaning, is absurd, irrational. Novels are filled with meaningless acts, evasions of the essential drama and we are cheated of *reality*. No life, no history, no human being, no event is without meaning. But it takes a certain training to penetrate the surface and we mistake *superficiality* for realism.

Our psychological reality, which lies below the surface, frightens us because it endlessly surprises us and drives us in a direction which society's rules and organizations define as wrong or dangerous. When experiencing such fears, the conscious mind tries first of all to control the unconscious by repression. When it cannot be repressed, it rebels. When it rebels, it may lead either to madness or to life.

CHAPTER THREE

Writing Fiction

IN FICTION I dwell on the pursuit of the hidden self. I give much importance to the Walter Mitty in all of us, to our dreams and fantasies, because I am convinced of their importance, their influence, and their revelatory character. What may seem unreal or invented in my writing is the natural outcome of dramatizing the conflict between the conscious and unconscious self. What we are accustomed to accepting as familiar is the external appearance of reality. *The external story is what I consider unreal.*

Even as a child I had an unusual awareness of what people felt. I had intuition about what went on behind appearances, and I trusted it and spoke out, as most children do, on the basis of that. Later I developed this intuition and gave it a sounder basis by the study of psychoanalysis. Psychoanalysis may be the study of neurosis, but while studying illness, it has given us techniques for discovery of the hidden self. I have dwelt much on the study of dreams, with emphasis on the image rather than intellectual smoke screens, returning always to the origin of the emotional attitude: *I feel* . . . the realms not controlled by the mind were ruled by a fusion of observation, emotion, and experience passing by the intellect and using the senses, the instinct.

There could be no true intimacy with a character without a knowledge of this *other* self. In *Webster's New Twentieth Century Dictionary* we find this definition of intuition. "To know instinctively; to acquire knowledge by direct perception or comprehension. Perceived by the mind immediately without the intervention of argument or testimony, having the power of discovering truth without reasoning."

Intuition can be fallacious or accurate according to how often it is checked against reality and developed. It can be a strong basis for understanding. As my aim is a deeper intimacy with people and countries (as demonstrated by the probings of the diary), I became more and more interested in the science of human nature, which is psychology. So in fiction I began with characters I knew well, intimately, knew in depth. They retained a psychological authenticity even though by the necessities of fiction they became composites (either to protect them from identification or because a theme sometimes necessitates emphasis, expansion, a stretching of facts, a more cumulative impact, and leads one into variations, ramifications, away from the facts). All my stories are based on reality. Somewhere in the course of them, I may feel the necessity of entering the character's dreams, symbolic acts, fantasies. I do not always put up a road sign: "here we enter a dream."

Many of those relationships so carefully documented by the realists are untrue to the deeper ones running beneath like an underground river; they are "games," diversions, and camouflage for other dramas. It is to reach a greater *reality* (authenticity) that I abandoned realism. Even Henry James, so meticulous a describer of "realism," wrote somewhere that if you describe a house too thoroughly, in too great detail, in too solid a presence, certain events can never take place in it. The house obfuscates or determines the "scene."

A reviewer said when I wrote *Stella* (novelette included in the collection *Winter of Artifice*): "Stella is not real because she does not go to the icebox for a snack." This kind of reality I take for granted and would distract me, the author or the reader, away from some other more important observation. For this kind of absentminded observation of some fact overlooked by the police, study detective stories! So I overlook the obvious and I concentrate on some other scene. How did Stella feel when she sat at the top of the stairs not answering a telephone call which would recapture her and pull her back into a painful relationship? It is not the homely familiar touches which would lead us to the reality of Stella but how she *felt*.

Stella, pp. 25–26:

In her movie star apartment there was a small turning stairway like that of a lighthouse leading to her bedroom, which was watched by a tall window of square glass bricks. These shone like a quartz cave at night. It was the prism which threw her vision back into seclusion again, into the wall of self.

It was the window of the solitary cell of the neurotic.

One night when Bruno had written her that he would telephone her that night (he had been banished once again, and once again had tried to reconquer her) because he sensed that his voice might accomplish what his note failed to do, at the moment when she knew he would telephone, she installed a long concerto on the phonograph and climbed the little stairway and sat on the step.

No sooner did the concerto begin to spin than the telephone rang imperatively.

Stella allowed the music to produce its counter-witchcraft. Against the mechanical demand of the telephone, the music spiralled upward like a mystical skyscraper, and triumphed. The telephone was silenced.

But this was only the first bout. She climbed another step of the stairway and sat under the quartz window, wondering if the music would help her ascension away from the warmth of Bruno's voice.

In the music there was a parallel to the conflict which disturbed her. Within the concerto too the feminine and the masculine elements were interacting. The trombone, with its assertions, and the flute, with its sinuosities. In this transparent battle the trombone, in Stella's ear and perhaps because of her mood, had a tone of defiance which was almost grotesque. In her present mood the masculine instrument would appear as a caricature!

And as for the flute, it was so easily victimized and overpowered. But it triumphed ultimately because it left an echo. Long after the trombone had had its say, the flute continued its mischievous, insistent tremolos.

The telephone rang again. Stella moved a step further up the stairs. She needed the stairs, the windows, the concerto, to help her reach an inaccessible region where the phone might ring as any mechanical instrument, without reverberating in her being. If the ringing of the telephone had caused the smallest tremor through her nerves (as the voice of Bruno did) she was lost. Fortunate for her that the trombone was a caricature of masculinity, that it was an inflated trombone, drowning the sound of the telephone. So she smiled one of her eerie smiles, pixen and vixen too, at the masculine pretensions. Fortunate for her that the flute persisted in its delicate undulations, and that not once in the concerto did they marry but played in constant opposition to each other throughout.

The telephone rang again, with a dead, mechanical persistence and no charm, while the music seemed to be pleading for a subtlety and emotional strength which Bruno was incapable of rivalling. The music alone was capable of climbing those stairways of detachment, of breaking like the waves of a disturbed ocean at her feet, breaking there and foaming but without the power to suck her back into the life with Bruno and the undertows of suffering.

This emotional reality which underlies superficial incidents is the keynote of my fiction. In *Children of the Albatross* (pp. 173–74) I describe this realm:

> Djuna walked back again into her labyrinthian cities of the interior.
> Where music bears no titles flowing like a subterranean river carrying all the moods, sensations and impressions into dissolutions forming a reforming a world in terms of flow . . .
> where houses wear but façades exposed to easy entrances and exits
> where streets do not bear a name because they are the streets of secret sorrows
> where the birds who sing are the birds of peace, the birds of paradise, the colored birds of desire which appear in our dreams
> there are those who feared to be lost in this voyage without compass, barometers, steering wheel or encyclopedias
> but Djuna knew that at this surrender of the self began a sinking into deeper layers of awareness deeper and deeper starting at the topsoil of gaiety and descending through the geological stairways carrying only the delicate weighing machine of the heart to weigh the imponderable

through these streets of secret sorrows in which the music was anonymous and people lost their identities to better be carried and swept back and forth through the years to find only the points of ecstasy . . .

registering only the dates and titles of emotion which alone enters the flesh and lodges itself against the flux and loss of memory

that only the important dates of deep feeling may recur again and again each time anew through the wells, fountains and rivers of music . . .

THE CHRONOLOGY OF EMOTION

When I was being analyzed by Dr. Otto Rank in Paris in 1933, I began to perceive a new order which lies in the choice of events, an order made by memory, by a chronology of emotion, not of dates. No one who is familiar with the mechanism of the unconscious which dictates our conscious acts denies that the rational was a superstructure of the intellect to control and repress the nonrational (primitive instinctive nature in us), and no one today would deny, in the face of recurring war, that this attempt to repress the nonrational was a total failure. Man used his intellect and reasoning only to mask the presence of that which he feared (nature in himself). The science of psychoanalysis demonstrated that it cannot be repressed, but that it can be brought to the surface and controlled and directed by the intelligence. Attempts to repress, as Freud demonstrated, result in unbalance and deformed or destructive eruptions. We had to learn how to coexist intelligently with our irrational or natural primitive self. We could not do away with it.

In my own talks with Dr. Rank, I was struck by the seemingly capricious or erratic course they took. Many writers had found it difficult to follow such free-form analytical talks. Among the analysts who wrote skillfully, brilliantly, and with unusual insight was Dr. Robert Lindner. In a collection of short stories under the title *The Fifty-Minute Hour* he reconstructed perfectly the peculiar pattern of the unconscious, as well as giving the best interpretations I have read of fascism and communism. The rational mind, or rather the mind in need of rationalizations, constructed rigid patterns as ill-suited to deal with human nature as our archaic legal system. It was a wish-fulfilling order which could at any time be found full of paradoxes, contradictions, and absurdities.

With more and more rules and regulations as to what constitutes a novel, the novel became more mechanical, dealing with clichés, until the most limited critics of writing admitted to a certain deadness in the novel and attributed it to the catatonic effect of the war. With the same obtuseness, they closed the door on the only direction the novel could go to free itself of conventional dead forms: they asserted that the way of Joyce, Virginia Woolf, Kafka was a dead end. Such critics, hand in hand with the old-fashioned critics of the thirties such as Maxwell Geismar, who condemned Hemingway for not living in the United States, and the moralists who confused sermons with literary criticism, declared that the novel was in an impasse. All this was done piously (like the damage done by the missionary to other cultures) in the name of realism.

For a while surrealism was, like symbolism, considered past history. But the theory remained and inspired American writers. Today the first course in surrealism is being taught at New York University by Anna Balakian. Not because it is past history but because it played such a vital part in the freedom of such American writers as Nathanael West, Henry Miller, Daniel Stern, Marguerite Young, Djuna Barnes, John Hawkes. André Breton's emphasis was on *freedom*. Freedom led to a state beyond and above realism.

The only path to freedom of the imagination was to follow the lead of images, no matter how absurd they seemed in their correlations, to wherever they journeyed. Again psychoanalysis came to confirm the soundness of this method by the researches of Dr. Desoillé in the *Waking Dream*. A person lies down and relaxes. As soon as his eyes are closed he sees an image. Dr. Desoillé asks him to continue to follow this image (dreaming while awake). Such journeys usually lead to the untying of a knot in the psyche, the opening of passageways into the richness of accumulated experiences which, like contraband, had been sealed off by fear or a trauma.

A writer who speaks of the world as an "untranslatable language" but is skilled in translating his impressions and sensations with kaleidoscopic language is Daniel Stern in *The Suicide Academy*.

Daniel Stern explores new ideas and new sensations with wit. His books are always full of surprises. "Suicide is, in short, the one continuous ever-present everyday problem of living. Suicide was a grand, dark continent to be charted and I was its cartographer." He has a humorous and imaginative play on "circle fatigue": "I was a metaphysical investigator of the reverberation of blackness in the human and inhuman soul . . . a victim of language and imagery improvisation on blackness . . . liberating the idea, the reality, the thing of blackness from its bonds of image imagination, metaphor and myth—that too would be a great liberation."

He depicts a fascinating character, Jewel, "with her allergy to truth."

He has a playful fantasy on our need of foreigners. "The sufferings of others are always a foreign language."

The quest for other dimensions here is reached by originality of expression and thought, a play with images:

In my cold fever, whether due to the heightening of my fears or to alcohol, I saw the landscape as a calligraphic wonder. The thinking line of trees casting elongated shadows on the snow, like a prayer book in a foreign language, but which one knew by legend to hold a famous and beautiful verse; the long line of uneven rocks scattered in a shaky hand, stretching from grass's end to the shore. First larger then smaller, light burnished colors then blackened gleaming shades all straggled with sea-weed, strophe and anti-strophe, unfinished statement of stone and sand. And the flights of sandpipers hurled at the sibilance of shore-froth hissing them back then enticing them to return to the edge, fragments of alien texts, scared letters whose meaning had been forgotten, old feathered prophecies, creations of inspired Astrologists of earlier generations. In the midst of these winter hieroglyphs I found Jewel, calm as stone; clearly resolved to live, or at least not to die this day. I told her, then, of my reading the landscape the way I had read the sky when I was a child. Stuck with *logos* from the start that was me. The world as untranslatable language. . . . Memory is the characteristic art form of those who have just decided to die and those who have just decided to live.[9]

The quest for other dimensions led by the poets and by the surrealists was constantly being paralleled in the science of human nature. Literature and psychology were penetrating the same realm and would have come to a total harmony except for our culture's fear of the inner-directed. The other-directed, because they would fit in the collective patterns more obediently and cause less trouble, were constantly encouraged.

In *Winter of Artifice* (pp. 124–25) I attempted such a fusion of external details interpreted simultaneously as symbolic dramas:

It is as if she were in an elevator, shooting up and down. Hundreds of floors of sensations varying faster than temperature. Up into the sun garden, no floors above. Deliverance. A bower of light. Proximity to faith. At this height she finds something to lean on. Faith. But the red lights are calling: Down. The elevator coming down so swiftly brings her body to the concert floor. But her breath is caught midway, left in midheaven. Now she is breathing music, in which all anger dissolves. It is not the swift changes of floor which make her dizzy, but that parts of her body, of her life, are passing into every floor, into the lives of others. All that passes into the room of the Voice he pours back now into her, to deliver himself of the weight. She follows the confessions, each anguish is repeated in her. The resonance is so immense, resonance to wind, to lament, to pain, to desires, to every nuance of sensibility, so enormous the resonance, beyond the entire hotel, the high vault of sky and the black bowl of hysteria, that she cannot hear the music. She cannot listen to the music. Her being is brimming, spilling over, cannot contain its own knowledge. The music spills out, overflows, meets with overfullness, and she cannot receive it. She is saturated. For in her it never dies. No days without music. She is like an instrument so tuned up, so exacerbated, that without hands, without players, without leadership, it responds, it breathes, it emits the continuous melody of sensibility. Never knew silence. Even in the darkest grottoes of sleep. So the concerns of the Hotel Chaotica Djuna cannot hear without exploding. She feels her body like an instrument which gives its strongest music when it is used as a body. Ecstasy reached only in the orchestra, music and sensuality traversing walls and reaching ecstasy. The orchestra is made with fullness, and only fullness rises to God. The soloist talks only to his own soul. Only fullness rises.

Like the fullness of the hotel. No matter what happened in each room, what diversions, distortions, hungers, incompletions, when Djuna reaches the highest floor, the alchemy is complete.

This might be considered a poetic statement of the theories I am expounding. Or in contemporary language: a description of turning on! Of multimedia, if you wish.

The unconscious does not see, does not clutter its vision with objects or details which do not play a role in the abstract drama. Psychic states select their stage set with great economy. Observe the voids, blanks, dark spaces in dreams in which there never appeared a completely *furnished* room. There are physical gestures, and objects which reverberate in our sensory computer because of the emotional experience associated with them.

In *The Diary* I describe "certain gestures made in childhood [which] seem to have eternal repercussions":

"Such was the gesture I had made to keep my father from leaving us, grasping his coat and holding on to it so fiercely I had to be torn away. This gesture of despair seemed to prolong itself all through life, I repeated it, not physically, but emotionally, because I always feared that whatever I loved would be lost to me."

In Volume Two of *The Diary* (pp. 56–58) I questioned what motivated the selections made by memory (as Proust made them constantly and erected his long continuous novel upon such selections):

What causes certain events to fade, others to gain luminousness and spice? My posing for artists at sixteen was unreal, shadowy. The writing about it *sometimes brings it to life*. I taste it then. My period as a debutante in Havana, no flavor. Why does this flavor sometimes appear later, while living another episode, or while telling it to someone? What revives it when not lived fully at the time? During my talks with my father the full flavor of my childhood came to me. The taste of everything came back to me as we talked. But not everything came back with the same vividness; many things which I described to my father I told without pleasure, without any taste in my mouth. So it was not brought to life entirely by my desire to make it interesting for him. Some portions of my life were lived as if under ether, and many others under a complete eclipse. Some of them cleared up later, that is, the fog lifted, the events became clear, nearer, more intense, and remained as unearthed for good. Why did some of them come to life, and others not? Why did some remain flavorless, and others recover a new flavor or meaning? Certain periods which seemed very intense at the time, like the posing, violent almost, have never had any taste since. I know I wept, suffered, rebelled, was humiliated, and proud too. Yet the story I presented to my father and to Henry about the posing was not devoid of color, humor, and drama. I myself did not feel it again as I told it. It was as if it had happened to someone else, and the interest I took in its episodes was that of a writer who recognized good material. It was not an unimportant phase of my life, it was my first confrontation with the world. It was the period when I discovered I was not ugly, a very important discovery for a woman. It was a dramatic period beginning with the show put on for the painters, when I was dressed in a Watteau costume which suited me to perfection, and received applause and immediately engagements ending with my becoming the star model of the Model's Club, a subject for magazine covers, paintings, miniatures, statues, drawings, water colors. It cannot be said that what is lived in a condition of unreality, in a dream, or fog, disappears altogether from memory, because I remember a ride I took through the Vallée de Chevreuse many years ago, when I was unhappy, ill, indifferent, in a dream. A mood of blindness, remoteness and sadness and divorce from life. This ride I took with my senses asleep, I repeated almost ten years later with my senses awakened, in good health, with clear eyes and I was surprised to see that I had not only remembered the road but every detail of this ride which I thought I had not seen or felt at all. Even to the taste of the huge brioche we were served at a famous inn. It was as if I had been sleep-walking while another part of my body recorded and observed the presence of the sun, the whiteness of the road, the billows of heather fields, in spite of my inability to taste and to feel at the time. And all as clear as leaves after the rain. Everything very near. It is as if before I had a period of myopia, psychological blindness, and I won-dered what caused this myopia. Can a sorrow alone, an emotional shock cause emotional blindness, deafness, sleepwalking, unreality?

Everything today absolutely clear, the eyes focusing with ease, focusing on the outline and color of things as luminous and clear as they are in New York, in Switzerland under the snow. Intensity and clearness besides the full sensual awareness.

Neurosis is like a loss of all the senses, all perception through the senses. It causes deafness, blindness, sleep or insomnia. It may be that this is the state which causes anxiety, as it resembles death in life, and may seem like the beginning of death itself. But why do certain things come to life and others not? Analysis, for example, reawakened my love for my father which I had thought buried. What were the blocks of life which fell completely into oblivion? What was lived intensely sometimes disappeared because the very intensity was un-bearable. But why did things which were not important return clear and washed and suddenly embodied?

Neurosis causes a perpetual double exposure. It can only be erased by daylight, by an isolated confrontation of it, as if it were a ghost which demanded visibility and once having been pulled out into the daylight it dies. The surrealists are the only ones (in art) who be-lieved we could live by superimpositions, express it, layer upon layer, past and present, dream and actuality, because they believe we are not one dimensional, we do not exist or experience: on one level alone, and that the only way to transcend the contradictions of life is to allow them to exist in such a multilateral state.

I quoted this fully because the questions it raises were answered by psychoanalysis, and because the description of dead areas could be applied not only to a personal neurosis but to many of the novels which are written in this state, novels which are not alive. Some novelists have confused this deadness with objectivity. They are boring. They read like case histories. It is as dangerous to write in that state as to write in a mood of boredom about boredom. *To write without feeling is to miss the one element which animates every line with life.*

Some of these catatonic novels may be written by victims of Puritanism, of Calvinism, or of the English complex that all personal matters should be avoided as bad manners. The dogmatic social critics compounded this by insisting on social consciousness as if personal consciousness were not a part of humanity in general. This hypocrisy about the presence of the self reached the maximum absurdity in the belief that the self, if present, would destroy objectivity. It reached such absurdity, that to relieve the tedium of monotony in character and situations, America developed an obsession with biographies, personal interviews, indiscreet photographers, candid cameras, a hunger for intimacy with its historical or theatrical figures, so amusingly ironic after so much had been done to eliminate, standardize, demoralize, discard, ignore the real *individual.*

Analysis has been revealing for many years how little objectivity there is in man's thinking. Even in the most rational man, there is an area of irrational motivations (follow the political scene for a day) which are personal, belong to his personal past. And only the knowledge of this would give him control over them, over their power to destroy and negate. What matters is the essence of a person, not his literal deeds. I was driven into the subconscious to search for this essence.

Recently a writer trying to write a screen treatment of *A Spy in the House of Love,* searching for a realistic detail (to make Sabina real!) added what he considered a most realistic touch: He made her appear with a few curlers in her hair! Sabina, obsessed with charming and seducing men would never appear in the presence of a man in such a revolting state. If she did wear curlers at some time or other, which I do not doubt, she never did in public. The detail was not realism, it was an effort to make Sabina like other women, and not true to the character of Sabina.

The novelist seeking to capture an essence, an abstract drama, stands more alone than the playwright or film-maker dealing with the same subject. After I had finished writing *Stella*, I showed it to the two people whose judgment I most trusted. They felt it was too abstract, that too much was left out, that in stylizing and selecting I had made her seem *unreal*. At this point, as a mature writer, I felt I had to continue my experiment in spite of their opinion, that I could no longer change my course. My destiny as a writer might have been much easier if I had listened. The interesting fact was that these people, ten years later, had become, one, an original and brilliant film-maker, and the other, a sensitive and accepted painter. Both were sincere and genuine enough to say that now they handled their painting and their film-making in the same way I handled *Stella*.

INTERIOR FATALITY

With my habit of going backstage always, I did not find that the drama lay in tragic incidents of a person's life, but in the hidden motivations which lay behind these incidents, the "interior fatality." I was more curious as to what prevented a personality from developing, a talent from blossoming, a life from expanding, a love from being fulfilled. My personal obsession with a human being's potential drove me to seek the handicaps, blocks, inter-ferences, impediments. This meant finding the original wish by examining early dreams and fantasies, their progression, and their withering. All these observations which I had practiced upon myself as the guinea pig in the diary, I now applied to my friends, my characters. This is a different position from most novels which accept the influence of the environment, outer pressures, the effect of incidents and accidents caused by society, history, etc. The tensions I set up (drama) were the tension between potential and fulfillment, outer and inner forces of destiny, outer and inner pressures. For this I could not be content with registering *action* without reflecting on how this action came about.

Therefore my characters experience and reflect, experience

and analyze simultaneously. So that the progression or movement may be a further degree of awareness which, for me, is the pivot of dramatic development. From *The Four-Chambered Heart* (pp. 47–48):

The organ grinder playing *Carmen* took her back inexorably like an evil magician to the day in her childhood when she asked for an Easter egg as large as herself and her father had said impatiently: "What a silly wish!" . . . Now Rango was saying the same thing: "I don't understand why you should be so sad at not being able to cut my hair any longer." . . . He could have said: "That right belongs to Zora, but I do understand how you feel . . . you are frustrated in your wish to care for me as a wife . . ." She wanted to say: ". . . Beware. . . . Love never dies of a natural death. It dies because we don't know how to replenish its source, it dies of blindness and errors and betrayals. It dies of illnesses and wounds, it dies of weariness, of witherings, of tarnishings, but never a natural death. Every lover could be brought to trial as the murderer of his own love." It was never one scene which took place between human beings, but many scenes converging like great intersections of rivers. Rango believed this scene contained nothing but a whim of Djuna's to be denied. He failed to see that it contained at once all of Djuna's wishes which had been denied, all these wishes had flowed from all directions to meet at this intersection and to plead once more for understanding.

Exploring the emotional levels liberated me. My early affinity with D. H. Lawrence became more and more understandable. He had had faith in his intuitions and instincts. He was very fond of the word "flow," in fact, insistent upon it. This word I loved too, as pertaining to life, and it became even more meaningful when I found that in neurosis a person cannot *flow*, that neurosis itself is a kind of paralysis.

There is no mystery in the art of writing, but the miracle by which a living emotion is captured without dying in the process is a mystery unless one accepts that to translate a living emotion into words, the emotion must be strong enough to survive the transplantation, and this means strong roots in the base of our emotional nature. Only then is writing effective and contagious. The advantage of being *inside* of a character is that it is only when one is *inside* that one can begin to feel with and for the character. I wanted you, the reader, to know Sabina (in *A Spy in the House of Love*) better than you ever knew Tennessee Williams' Blanche DuBois in *A Streetcar Named Desire*. I wanted you to feel as if you had been intimately related to her.

In the film *The Champion* Anthony Quinn played a boxer; the camera was inside of his head. You saw the ring, the blow, the sudden swinging and swirling of the lights and crowd as he grew dizzy, his vision clouded. You could never have experienced this if it had been told in so many words by the onlooker.

Bergman used the same inside-of-the-camera technique for *Persona*, and Antonioni for *Blow-Up*. Why some believe that being inside of a character, seeing the world as he does, should cause claustrophobia and outcries of subjectivity, I do not know.

In *A Spy in the House of Love* (p. 15) I showed only the aspects of the relationship which Sabina could see, no more. The men who played a role in her life were not treated as rounded characters, independently of her, because they did not exist in that total way for Sabina. Passion, I meant to say, and illusion, are an intense but narrow lens.

It was always at this precise moment of diminished power that the image of her husband Alan appeared. It required a mood of weakness in her, some inner unbalance, some exaggeration of her fears, to summon the image of Alan. He appeared as a fixed point in space. A calm face. A calm bearing. A tallness which made him visible in crowds, and which harmonized with her concept of his uniqueness. The image of Alan appeared in her vision like a snap-shot. It did not reach her through tactile memory, or any of the senses but the eyes. She did not remember his touch or his voice. He was a photograph in her mind, with the static pose which characterized him: either standing up above average tallness so he must carry his head a little bent, and something calm which gave the impression of a benediction. She could not see him playful, smiling, or reckless, or carefree. He would never speak first, assert his mood, likes or dislikes, but wait, as confessors do, to catch first of all the words or the moods of others. It gave him the passive quality of a listener, a reflector.

At no time is Alan described otherwise than as Sabina sees

him. There is no other way to make one experience Sabina from within, know her.

It was Virginia Woolf who sought to restore to the novel not its familiar character structure, but the visionary insight of the poet. The novelist here becomes the one who sees character from *within*, catches the elusive flow of images which are the key to the character's inner reality and which are more revealing than his actions (and to me far more interesting than the mask created by family, environment, mores, national ambiance, class, and education, all of them imposed artificially over the natural self).

It was Proust who said: "Style is a matter of vision, not technique."

In my novels I wanted to enter and remain within the characters, to describe only what they saw and felt, hoping to achieve a more intimate knowledge of them. I followed the patterns of inner monologues, gave the flow, free associations, dreams, reveries. It was like a musical notation on five lines. From within, a character does not see all around himself or all around others. No one does this in life. The only one who seeks this global image is the biographer. And in general biographies are not taken from live models but partake of post mortems.

I started to write the first of my longer novels, *Ladders to Fire*, with Lillian as the central character. She was a living character, part of my life and very much in my consciousness. Which means that, like a detective given a perplexing problem or crime to solve, something about Lillian's life had aroused my psychological curiosity and desire to observe, annotate, and interpret. I thought of her as a vivid character, who had an interesting life, great dynamism, and I wondered what had turned all this into an imprisoned being, frustrated and as bound in a web of negations as the gladiators defeated by the net the enemy threw over them. She was the most bound person I had ever met. I describe her as impaled on the cross of puritanism. The paradox of paralysis in life together with such fire and energy at the center was mystifying to me. Could any love relationship liberate such a person? Could she be transformed into a feminine woman, could she be sensualized?

At times I chose a character first, and the character inspired the theme. As an opposite to Lillian I chose the "freest" and most "freeing" character I knew, Jay. It was against Jay that I pitted Lillian. His naturalness and relaxation against her high tension, his contagious sensuality against her rigid defenses. Her protective maternal qualities would appeal to him. Her activity against his passivity. If there were in Lillian what we have chosen to define as masculine characteristics, there were in Jay what we define as feminine ones. The novel, in my own terms of being able to flow along inspired by a theme and a mystery to be unraveled, grew and expanded. Lillian swung between Paris and New York, typical of the artist's life, an international geography and race of its own, the artists. She was a pianist, and Jay's painting and her music also confronted each other.

Paul Rosenfeld came to me once and said: "I want to write my biography and I don't know where to begin."

I suggested he begin with stating what his wishes were, his dreams, and then answer whether they were fulfilled or not. This may have been one way to begin a biography. But also a novel. With Lillian I was not so interested in recording her actions, as to find what prevented her from blossoming, *from reaching what she wanted.*

I ended *Ladders to Fire* on a theme which in a way seemed to give birth to the beginning of the book which followed. I end on the theme that Djuna felt (pp. 150–52): "The present was murdered by this insistent, whispering, interfering dream. The night and the Party had barely begun and she was being whisked away on a gold chair with a red brocade top by an abductor who would carry her back to the dark room of her adolescence, to the long white nightgown and hair brush, and to her dream of a Party she could never attend."

In the next book, *Children of the Albatross*, Djuna, a mature woman, seeks to contact her own adolescent self through a young man of seventeen. She is returning to adolescence, unconsciously, to discover what impedes her forward movement into experience. In Paul she sees her own fears, contractions, reticences, evasions. This kind of continuity, of emotional chronology, seems more important to me than that of factual chronology. In the timelessness of the unconscious (what dream ever recognized clock time, age, or period?) such returns, backtracking are frequent. In the case of the artist it is often an explanation of his youthfulness. Wallace Fowlie spoke of the poet's "retaining the sensibility of the child" in the mature man. It does not mean childish innocence, but a perpetual innocence toward experience, entering each one wholly with a sense of curiosity and no memory of past failures, past defeats. A child's forgetfulness helps him to live in the present.

UNREAL RELATIONSHIPS

When I dramatize the illusory quality of a relationship, it is not to say that Sabina or Lillian or Djuna are unreal, but it does mean that I believe many relationships we have are unreal. They do not have their roots in the reality of each one but in a fictitious persona made up of either memories, or training, or brainwashing by society.

The combination of elements is another interesting factor in composite characters. When I wrote the story of Artaud, titled "Je suis le plus malade des surréalistes," I had only the descriptions of Artaud I had made in the diary. I had not seen him for several years.

I did not know what Artaud had become. All I knew was that he was in an insane asylum. In another section of the diary I found an exact reportage of a preliminary questioning of a schizophrenic man. Jean Carteret, who was interested in psychiatry, took me to a public psychiatric hospital, a sordid place where they tried to "classify" the form of insanity before placing the madman in an asylum. The blundering questioning made a deep impression on me. Also the fact that Jean and I understood the symbolism of the man's fantasies, whereas the doctor was merely using the incoherence of them to prove his diagnosis, heightened the impression for me. On rereading this I felt: this might very well be Artaud speaking. There are resemblances in the poetic expressions (the madman was well read), in the nature of his fears, general similarities in the sexual puritanism. When I placed the two fragments together they seemed to be in harmony, one the outcome or development of the other. It was psychologically logical, consistent. A year or two later, after the story was published, I came across a letter written by Artaud from the insane asylum. The tone, the theme of the obsessions, the language, were almost exactly like the speech of the madman I had recorded. I had achieved a psychological consistency. Faithfulness to the inner reality of Artaud.

Combinations of elements are similar to composites. I have interwoven descriptions of Mexico with descriptions of Guatemala. If together they make a more complete landscape (as you might combine several colors to obtain a certain shade), I have given certain experiences to the character which seemed to be the kind of person who would engage in such an incident. The mind of the novelist is a storage house. Somerset Maugham always mentioned using the stories he had *heard*. Others take stories from newspaper clippings. I needed to be closer than that to my material. But there are no laws about this, no rules. I have friends who tell stories so well that I do not need to verify them. Renate told me about the man with the seals and, being herself an artist and very articulate, she made it so clear to me that I could write it as if I had been there, adding only my own poet's touches about beach, sea, skies, rocks, and seals I had seen.

This is why I object (as Proust did) to the process of unraveling and separating elements which the novelist has combined, because he is creating a psychological consistency, a psychological construction which may have a completely different intent. There is the truth of a character as others see him, there is the truth as the character himself sees it, and there is a third truth:

what the novelist has constructed with elements arranged in a different way to *signify something else.*

Everyone knows the story of Picasso's portrait of Gertrude Stein. Gertrude Stein said it did not resemble her. Picasso answered: "it will, it will."

Without going so far as to say I am portraying what people will become in their old age, or in a futuristic world, I may say that while Lillian did not recognize herself in *Ladders to Fire*, she did recognize the resemblance between my portrait and her Rorschach test. But I may have dramatized a completely different theme than that of Lillian's life, for so many actual lives in reality remain static at one point and cease to evolve, so many dissolve into dust, so many lead nowhere at all, that the novelist often has to take colors as the painter—using his own combination of colors, creating his own dramas.

Just as the novelist decomposes elements, and recomposes them to create another truth, I have the feeling that in our time (beginning with Proust, who by placing character under microscopic analysis revealed motions, ambivalences, emotions we were scarcely aware of) we are fragmenting the old concept of the unity of character in order to make a new synthesis. For example, the old novel assumed that we matured evenly, all in one piece, and never stopped to examine the asymmetry of our maturity. For a while we may have what may appear like formlessness. This accusation has been leveled at every new form. But we have to decompose in order to recompose in order to make a new synthesis at each *discovery we make about character.*

Because at first sight, at a casual glance, all X rays look somewhat similar, people have said all the women in the novels are me. This may have been because the *tone* in which I tell of the inner states is mine (like the style of a painter) because it happens that the language of the unconscious is similar. In other words, in our dreams, fantasies, stream of consciousness, there are fewer of the differences which mark our outer personality (nationality, class, accent, education) by which we categorize people. It is, in that sense, universal. You could hardly today distinguish the nationality of a painter by his work. Neither can you distinguish the difference between the dreams of one person from another. The image is the link.

I was asked why I used the same characters over a long period. The diary taught me the interest there is in watching development and growth. These cannot be telescoped in one novel if the character itself is rich, interesting, or adventurous. I kept many of the same characters not only to demonstrate organic, gradual unfolding, but even more to demonstrate the law of *relativity*, the contrast in behavior of the same character toward many others, in intimacy in contrast to behavior in the world. If people *are* interesting to begin with, they probably will continue to be so. And in speaking of characters, I was once reproached by a student because he said it was easy for me to write about interesting characters because I traveled and met interesting people all over the world. He had imagined that I selected them from an already glamorous source. But my characters were neither unique, foreign, exotic, nor glamorous.

The ones who became famous were not famous when I met them. Djuna and Sabina had humble ordinary beginnings, in poverty and in unglamorous sections around New York similar to Henry Miller's Brooklyn. The interest is in *depth*, it lies deep within the characters, not in their nationality, or status, or fame. What may seem to make them exotic, not average, is simply my preference for the artists: I found among painters, musicians, actors, writers, sculptors a common ground and a common language necessary to me as an uprooted person, a woman in a sense without a country, just as other professional people find such a common ground among their colleagues. The "exoticism" of artist's lives is merely that, not having a vested interest in the commercial aspects of life, they usually act with more honesty as they feel and see (the Emperor has no clothes on) and can defy hypocritical customs. In a culture dedicated to leveling and standardizing this becomes "exotic," but we need the one willing to risk all to keep his imagination and creativity alive for our own sake. The invention which keeps our world moving forward comes from what Alan Swallow called his "maverick writers."

REBELS

Pursuing the analogy with scientific analysis (Proust the psychological microscope), we find my characters did seem to go through a breakdown of their false synthesis in an effort to find a more authentic one, a new one. In that sense, they are rebels. Karl Shapiro pointed up my dedication to the rebels (Henry Miller among the writers, Dr. Otto Rank among the psychoanalysts, Antonin Artaud among the surrealists). A certain daring, a questioning of the cliché is necessary to creation and innovation.

This questioning never ends in the creative personality. There is never a point at which he can stop and say, it is done. This process is as continuous as that of the growing lobster which sheds its shell periodically as it continues to grow. Some people prefer to shrink themselves to fit the shell they are used to. We seem to have become aware of relativity of truth and character at the same time as relativity in science. In science a new discovery erases the old conclusions. Not so with the novelist. But science and art are far more related than the practicians are willing to admit, just as a person not familiar with a foreign language hesitates to speak fearing ridicule. The artist and the scientist do not today speak the same language. Someday they will.

It takes courage to face the mobility and fluidity of life. It means confronting the undiscovered areas and the ones we have stored in the attic for the sake of tidiness. As Tennessee Williams said: "If you touch upon their illness, they turn on you and destroy you."

We are all vulnerable in that perpetual motion which nature and life demand. We would like to find a finality, an absolute, a place to settle down where we no longer need to be disturbed.

But if there is distress in continuous evolution, there are also euphoria, lyricism, the excitement and adventurousness which the young seek in speed, in noise, in external action. Nature teaches creation and destruction, destruction and creation. Human nature has the same capacity. If the diary had not given me an almost meteorological interest in each new day, I might not have noticed each day anew, never accepting a final image as a painter does.

It is true that when you describe the flow and tides and ebbs of the unconscious, the boundaries become foggy (Edmund Wilson once noted that all of *Ulysses* sounded like the same person). In that realm the differences become more tenuous. But by this we also gain a universal language. Turkish, Syrian, Greek, Spanish, or American women can sit at breakfast and report dreams and a certain revelation would be exchanged.

The dreams in *The Tale of Genji*, A.D. 1000, dreams in ancient history, are clearer to us today than some of the traditional forms of behavior to which we have lost the key.

I eliminated what I considered misleading factors: age (because age is relative); nationality (because that would immediately implant a certain "type" which I feel people are outside of, beyond); misleading information such as background, education, race, color, status, class. I considered passport identification the most misleading of all simply because the true personality lies outside of these classifications. These are superficial classifications which compound errors about people. Whatever part of our self has been forced to fit into those molds is not the one which, as a writer, I am concerned with.

I became very conscious of character as geological strata. Levels. I began very early to say I would only include the furniture if it was part of the symbolic drama, that is if it was significant, if it too played a role in the revelation of character. I did the same with costume.

If, in Robbe-Grillet's novel *Jealousy*, the way the man's wife served the drink to her visitor was important to this drama of jealousy, then it was included. But the hundred repetitions of this mechanical daily gesture found in most novels I consider mere *filler*, as in grade B films, filling empty space while there may be something else of greater importance taking place unobserved.

There are some geological layers of the personality which are not created by environment, race, or position in life, profession, or economics. These have to do with the strata born of emotional experiences. Being uprooted may have contributed to my desire to take roots in something more permanent, more continuous, which is the spirit of man.

People say they cannot keep the characters straight, but what they should say is they cannot keep them apart. There is a deep level *at which personality traits merge*. The analysts too intent on obtaining a schema or skeleton of the structure of the personality often get bored with the monotony of it (when it is classified as parallel medical conditions!). But the novelist, the poet whose craft consists of breathing life and individuality into these patterns can easily keep both the differences and the mergings. Too much individuality makes eccentric or unique characters, but a pursuit of the essentials makes for something beyond the personal. The letters I have received about the diary almost all assert first of all that this is *their* diary. It is everyone's diary, barring a few differences of locale, education, or nationality. The stress is on the identification. Which means we communicate by channels which bypass the intellect, which are in a sense *subliminal* when we stay on those particular geological strata: the deepest.

By cutting out or disregarding the differences between human beings, whether a person was born in Brooklyn or Paris, I seem to have allowed the similarities to resound.

I do not mean this in any way as a defense of the novels, for they were experimental and they have many flaws. But they would have to be compared with parallel constructions: the novels of Giraudoux, of Pierre Jean Jouve, of Djuna Barnes and Marguerite Young. Liberation from categories makes freedom possible. When people are puzzled by the relationship of two extremes, such as Henry Miller and me, they forget the affinities of basic, essential things. Both Miller and I were concerned with freedom from old forms, with revolution in writing, and we met over the championships of two rebels: Buñuel in films, André Breton in surrealistic theory. Creativity is in itself a denial of categories, dogmas, and set values.

ROOTS IN DEPTH

Rootless as far as superficial details, one takes roots in depth, in deeper and more everlasting values. From the first writing I did I was seeking an inner world which could resist outer catastrophes, change, loss, and deprivation. When we are amazed at the passivity, or the lack of inner resources, of some of the young, and their inertia, and their alienation, we never connect this with the positive denial of transient values in favor of more enduring ones.

Because of this freedom from restrictions, dogmas, definitions, I could identify with characters unlike myself, enter their vision of the universe, and *in essence* achieve the truest objectivity of all, *which is to be able to see what the other sees, to feel what the other feels.* I am reversing the statement that all these women are me, from the fact that all these women are potentially in all women, just as the virus of tuberculosis lies dormant in all of us. I would say all women have in themselves potential Djunas (reflective), Sabinas (equivalents of Don Juan), and Lillians (blind action). Lillian is violent and cannot free herself by action because she has no awareness, Djuna becomes bound by her understanding and cannot rebel, Sabina seeks to act out her fantasies and is caught in a web of multiplicity. The illusory freedom of Sabina (we know she is bound up by guilt) is in conflict with the maternal protective Lillian (whose maternity is devouring and a substitute for sexual relationship). These aspects exist in varying degrees in all women.

The repetitions in the novels were intended to define the repetitions in life experience. People tend to repeat the patterns of their emotional lives. Though I follow the characters in different cycles, time or cities or relationships, Djuna continues to receive confessions and to be a diagnostician of the psychic life; Lillian continues to travel away from the confrontation of her secret self (it takes the death of the Doctor in Mexico to jolt her out of evasions). Developing character in the old, classical sense of the word is no longer feasible in a period of psychoanalytic principles. My intent was to dramatize new aspects of awareness, and this awareness was destiny, our only way to defeat fatality.

The classics were content to describe the romantic (neurotic) illusion which separated the lover from his love, but in our time it was illusion which had to be conquered to win love. I highlighted the obstacles which made an enduring relationship impossible (being a masquerade between two personas) or a duel between two people miscast by each other, each insisting on the other's playing the role assigned to him by the lover's need.

Lillian, for example, was too strong, too powerful and could not find a balanced relationship. The groove she followed automatically was that of mother and child. She carries within her a wish for the hero, but in life she falls in love with his opposite. The man of power needs no mother. One can see in the novel that she makes impossible wishes: she responds and relates to the childlike in man, and then laments that this child cannot be a husband. She is all contraries. She demands yieldingness and decries dependency. She is drawn to passivity and demands activity. These ever contradictory impulses end in a draw. The fear dictates certain choices which do not correspond to the deepest wish of all. She plays the piano with too much strength. She forces her strength into relationships which cannot contain it. Because of the inbalance in her selections (experiment with the unsuitable element in chemistry), she cannot find a mate suited to her true nature. Yet she is the only one who attains a fusion and balance at the end, in *Seduction of the Minotaur*.

Why? Because she was the only one who could receive the eloquent messages direct from nature. Through the senses (which she feared to yield to sensually) she was able to become at one with nature (her nature) through the Doctor's insights. She ceased defending herself against her own nature in Mexico.

Sabina is a different drama. She does not want to fall under the domination of man (as her mother submitted to her father). She wants to attain the sexual freedom of man (as her father did). She saw her mother trapped in devotion and pain, and she decided to avoid all similarities to her mother, which in her child's concept meant to be like her father. Her dichotomy was that she felt herself to be either the slave or the enslaved, the seduced or the seductress. She could not bear to be the wife. She lived for seduction.

I did not describe women at greater length because I was a woman, but because I knew more about them, and because most of the women characters in literature are done by men (not always accurately), either by men who loved them too much or not enough or hated them. I wrote out of empathy, identification, and mimicry, but that does not mean I *am* all of them, which would be quite a tour de force.

In the novels I swing between meticulous interest in the private and personal relationships, and the exposure of this relationship to the world. I use the close-up in counterpoint to the mob scenes (cafes, parties, streets). I enter the private world, but always it is confronted with the collective. The core of the two might be said to be relationships, of all kinds and on many levels.

Identification and empathy are the opposites of alienation and separation. They also achieve the opposite. They bring one inside a human being, in intimate contact with him so that one can understand his motivations, relate to him. This more closely resembles the way we live our relationships and friendships and loves than the way in which many produce insulation caused by pseudo-objectivity. In the pseudo-objectivity I am writing about, something takes place which resembles the process of embalming. The humanity is drawn out and a fluid replaced which has no power to give life, only to preserve its semblance.

Projection and identification are living ways of experiencing the life of another. They are familiar to the psychologist. They can create empathy (putting yourself in the skin of another). They can (like the best of our psychologist-novelists, Simenon) help us to reconstruct the motivation, the feelings, the impulses of others. They are a method of understanding. I learned this process from *The Diary*.

I spoke of "now I am becoming June." Or "I would like to be June." I saw in June some freedom of action which I wanted to have and, as a young woman, could only achieve by identifying with it. Actors understand this. In *House of Incest* the poetic image of two aspects of woman was pursued and became the two faces, the night and day faces, of woman, one all instinct, impulse, desire, impetus without control, the other who had sought control by awareness. The only danger, of course, is that one strong personality can submerge the other; one can feel the loss of himself in the other (as frequently happens in love), but there is no life without danger, and the *other* danger, the danger of alienation (and through alienation, nonlove, or hatred, or destructiveness, dehumanization), I consider far greater. In order to *be with* a character, in order to see him in his own terms, I may have blurred the outlines. In the case of proximity, where the danger of losing one's self occurs, the psychological drama becomes one of disentangling the confusions, as in *Winter of Artifice* (p. 92) in which the daughter feels in so many ways identified with her father (through love) that she is forced to examine in which way they were not alike:

It was a struggle with shadows, a story of not meeting the loved one but loving one's self in the other, of never seeing the loved one but of seeing reflections of his presence everywhere; of never addressing the loved one except through a diary or a book written about him, because in reality there was no connection between them, there was no human being to connect with. No one had ever merged with her father, yet they had thought a fusion could be realized *through the likeness between them* but the likeness itself seemed to create greater separations and confusions. There was a likeness and no understanding, likeness and not nearness.

This is a direct statement. Now I resort to images to convey the complex feelings:

One day down south, while they were driving, they stopped by the road and he took off his shoe which was causing him pain. As he pulled off his sock she saw the foot of a woman. It was delicate and perfectly made, sensitive and small. She felt as if he had stolen it from her: It was her foot she was looking at, her foot he was holding in his hand. She had the feeling that she knew this foot completely. It was her foot—the very same size and the very same color, the same blue veins showing and the same air of never having walked at all. To this foot she could have said: I know you. She recognized the lightness, the speed of it. 'I know you, but if you are my foot I do not love you. I do not love my own foot.' A confusion of feet. She is standing there pitying his foot, and hating it too, because of the confusion. If it were someone else's foot her love could flow out freely.

What makes us human is empathy, sympathy. The novels born of repulsion, revulsion, hatred are those I consider war novels. They encourage war among human beings and, consequently, universal war.

In my first published diary there is a study of my identification with June, a model of the free woman I wished to be. But that is the beginning of all growth. Young people have their hero worship (today mostly a worship of the nonhero, of the criminal). Maturity brings the natural distinctions; it is adolescence which is fearful of confusing the boundary lines.

I always made fun of the "ten foot pole" school of writing. I read a novel once in which the observer was posted in a house next door and all he reported was what he could see from his window. This voyeurism was no preparation for experience. It was no wonder that by reading "do not touch" novels before the war, many young Americans who went to war collapsed at the reality of war. They had been fed on unreality, on placebo novels.

This Calvinistic persecution of the personal, of the intimate life, of the personal relationship to all things operates under two false premises: one, that it is more virtuous to give this self to the collective life; two, that it is even more virtuous to have no self at all. The taboo was on the ego, as they miscalled it, not having read the definition of ego correctly. The philosophical definition: "The entire man considered as union of soul and body." The metaphysical definition: "The conscious and permanent subject of all experience." The psychological definition: "The self, whether considered as an organization of systems or mental states, or as the consciousness of the individual's distinction from other selves and so as contrasted with an alter or alter ego."

Wallace Fowlie writes in *The Age of Surrealism:* [10] "In his solitude, which is his inheritance, the modern artist has had to learn that the universe which he is going to write or paint is in himself. He has learned that this universe which he carries about in himself is singularly personal and unique as well as universal. To find in one's self what is original and at the same time what can be translated into universal terms and transmitted, became the anxiety and the occupation of the modern artist."

This surrender of the self, self-knowledge, led to a grave loss of identity and became the cause of alienation. Alienation from self means alienation from others. You cannot relate to others if you have no self to begin with. In order to respond, to exist, to participate, to love, or serve, or create or invent, there had to be a self to generate such emotions. Introspection, which was the only way to achieve self-knowledge, was disparaged. Yet no one connected this absence of self with the origin of the unfeeling, unreflecting, unthinking "gangs" and hysterical mass movements. The young today have repudiated this imbalance. They are searching for the self within, which has been atrophied. As a result there has been, in the last few years, a tremendous liberation of the imagination, along with the flowering of originality, individuality, creativity, involvement. When I lectured in the fifties, I had the feeling that the students had no reflexes. And educators agreed with me. Then all concern with personal conflicts was taboo and regarded as narcissistic. Youth had to break down before they would pay any attention. When I began the novels in 1946, there was an outcry against fiction that dealt with neurosis. Yet at the same time Auden's *The Age of Anxiety* theme was presented as a ballet. Today everyone agrees we are a sick society. What the novelists and playwrights were giving us years ago were premonitory signs. The novelist is, after all, but a gauge of what is happening, a mirror. He can articulate what is not yet visible to the unobservant eye. By confronting neurosis he can also indicate a way out.

Only a full-blown, mature, intelligent self can contribute to collective interests. But first of all it has to be encouraged to *exist* before it is asked to make a choice. The loss of personal identity has led to a most dangerous state of dehumanization.

The people who turn to the diary are seeking themselves, the tracing of a route toward expansion and awareness, the road to creativity. All this has become lost in a vast, blind, anonymous mass unthinkingness, what Frank Lloyd Wright called "mobocracy," so dangerous to human life and humanity.

I did concentrate on conflicts between individuals in their search for themselves through others. In *Ladders to Fire* I explored whether one human being could liberate another, whether we could, through the association of love, learn to be liberated of false values and false roles, whether through love we could create one another. I used as an illustration of such dependence in love the painting by Picasso which represents two figures breathing through one lung.

Even when a character as entangled in inhibitions, fears, anxieties as Lillian was thrown into the life of Jay the painter, in Paris, she did not acquire freedom within herself. It simply made her overdependent on the person who gave her this "freedom." She felt she could not live without him; it was a vicarious freedom. I discovered that we cannot let others act for us what we cannot act ourselves because we are merely living through them. This freedom must come from within and must be self-generated. But in the recognition of that inhibited part of ourselves in the other lies the first step toward becoming free.

Marguerite Young and I talked about the feminine awareness of these connecting links. I had spoken of her work as cellular, organic, in the way it grew from one unbroken cell to another. She told me of an episode in her childhood. She had once wanted to knit a scarf that would go all around the block, link by link, to enclose, surround, encompass more than her personal world. Was it a feminine tendency, to relate, unite, connect, organically, cellularly, while the masculine mind wanted to separate, to become independent? If there are obscure moments in my novels, they must come from this attempt to describe a total, organic, multiformed expansion, rather than a separation which the intellect attempts, dividing one element from another, analyzing them as independent functions. Relationship is the outcome of growth, expansion, unification; alienation the result of separation.

One of the aims and purposes of intimate relationships is to remove the mask, to penetrate through the persona, and beyond, to find the emotional self. All my characters seek that, as I did in *The Diary*. In *Ladders to Fire* I portrayed Jay humorously going about with a notebook putting down facts. I felt one could not seize upon the real meaning of a person except through his symbolic acts which are the key to his essence.

It was not a conscious, premeditated plan that made me spend more time upon the women characters than upon the men, though it is true that most masculine literature gives a man's point of view of woman, and that very few (with the exception of D. H. Lawrence) had an intuition of women's feelings. (According to Harry Moore's *The Intelligent Heart*, Lawrence had access to his love's diaries!)

I spent more time on the women characters because I understood them better, because I felt they had more conflicts than men, and above all because I felt that a great part of woman was as yet inarticulate. Dr. Otto Rank confirmed this feeling when he said that we knew little about woman's psychology because a man had invented psychology, and because woman imitated man's intellectualizations and rationalizations and did not trust her way of perceiving which was related to the artist, rather than the intellectual. "Man invented the soul," said Dr. Rank. D. H. Lawrence said that men designed the patterns followed by women. So, in a natural way, I situated my vision within various women, to see men in relation to them and seeing the reflection of these relationships in feminine terms. My act of placing my "camera" within women and elucidating woman's feelings was immediately met with tantrums by certain critics. They behaved like exasperated men when they feel they "cannot reason" with a woman! All I was saying was that the psychology of woman was different and could be understood if we were willing to look at it; that the emotional reactions of neurotic man crystallizing into complexes enabled us to understand woman crystallizing through her reaction to certain social, historical, and personal constrictions.

There was no declaration of war between the sexes in my work. There was a desire to show that relation is only possible if one understands the emotional crystallizations of both men and women. I always described the moment of relationship between men and women, but I did not follow the men in their lives outside of those moments. My camera was inside of the women. It was not a parti pris. I think we should always write about what we know, or what we wish to know. I think this was taken as a personal offense by some critics. *I wanted them to know women better.* In a true relationship there is no taking sides, no feminine claims in opposition to masculine claims, no reproaches at all. There is an effort to confront together what interferes with genuine fusions.

War is a declaration of differences and a breaking of bridges. I was always building connections, interrelations, and bridges. That was why I never described the broken connections as Tennessee Williams did in *A Streetcar Named Desire.* My women did not break. They sought by every means to walk the tightrope between various roles, conflicts, and dualities of the personality. Neither did they go to war as Martha and George did in the monstrous play *Who's Afraid of Virginia Woolf?*

I have never understood the war of the sexes anymore than I understand war between nations.

In my work we have the close-up, intimate relationships, and then, in counterpoint, we also have the connection of these relationships to the world at large. At the end of *Children of the*

Albatross (pp. 164–65) the characters meet in a cafe scene. In *The Four-Chambered Heart* they merge into the historical events of war in Spain. When people fail in intimate relationships, they return to the world at large to find a new one. When they fail in the world at large, they return to the cities of the interior, the meditation place of Oriental philosophy, or the psychoanalytical examination of their defeats.

"Elbows touching, toes overlapping, breaths mingling, they sat in circles in the cafe while the passers-by flowed down the boulevard, the flower vendors plied their bouquets, the newsboys sang their street songs, and the evening achieved the marriage of day and night called twilight. . . . They sat rotating around each other like nearsighted planets, they sat mutating, exchanging personalities."

Ladders to Fire ended with a big party. *A Spy in the House of Love* has intermittent returns to the bar.

Part of our reality is that we invest others with mythical qualities, and we force them to play the roles we need. If we do not take into account the force of these myths, we overlook one of the most powerful motivations in human nature. Many people invent situations, invent each other, to satisfy some obscure psychological need. These imaginary relationships, acted in a void, not only may take a great deal of our energies, but are doomed to frustration. I wanted to expose these substitutions (as in dreams), these efforts to correct the past, such as the scene in *Winter of Artifice* (p. 116) in which the daughter realizes that the dialogue taking place with her father is not truly between herself and her father but between her father and her mother. He has made her an understudy for the mother. He is justifying himself to the figure of the mother which for a moment has been superimposed over the daughter. These realities lie beyond and above reality.

"But suddenly she stopped. She knew her father was not seeing *her* any more, but always that judge, that past which made him so uneasy. She felt as if she were not herself anymore, but her mother, her mother with a body tired with giving and serving. She felt her mother's anger and despair. For the first time her own image fell to the floor. She saw her mother's image. . . . *It seemed to her that her father was not quarreling with her but with his own past.*"

THE THEATER OF THE ABSURD

We accept this image-making in the theater. The theater of the absurd, the works of Ionesco and Beckett dramatize or satirize the irrational elements of our behavior. This makes the irrational visible and capable of being understood.

People are concerned about what is left out of a personal vision, but the personal vision is closer to the laser light, more intense, more effective, and the reaches of its intensity are concentrated. One is not trapped by a subjective vision. No one is trapped backstage. The objective novel has an illusory range, like Cinerama, a big screen, but does not indicate a deeper drama. Thomas Wolfe's listing the name of every river in the United States does not give any truer measure of its immensity than the sense of space in Whitman's poetry.

Intimacy comes from the novelist who has had his passionate experience first, as with D. H. Lawrence, and then examines it, dwells on it.

Our American culture decided at one point to trust the "objective" vision of the many against the one, the "subjective."

There is a concept that objective listing of facts allows you to form your own interpretation. But that was not the function of the novel. It was to make you *experience* it. It is not a mathematical listing of facts which will give you experience. Experience means to feel, it comes by way of the senses, not the intellect. Stressing objectivity by way of intellect or humor is a fear of experience. It is a scientific, theoretical attitude, rather than an immersion into life.

You can take a "trip" inside of a character, in a subjective fashion, and then walk off and make all your deductions and dissections. To look upon *In Cold Blood* as objective reportage is an absolute fallacy. Truman Capote's entire orientation toward the story masks a personal, psychological attraction which would be more interesting to investigate than the sordid crime which he only tells partially, leaving out the most significant factor which would have created emotional revulsion, that the criminal castrated the father. The pseudo-objective tale masked the subjective one in a way which Genêt never practiced.

Zen Buddhism teaches this immersion in the object you wish to *experience*. You look at a tree until you feel yourself *becoming* the tree. This is the participation mystique.

The more you *feel*, the more you experience what it is like to be a tree or to be Sabina. Many of the young seek this "to be with it" through drugs, when it can better be achieved by cultivating feeling.

People do not reveal themselves to an objective spectator. They reveal themselves in moments of flare-ups in relation to others.

To pretend that one is not there in a moment of revelation of character is an affectation. The presence of the novelist is no different than the presence of a camera or a reporter, except that the reporter, having no personal relationship with the person he interviews, may ask the wrong questions, the questions which will close up the subject.

I wanted you to know more about Sabina than you were allowed to know about Madame Bovary or Blanche DuBois.

Wallace Fowlie comments on the kind of surreality I am seeking: [11] "Reality, then, as demonstrated by the realists and as seen by man's limited conscious self, entered upon a period of disfavor when it was considered imperfect, transitory, impure. And many of the new writers are characterized by their refusal of reality. . . . A new kind of absolute is in sight, which, although it contains a refusal of what we logically call logical intelligence, is an elevation of the subconscious of man into a position of power and magnitude and surreality."

Form and style are born of the theme, inspired by the theme.

I proceed in reality as a poet does. I often begin from one phrase. I hear one line, like the first line of a sonnet, and the rest is development. Or to put it in terms of music, I hear a melody, a few bars, and on this I improvise until the theme is fully developed and complete. One image, one observation may be the starting point. I have no plan or construction in advance, but once I possess a theme, it seems as if all my other faculties enter into play. Free association might be compared to a trapeze from which one can leap from one idea to another, one image to another. The language which I was always practicing is ready to be used. The information (such as information on the habits of seals, or the names of trees in Malaysia) all falls into place. I have no ready-made plot, but I do have a theme.

When I wanted to write about adolescence in *Children of the Albatross*, I chose words, images which would render this quality of evanescence, fluidity, and elusiveness of adolescents. I used the structure of the ballet as a pattern, suitable to the theme, for an over-all design to express quick entrances and exits and light mobility of the young. I selected objects—a white scarf, a measuring tape, chopsticks, a knitted blanket—they favored.

Long before psychedelic luminous paints, I described Paul and Lawrence as touching up every object in the room with luminous paint. Then, when they turned off the lights, a new room appeared (*Children of the Albatross*, p. 65):

"Luminous faces appeared on the walls, new flowers, new jewels, new castles, new jungles, new animals, all in filaments of light. Mysterious transluscence like their unmeasured words, their impulsive acts, wishes, enthusiasms. Darkness was excluded from their world, the darkness of loss of faith. It was now the room with a perpetual sparkle, even in darkness. (They are making a new world for me, felt Djuna, a world of greater lightness.)"

In several books I have tried to describe the luminosity of children's faces, of adolescent faces which are so often lost. A transparency. I used the symbol of the albatross because it was phosphorescent. I used objects and textures and words as a painter does to create an atmosphere which reveals the invisible, the psychic life.

When I started the portrait of *Stella* (p. 8) I had no plan. It was the character of Stella herself which suggested a theme: the confrontation of the actress and the human being and the conflict between them. Her own body, voice, gestures, and way of dressing gave me the style and words I needed. I sought equivalents for her voice. I remember standing in the room shaping my lips as she did, whispering as she did, to see what shape or what weight her words most often took.

Some word was trying to come to the surface of her being. Some word had sought all day to pierce through like an arrow the formless, inchoate mass of incidents of her life. The geological layers of her experience, the accumulated faces, scenes, words and dreams. One word was being churned to the surface of all this torment. It was as if she were going to name her greatest enemy. But she was struggling with the fear we have of naming that enemy. For what crystallized simultaneously with the name of the enemy was an emotion of helplessness against him! What good was naming it if one could not destroy it and free one's self? This feeling, stronger than the desire to see the face of the enemy, almost drowned the insistent word into oblivion again. What Stella whispered in the dark with her foreign accent enhancing strongly, markedly the cruelty of the sound was:

ma   soch   ism

Soch! Och! It was the och which stood out, not ma or ism but the och! which was like some primitive exclamation of pain. Am I, am I, am I, whispered Stella, am I a masochist? She knew nothing about the word except its current meaning: "voluntary seeking of pain." She could go no further into her exploration of the confused pattern of her life and detect the origin of the suffering. She could not, alone, catch the inception of the pattern, and therefore gain power over this enemy. The night could not bring her one step nearer to freedom. . . .

Her image on the screen was imponderably light, and moved always with such a flowering of gestures that it was like the bloom and flowering of nature. This figure moved with ease, with illimitableness towards others, in a dissolution of feeling. The eyes opened and all the marvels of love, all its tonalities and nuances and multiplicities poured out as for a feast.

If the pattern of the new novel is to be one in which every-thing will be written as it is discovered by the emotions, the form will be similar to that of life in which memories, reveries about the future, and present action interweave. The subconscious will determine the theme and the theme will determine the form. The subconscious is not the place of chaos it may seem to those accustomed to an artificial order. Yet only when its message is grasped by contemplating its natural order does its meaning become clear. There is a rigorous pattern in the unconscious but it only appears at the end, as in a message written with invisible ink suddenly captured by the proper chemical powder. After all the moods, dreams, fantasies, symbolic acts, and atmosphere are registered, a design appears, as in the highly sophisticated doodling of a good artist.

The development of the theme bears a similarity to jazz, which by continuous improvisations and variations finally creates a piece of music never before played, much less written.

Jean Giraudoux, known in America only as a playwright, and chiefly for *The Madwoman of Chaillot*, wrote many poetic novels and agreed with those who said they were not novels. According to Pierre Brodin, he "insisted on the role of play and chance. He insisted on the role of fortuitous circumstances. He compared himself with a musician who within his improvisations acknowledges no law but that of unity of *tone*." [12] His com-positions elude traditional rules. An episode to which we are accustomed to give much importance, such as the death of one of the principal characters, might well be expedited in five lines; whereas a detail might be treated at length and in full develop-ment." This, according to Giraudoux, is because the values, the emphasis in our subjective life do not obey the rules of our conscious life. *They are dictated by feeling.* If a death is not felt as important to the emotions, it is not objectively important. This is the reality (and the sincerity) of our emotional life. It is not a symmetry created by conventions (one should be sorrowful at a death and joyous at Christmas) or conventional feelings, the *feelings we should have*, but it is the asymmetry of the feelings we do have. The writer who developed this most thoroughly was Marcel Proust. He made this very clear when he stated briefly the fact of the death of his grandmother but only described it at length when Proust himself, some time later, became fully aware of the pain it had caused him. Only when reliving it emotionally does he describe it in the fullness that he was then experiencing (and making us experience). This happens when the novelist remains true to human psychology rather than to chronology of events. Many of us have experienced such delayed reactions. The closer a writer keeps to emotional reality, the more alive the writing will be.

The structure dictated by a plot à la O'Henry, designed around action in the external world, could not run parallel to the inner plot.

Many writers (James Joyce, Virginia Woolf, Franz Kafka, Marguerite Young) have sought to reproduce the true flow of man's thoughts, feelings, reveries, but they found the old forms too inflexible. They were forced to adopt the technique of Freud to track down the sinuosities of these underground rivers: free association, dream imagery, study of symbolic acts. The external world is familiar and protects us from an awareness of our feelings, from an elusive and intangible world whose laws we do not yet know completely. When we fear to recognize this inner world which escapes the rule of our intellect, bypasses our artificially set-up barriers, we turn against the writer who reveals them and say that this exists only in the mind of the writer, thereby denying a part of ourselves.

When I am told that my novels have no form, I always remember the story about Erik Satie. When Satie was told his compositions had no form, he composed a piece which he entitled *Sonata in the Form of a Pear*.

The Four-Chambered Heart, for example, has the shape of a river! The survival of the houseboat on a troubled river is the symbol of Noah's Ark in the flood of events. Two people are able to *flow* in rhythm because of the harmony of their love, but they are constantly arrested, prevented from flowing by the static, paralyzed life of the third character who represents death in life. The houseboat, anchored to the shore for good, is a symbol. The flowing of water has always been a symbol of the unconscious. The book takes its lulling rhythm from the river; its beauty and its moments of arrest are expressed in the houseboat's inability to break away from its moorings, to go on a long voyage. Only in their dreams at night do they see themselves traveling, wandering, free of such burdens.

In *A Spy in the House of Love* I presented the male characters only at the moment they passed through the intense searchlight of Sabina's vision or desire of them. I intended to dramatize both the limitations and the intensity of passion, intensity rather than completeness in relationship.

The form of this novel was inspired both from Schnitzler's play *La ronde* and from watching a colored stage light turning and casting now a yellow light upon a scene, now red, now green, now amber, now white, enclosing each scene in a circle of light.

The old concept of chronological, orderly, symmetrical development of character died when it was discovered that the unconscious motivations are entirely at odds with fabricated conventions. Human beings do not grow in perfect symmetry. They oscillate, expand, contract, backtrack, arrest themselves, retrogress, mobilize, atrophy in part, proceed erratically according to experience and traumas. Some aspects of the personality mature, others do not. Some live in the past, some in the present. Some people are futuristic characters, some are cubistic, some are hard-edged, some geometric, some abstract, some impressionistic, some surrealistic! Some of their insights remain relative, and we can no longer think of a character as good or bad but a combination of characteristics which vary according to relationship and the point in time. We know now that *we are composites in reality*, collages of our fathers and mothers, of what we read, of television influences and films, of friends and associates, and we know we often play roles quite removed from our genuine selves.

FREEDOM PRESENTS NEW CONFLICT

Freedom has posed a new conflict in American writing. The emergence of the self-educated man seeking more and more naturalness and freedom created informality. This is best expressed in the informality and naturalness of a writer like Henry Miller. In many other writers this naturalness has been accompanied by an overthrow of all aesthetics. Beauty was associated with the bourgeois past, with romanticism and wealth. Reality, they asserted, is *ugly*. Beauty and aesthetics are artificial. All *art* was artificial. This reached a climax in pop art which brings all the monstrous objects we do not wish to see right into our home, a complete reproduction of a service station or a diner into museums.

A great confusion set in among freedom, informality, and sloppiness. Some of the beat writers such as Ginsberg and Kerouac were marvelously spontaneous, and many were absolutely sloppy.

Spontaneity belongs in the first jet of writing, but some disciplined selectivity and cutting should follow in editing. While I have enjoyed the informality of the diary writing, I also enjoyed compressing and cutting the short stories in *Under a Glass Bell* until they were gemlike. I would not change one word today, twenty years later. But the disciplines I practiced in my fiction no doubt had an influence on my spontaneous writing.

I have often said that it was the fiction writer who edited the diary.

A Hindu philosopher once said to me: "I am very concerned about America. In the East, when we let the unconscious rule us, we have the disciplines and rituals of religion to contain it. Europe has the discipline and rituals of art. The artist gives it shape, meaning, form. But America . . .?"

Henry Miller always refused to cut anything out of his books. He accepted himself, the good and the bad writing. He did not feel that perfection was natural.

But, of course, distillation and selection are necessary to poetry, and if it is true that we have no wish to return to the formalities of nineteenth-century English, it is also true that not all are born in the slums, and everyone should not try to adopt speech and writing which is not natural. To Henry Miller who advocated naturalness and teased me for not adopting colloquial English, I once answered: "but it is not natural to me." A writer should use the language most integral to what he is, natural to him.

In my own work I can observe a change from *Under a Glass Bell*, the result of much polishing, to the style of *Collages* written twenty years later. It is written in a more casual, informal style because I was more at ease and relaxed in my own style of writing; but this ease did not come from careless, lazy writing; it was the product of intensive years of work and discipline.

Margaret Mead has some pertinent things to say about discipline in connection with LSD in an article [13] which is important enough to quote at length. (For the writer read *creative* in place of *religious*.)

The question put to her was:

Users of LSD claim that with it they have valid mystical experiences, comparable to those previously known by holy men and saints. Is there any clear difference between the two experiences? And if not, what right has society to deny anyone this new access to age-old spiritual experience?

Margaret Mead answers:

The question of validity has troubled every religious group that has accepted the possibility of mystical experience. As in the case of miracles, visions are subjected to the most intense and severe scrutiny. Those who claim, or have claimed for them, a unique relationship to God may be admitted to sainthood only a very long time after the event. Joan of Arc was burned at the stake as a witch in 1431 and was not canonized until 1920. In the Christian Western tradition, validity turns essentially on the relationship between an individual's mystical experience and the religious beliefs of others. That is, it is the miracles, the stigmata and the visions that come to have relevance to the community of the faithful that are judged, in the end, to be valid. In this sense the question of whether or not LSD users have *valid* mystical experience is beside the point.

The central issue is that LSD changes the state of consciousness of the user for a shorter or longer time. Puritanical Americans disapprove of all drugs of this type, even mild ones like nicotine and alcohol. Moreover, they take the stand that individuals' private lives are within the jurisdiction of public legislation. At present their zeal for total abstinence is concentrated on drugs. It is expressed also in the refusal to regard addiction as an illness instead of a crime or a sin.

The problem of LSD is further complicated by the claim that it produces a state comparable to psychosis and that controlled experimental use of this drug can give psychiatrists new access to an understanding of their patients. For many persons it is only a short step from this claim to the belief that young people, students, are being allowed to take a drug that may make them insane . . .

At the same time there are others who claim that certain drugs such as marijuana, mescal and now LSD open the doorways of perception and give the user an extraordinarily vivid sense of himself and his relationship to the universe. This was the viewpoint of Aldous Huxley in his book *The Doors of Perception*. . . . In his interpretation, psychedelic drugs become adjuncts to religious experience comparable to but more effective than fasting, isolation, prayer, meditation and highly controlled exercises in breathing or in taking special physical postures. The means are new, but the quest for religious experience is part of an ancient tradition in which the individual who feels a vocation makes a long, disciplined effort to attain a closer relationship to the supernatural. Even when the vision comes to an unbeliever like Saul of Tarsus, who neither sought it nor prepared for it, the experience is within a living tradition.

Certain cultures—for example, Balinese culture and the peasant version of Haitian culture—have encouraged religious-trance experience for many individuals. In these societies people take a great many precautions in selecting and ritually training those who will engage regularly in trance and in controlling where and under what circumstances trance may be induced. Individuals who go into trance at the wrong time and in the wrong place are exhorted to stop these activities or stay away from the community.

It is quite possible that the use of psychedelic drugs, whether in an old or a new religious context, may be able to facilitate mystical experience. But all we know about religious mysticism suggests that very careful disciplines and rigorous forms of training would have to be developed on which those who used the psychedelic drugs as an adjunct to religious experience could draw. It also seems clear that in our own American tradition, one test of whether such a development was in fact a religion would be its social relevance. For unlike those Eastern religions in which mystical experience is a purely individual spiritual belief, Western religions contain the expectation that religious experience benefits not only the visionary but also others who share his faith. . . .

It must also be recognized, however, that there is no necessary relationship between the use of drugs and religious experience. The ordinary LSD "trip" has no more necessary relationship to mystical experience than the drinking of ten cocktails. . . .

From one point of view the battle between those who wish to enlarge their experience through the use of LSD and other drugs and those who are exercising all their powers to prohibit this use is a very old one in Western cultures. On the one side are those who believe that control over consciousness is crucial to human living and that loss of control inevitably leads to the emergence of dangerous, bestial impulses. On the other side are those who believe that control of consciousness is itself inimical to true spirituality.

I am quoting this because it is important to the modern writer. The whole theme is as important as the emergence of psychoanalysis. In spite of its enemies, in spite of that sector of the people who remain prejudiced, it has altered the consciousness of our time, influenced us even against our knowledge. It has penetrated, infiltrated, affected all our thinking, arts, and living. The same is true with LSD. Whether we use it or not, are for or against it, it has already changed and altered our consciousness and our vision. There is a parallel between the problems of religion and the problems of creation, imagination, and poetry.

Freedom of the subconscious for the artist is equally crucial. The enrichment and the risks are equal, the belated canonizations similar. The fact is that even hostile antiart elements are subliminally influenced by the artist. And the real issue—of who, and how, and when we used means of expanding consciousness—has the same answer: The only one who can allow his unconscious to be free is the one who can understand its meaning and control its destructive aspects. After all, the most bestial and dangerous human being we have known in our time, Adolf Hitler, did not take LSD.

In short, every form of experience has its negative and positive side. Religion and art can supply experiences without use of drugs if one does not believe in them.

A good substitute for drugs would be the artist's vision. The artist, by a long discipline of fighting rationalizations, conventions, and clichés, achieves a freedom of vision which is exactly the one sought from drugs. Drugs merely remove the conscious controls, the built-in defensive masks. The poet, film-maker, painter have a natural access to his unconscious, and if one trusted him, one would share his visions. I took LSD to see if the world I described in my poetry resembled the world of LSD, if it was a different world from that of the images inspired from dreams or poetic states. It was the same, only intensified and concentrated in a way that would ultimately consume or unbalance a human being.

One might translate Margaret Mead's words for the writer: The question of validity has troubled every artistic group that has accepted the possibility of creative artistic experience.

The most valuable contribution of American writers has been in the realm of rhythm. There was rhythm in Kerouac's *On the Road*, rhythm in Daniel Stern's *After the War*, a rhythm taken from jazz in Stanford Whitmore's *Solo*, as well as an original attempt to write the equivalent of jazz. There is a long, tidal rhythm in Marguerite Young's *Miss MacIntosh, My Darling*.

But the danger for American writers is that while in motion they are effective, but when depth and reflection are necessary or inevitable, they occasionally flounder because they have not learned to stop the physical action and watch the psychic action.

Every new development in one art is often paralleled in another medium. Jazz, collages, mobiles, animation in films, the combination of several arts have all indicated ways of renewal for the novel form.

Jazz was bound to have its effect on writing. The fluctuations and rotations of mobiles were bound to affect writing. From the early days when it was found that the drumbeat affected soldiers because it paralleled the beating of the heart, rhythm has been a way to influence impetus. Rhythm in poetic prose has the same intent.

The use of rhythm as magic in writing is similar to the drumming in jazz. Rituals, costumes, gestures at ceremonies all are intended to move and sweep us into experience. We have observed Indian and Mexican fiestas in which music, color, and rhythm create a contagious, engulfing atmosphere, never realizing that we ourselves have banished from our civilization the arts which have the power to move our senses and our emotions, to heighten our sense of life. It is this lack which I believe to be at the base of the fascination for drugs.

To demand of the novel an objectivity which condemns us to be mere spectators is to deprive ourselves of the original intent of the novel derived from the Italian word *novella*—the never-before-experienced.

Rhythm is what animates poetry, sets it in motion, gives it levitation. It is rhythm which appealed in jazz, the rhythm of life, the pulse, the beat. Rhythm is inseparable from life, from the senses, from a sensory way of perceiving and feeling life.

The rhythm of *Seduction of the Minotaur* which takes place in Mexico is slower than the rhythm of the descriptions of New York in *The Diary*.

The importance of rhythm in my estimation is a measure of the difference between a live book and a dead one.

My brother, the composer Joaquín Nin-Culmell, told me once that when people approach him he *hears* them in terms of *sound*. They make a sound impression, a musical impression. This may be valid for a composer. But each art I became familiar with I felt related to the art of writing. When I first frequented painters (as a model), I watched the mixing of paint and discovered the range of colors. Then I began to observe people in terms of their coloring, the colors they wore and lived with. From painters I learned the difference between transparency and opaqueness. When I was with musicians, I learned from my brother to think of people in terms of the music which expressed them. When I studied dancing I became more observant of people's way of moving and standing and sitting, the way they handled their bodies, hands, and feet.

A new novel by Daniel Stern, *After the War*, has a definite tempo which is sustained throughout, perhaps because he is an excellent cellist.

Not all rhythm can have the swift pace of jazz. In my novels movement is not always a matter of tempo but also may be a matter of gradations of awareness, emotional fluctuations, immersions into experience and drawings away, flashbacks, and futuristic descriptions of potentials in character usually seen by the lover. The illusion of romantic lovers in our modern times becomes the vision into the potential of the loved one. A fast tempo is not possible to reflection.

A constant rhythm expressed in the lyrical passages can create another kind of rhythm that asserts the power of the imagination to rescue itself from tragedy, from ugliness, from anxiety, or from the neutral becalmed regions of nonexperience.

BIGNESS IS NOT GREATNESS

Americans, accustomed to thinking predominantly in terms of high numbers, with a great many digits, applied the same measurements to the novel. A novel was *great* only if it was *big* and crowded with people, numerically and geographically immense, historically all-encompassing, a Cecil B. De Mille epic. The close study of one human being is as important to a community as the study of mass movements.

What determines the length of a fictional piece is not always easy to say. Occasionally I have dwelt on a character who I believed would be material for a full-length novel. When I began to write *Stella* in *Ladders to Fire*, I thought I would have more to say. But at a certain point, I had said all I wanted. It remained a novelette. Some characters cannot be stretched, expanded beyond their capacity.

Why does a painter choose a small or a large canvas? The short pieces in *Collages* I felt could not be developed at length. Marguerite Young thought each episode would make a book. But I felt that it was the fantasy I wanted to emphasize, and I would lose the collage spirit of many small pieces assembled to form an impression, I would lose the lightness of rhythm, touch, and textures, the transparencies. Thus, sometimes briefness, a semiabstraction can express mobility, a lyrical levitation which a full development might weigh down, even destroy. In this case I wanted to achieve levitation, and I was attracted to the charm of short tales which would sparkle and be more like a collage or a mobile than a full solid novel.

If diary writing taught me the authenticity of one's reaction to experience, it also taught me to record these emotional levels. A young writer from Black Mountain College who had developed a terse, nervous, wiry, slick-surfaced writing, as brittle as lacquer, with a racy style of its own, could not find the loophole by which he could reach the other dimension which worried Hemingway. I suggested he think of his writing as skating and to watch for a place where he might make a hole in the ice to fish on the bottom.

Naturally this slows down the "action." But it also enriches it. *Blind* action only contributes to our emotional atrophy.

Movement, motion are expressed in novels in the constant flux of personal relationships. In *Children of the Albatross* the image of swirling constellations and planets, (p. 169):

At the same hour at the tip of the Observatory astronomers were tabulating mileage between planets, and just as Djuna had learned to measure such mileage by the oscillations of her heart (he is warm and near, he is remote and cold) from her first experience with Michael, past master in the art of creating distance between human beings, Michael himself arrived with Donald and she could see that he was suffering from his full awareness of the impenetrable distance

between himself and Donald. Hello, Michael! Djuna said, and the
100000000000000000000000000000 miles between himself and human
beings became like a small pencil addition on a note paper and not a
state of being. They were laid aside like a mathematic student's
abstractions.

In this way I give the measure of distance between human beings as a psychological reality.

LANGUAGE

I do not believe that we can communicate with banalities.
Ionesco's *The Park Bench* illustrates this. An old man and an old
woman are sitting on a park bench. They engage in a typically
corny conversation about weather, rent, politics, servants, new
taxes, high cost of living, bad telephone service. Casually the old
woman mentions that she is waiting for her daughter to join her.
They keep up this exchange of clichés for a long time. After a
while someone arrives and greets the old lady. It is not a girl but
an effeminate young man! The most important, the most startling information had been ignored: that this woman considered
her son as a daughter.

For this reason I stress the expansion and elaboration of language. In simplifying it, reducing it, we reduce the power of our
expression and our power to communicate. Standardization, the
use of worn-out formulas, impedes communication because it
does not match the subtlety of our minds or emotions, the multimedia of our unconscious life. The concept that we communicate
by simplicity, by denudation is erroneous. The writer's role is
to express what we cannot express. He is our virtuoso; he can
help us out of our prison of inarticulateness. Man's thoughts and
feelings are far more subtle than those he can usually formulate
himself if the writer fails to endow him with the fullest range of
expression. The writer was at one time the magician who broke
through the silence barriers until he chose to talk in the way
everyone talks (the man in the street), a language that conceals
more than it reveals, clutters and finally paralyzes exchange between human beings.

Elaborate language, said the action novelist, was not necessary for our daily relationships. It was a luxury and an affectation we could dispense with. Simplifying it to basic English would lead to better communication. What it led to was an almost total atrophy of verbal expression. The Calvinist puritanism of speech weighed heavily also on color, rhythm, musicality of language which were equated with romanticism, baroque architecture, and aristocracy. This constriction caused a whole trend of gray, lifeless novels, pedestrian and without effectiveness, for our senses participate in our reception of words, and our senses were undernourished. In this generation we see the explosion of color, too long restrained, and like all things too long repressed, rather garish.

People may not speak as artfully as the novelist occasionally reports they do, but since the manner in which they speak is created to reveal nothing, the more daring novelist takes the liberty of speaking as they *should*.

We use outworn words and outworn definitions that no scientist at work upon a new discovery would use, and yet we have opened realms of the mind which are completely new. Every discovery in science coined a new language. Every profession in the past created its own language (the language of fishermen, of deep-sea divers, of farmers, soldiers, tailors, for example). The writer's role is not ornamental; it is to teach us to speak as we feel and as we see.

I do believe in richness of language when it is used to create an atmosphere, to heighten meaning, but I want to stress the difference between preciousness and richness. Preciousness is an elaboration which is not essential to meaning. Richness is what is essential to the meaning, texture, mood, atmosphere, rhythm, and color. The language of action may be simple and direct, but the language for our sensations, emotions, intuitions, instincts, for our psychological states is not. Triteness is far more dangerous than richness, for it is the use of a *dead* word. The only artifice in literature is insincerity. The only decadence is automatism and imitation. Poetry is not an aesthetic luxury; it is our relation to the senses, as art is.

Standardized speech and writing may have come out of a misunderstanding of democratic education. We talked down to our audiences to reach their untutored limitations rather than exalting them to the difficulties of following our highest reaches. To be popular with the many, we failed in our less popular role of educators. My greatest reward for my austerity in this realm was to hear today's students say to me: "You never talk down to us. You always take for granted that we are going to follow you."

Our admiration of the self-made man turned perversely into admiration of the unskilled, the amateur, the imperfect, the childish, the unformed, immature, incomplete, with a prejudice against the virtuoso, the original, inventive, talented individual.

The writers I recommend are those who can manipulate the entire range of musical notation which, in the English language, is one of the richest.

When it comes to choosing the words, the language for a particular experience, I would say that this art is born of preparation, exercises in craftsmanship, a love and interest in language itself. When I hear or read a word I like and have never noticed before, I write it in my notebook and do dictionary research. I love the dictionary. Henry Miller and I once wrote new words in very large letters on a large piece of cardboard or paper and hung them up on the wall to enjoy.

I am curious about science, the world around us, fashions, textures, lighting, theater, all the other arts and their particular language. This work is for me, like the scales of the musician.

When I first talked with Dr. Timothy Leary about the experiences of LSD, he maintained that we had no language with which to express such "states." This is the same attitude taken by the mystics about their experiences. They say: "There are no words for it." I said that I felt there is a language for every "state," the language developed by the poet whose very craft consists of searching for the language in which to describe the most intricate and subtle moods. I mentioned Henri Michaux and many of the French poets who described dreams induced by drugs. Dr. Leary did not seem to agree with me. But my feeling was re-enforced by a meeting with Henri Michaux, whose *Miserable Miracle* was translated by Louise Varèse (City Lights Books). He said to me: "People have the impression that I take drugs all the time, every day. But that is not so. I may take drugs at intervals of a year or two, and spend the whole time in between working on the description of the experience, struggling with the defining of it."

Such literary craftsmanship is the responsibility of the writer. In the case of Henri Michaux, one might say that he was a skillful, mature poet before he engaged in the description of profound psychic states by way of drugs.

Alan Watts is one of the best writers on psychic states, ecstasies, and mystical experiences, which may be due also to his literary discipline in writing about religions long before he became interested in the mystical states induced by LSD.

As in this realm the language of the poet is more than ever necessary. The subtleties and magic power of language had been so much disparaged by the school of clichés and basic English it is understandable why more has been written *about* LSD by intellectuals than by any outstanding poet. There has been more commentary, more analysis, more dissection, more taxidermy than actual poetic statements. There has been no work equal to the utterances of Henri Michaux.

The language of the poets is like a hexagon or a kaleidoscope. It can fuse together many dimensions and aspects without discarding the symbolic and mythical quality of the image or sensation. As soon as one wishes to deal with states of emotion or with visions and psychic experiences and with psychological reality, one must turn to the poets.

I fought a rather bitter battle for the enrichment of language. For many of the foreign-born, studying English means discovering the extent and possible expansion of it, not taking it for granted. I was as fascinated with the range of English as a musician would be with hundreds of new chords, new instruments. I resisted colloquialisms not per se but because they are limited, flat, and inexpressive (jazz language stands as one marvelous exception). There is nothing to equal the fervor of a foreign-born for a new language. Every word is *new*. Every word is reconsidered, reborn. I was studying at Public School No. 9 when my English teacher advised me kindly to go around the corner and buy up an armful of magazines to learn everyday English because she was alarmed by my "affected" use of literary English. My reaction to this was to revolt and to drop out of school. I felt I could educate myself more by reading than by the methods employed at the time.

It was not the writers but the film-makers who opened the way to the language of images which is the language of the unconscious.

Because our culture demoted the artist, it lost its contact with the means of expressing imaginative and subtle experiences. When a nonartist attempts to describe dreams, visions, hallucinations in a film such as *The Trip*, the absence of artistic means can only create vulgarity and garishness. Only poetic writers or filmmakers who are able to handle rhythm, music, cadences, tones, textures, color, atmosphere, superimpositions could have succeeded in making such a film—artists like Fellini, Antonioni, Cocteau.

Two great poets expressed a wish to be the first visitors to the moon, Blaise Cendrars and Antoine de Saint-Exupéry. If they had gone and returned to write about the trip, we would all have been able to *experience* a voyage to the moon. But the brief, staccato, factual problems, emergencies, technicalities in which the scientist reports his current adventures do not communicate this experience to us. The astronauts said there were no words to express what they felt. Imagine a poet writing (in advance of our going there ourselves) of his trip through space to the moon. What we get now of this marvelous adventure, or the

adventure of walking in space, is the length of the hose, the composition of the space-men's clothing, the position of the vehicle.
Poetry, far from clashing with science, would enable us to share
the adventure of the astronauts (as we shared the experience of
the first transcontinental mail flight with Antoine de Saint-
Exupéry in *Nightflight*).

A deep-sea diver who was also an exceptionally skillful writer,
James Dugan, in *Man Under the Sea* brought us the vivid images
of the undersea explorations of the first skin divers, the first
aquanauts.

The poet brings the dissected plants to life, because the poet
is primarily *the lover of the world*, and therefore he alone can
make us fall in love. Very few of us are necrophilic and fall in
love with dead matter after it has been dissected by the intellectual.

Long before the scientists made flights in space possible, the
poets conceived of the emotional adventures in flight, timelessness, levitation. Shelley was known as the poet of flight. Only
when the poet and the scientist work in unison will we have
living experiences and knowledge of the marvels of the universe
as they are being discovered, not yet embalmed in museums.

A limited language does not prepare us for unusual experiences.
Words acquire, every moment, totally different meanings. A
word like "moon" meant something to the romantics which it
does not mean to us. Often new words become necessary in order to express a novel experience accurately and completely. As
one expands and experiences, the experience expands the individual, demanding more than a limited skill in language.

When people stress simplicity in language, they do not mean
simplicity but standardization. Words are living organisms and
have enormous power when alive, but when dead not at all. The
way to recognize a dead word is that it exudes boredom. When
expressions become mechanical, standardized, they lose their life-
giving quality. We each need a broad range of expression to do
justice to all the levels of his personality.

The writer must also look into the language he uses for what is traditionally called characterization. He must consider whether he wants an imitation of colloquial speech or of provincial or local mannerisms. This approach belongs again to the school of realism. To me these characteristics become less important when people focus on emotional experiences. The imitation of reality creates separation and classifications (southern, northern, middlewestern, western, middle class, upper class, lower class, racial tonalities, which unconsciously type and limit), whereas the creation of an inner dialogue, a speech closer to the universal subconscious, annihilates these external characteristics and becomes another language, common to all emotions. Someone said to Shakespeare: "That is not the way people talk." Shakespeare answered: "No, but it is the way they *should* talk."

I do not register local idiosyncrasies. They are ephemeral, like fashions, and they change and date with whims and fads. Slang changes. It is a short-lived language. It is transient. There is a language we can speak which is not subject to fashion or time. It is the eternal language of the poets, because the best ones have always extracted the essence of language, distilled it, and thus made it permanent.

If I never showed much interest in the lingo of the moment, I did take an interest in the *key words*, the words which appear and reappear most frequently in a person's speech, the words which compose his private vocabulary. This seemed of interest to me because it was revelatory. A Southerner's speech only revealed that he was born in the South, but a person's repeated use of certain words can lead one to vital discoveries.

KEY WORDS

D. H. Lawrence used over and over again the words "livingness" and "flow," and I wrote about his language (*D. H. Lawrence: An Unprofessional Study*, p. 60):

Lawrence's language makes a physical impression because he projected his physical response into the thing he observed. . . . His sensorial penetration is complete. That is why his abstract thought is always deep reaching: it is really concrete, it passed through the channels of the senses. . . . Lawrence attempted some very difficult things with his writing. For him it was an instrument of unlimited possibilities; he would give it the *bulginess of sculpture*, the feeling of heavy material fullness: thus the loins of the men and women, the hips and the buttocks. He would give it the nuances of paint: thus the efforts to convey shades of color with words that had never before been used for color. He would give it the rhythm of movement, of dancing: thus his wayward, formless, floating, word-shattering descriptions. He would give it sound, musicality, cadence: thus words sometimes used less for their sense than their sound. It was a daring thing to do. Sometimes he failed. But it was certainly the crevice in the wall, and opened a new world for us.

Madmen who lose contact with reality usually regress to their primitive animal behavior and use primitive animal language. Some of our writers favor lavatory writing, graffiti, gutter language, army barracks or clinical expressions. At first this seemed an inevitable consequence of the age of the common man, of uneducated writers, of proletarian social realism and the naturalistic novel. But now I see another aspect of it. It may well be a sign of neurotic lack of sense of reality, that is, an effort to make one's experience real by use of brutal expressions, to shock one's self into feeling by the senses, again a perversion born of puritanism. To write aesthetically or emotionally about sensuality was *not real*. To be real, language must be violent, vulgar, and crude.

When it is not necessary (as when Zola transcribed the speech of the laundry women), then it becomes as much of an affectation of masculinity and reality as the affectation by ornamentation of aristocratic speech. Some gutter language may be natural, but it is not universal. The age of the common man was a democratic ideal; the speech of the gutter is not. It has become, unfortunately, a symbol for rebellion against authority and order, but its use had the opposite effect: it is not a sign of freedom; it is a sign of inarticulateness and anarchism. Deeper down, it is a degrading of the senses.

To my mind the only artifice in literature is insincerity, particularly when this insincerity is an affectation of simplicity. The true decadence is automatism and imitation. The only effete people, I feel, are those who consider every new word unknown to them indigestible and precious. There still remains to be achieved the enormous task of convincing man that poetic language is not merely an aesthetic luxury or a baroque ornamentation, but that it is the only expression we have for the complexities and subtleties of our emotions and perceptions as we know from the study of our dreams. The only unnaturalness of speech is a literal imitation of common speech. There is no language of the common man. There is the problem of inarticulateness common to all of us. Inadequate expression communicates only dim perceptions. The writer who was to have been the magician delivering us from our limited formulations chose to imitate our stutterings and fumblings and awkward silences.

What I am stressing is the use of language as magic, the use of rhythm and image. The fear of using the full span of language would be like denying ourselves the use of an orchestra for a symphony. James Joyce tried to tell us in so many ways that man's life does not take place on one level only but on several simultaneously. And we cannot express this with one string.

Every writer experiences moments of paralysis, blocks. Some react with anxiety. They feel they may never write again, that the source has dried up. Others take it philosophically and wait. Others, like me, seek the psychological origin of the paralysis. I am assuming that writing comes from a source which does not dry up, and I deal with the temporary obstruction. Having studied psychoanalysis deeply, I have observed that the flow of life is often interrupted by obstructions. In writing, a little sleuthing will lead us to the obstacle, and a little analysis will remove the obstacle.

I examine myself: Have I touched upon a taboo, a traditional taboo (religious, racial, social) which still operates in me, controls me without my being aware of it? A taboo subject? A taboo feeling? Have I come upon an experience which might expose me, the author, to ridicule or misunderstanding?

Much of the time I found either a taboo or an inhibition (such as the personal inhibition Dostoevski revealed in his notebooks when he contemplated the possibility that Raskolnikoff was not killing the old moneylender but his mother, yet would not include this in the novel). But the most frequent diagnosis I ran into was *insincerity*. I was writing something I did not feel, did not believe, did not care about. This was the most frequent cause of impotence.

Another frequent cause of blocking is looking at one's work through the eyes of a hostile world. When we lose our own inner vision, our self-confidence, and our faith, we begin to see our work through the eyes of the enemy. We adopt the vision of the enemy. We believe him. This is fatal to a writer, as fatal as it is for the personality who lives to create a false image invented by public relations. Falsity in writing destroys the source of inspiration.

The blocks are more often psychological than technical. I ask myself: what am I afraid of—of transgressing taboos which will bring retaliation, criticism, unpopularity, vilification, loss of one's family loves? Do I feel the theme is beyond my power and technique? Is it a childhood fear of the consequences of being truthful? hurting others? revealing secrets which do not belong to me? There are so many fears. Some are born of guilt. We fear exposure of the self even when we are not writing about ourselves. Technical difficulties are often bound up with psychological difficulties—timidity, ambivalence, indecision, conflict.

The younger generation of writers has overthrown many taboos, social, historical, racial, but have not yet developed an acceptable way to express this new freedom. The solution to many of these problems lies in the use of art. There is always a way of saying even the most offensive things in a palatable way, of revealing the most profound secrets of the personality without inspiring repulsion or recoil. Symbolism is one of them. Another is writing with a sense of beauty, of style, aesthetics, poetry. A sense of organic meaning, sincerity, and grace can make any subject possible.

Without any use of explicit language, Maude Hutchins, who is the equivalent of Colette in descriptions of erotic relationships, describes vividly and cinematically love scenes which are far more effective than those of many plainspoken writers. She is one of our most aristocratic of writers, in the broadest sense of the word, which I use for quality and elegance. Any of her books can be read for a lesson in style, in sensual grace.

When Daisy Aldan teaches her poetry class at the School of Art and Design in New York, she uses the stories in *Under a Glass Bell*. One of the parents protested the birth story. The mother thought her teen-age girl should not read such a tragic story about birth; it might frighten her away from bearing children. Daisy Aldan's answer was: "Your daughter will sooner or later read something about birth told in a brutal, violent or ugly way. Better for her to prepare for life by facing experience told in terms of beauty and emotion by an artist."

An example of an indirect way of describing the feminine element in a man is found in *The Mohican*, one of the short stories in *Under a Glass Bell* (p. 45):

His talk was spherical, making enormous ellipses, catching the Turkish bath in Algeria where the beautiful boy massaged him so effectively that the Mohican had to run away from him—the Mohican's whole face expressing that he had not run away, a reminiscent mockery of the experience, something like the criminal's desire to return to the scene. If I pressed him I might discover that he had seen the boy again, but I would never know more than that. Yet while the Mohican talked, his very way of standing, of placing his weight upon one foot, of crossing his arms like a woman to protect the middle of his body, the trellis of shadows tabooing the middle of the body, while the eyes acknowledged perversity, everything helped one to imagine the Mohican and the boy together.

A very proper Frenchwoman who was translating this passage into French did not immediately realize what I had said; it had slipped by the censor!

It was H. L. Mencken who said we had no critics, we had only moralists. I do feel we have very few objective critics. Many of them are entirely motivated by their adhesion to political groups, others are academic and only apply the standards they learned in the past, still others are moralists. Very few are trained professional reviewers. The assignment of book reviews sometimes is done casually, accidentally, and with little orientation.

We train and screen men for all professions except that of book reviewing. Anyone is allowed to write about books. The destructive consequences of this negligence are incalculable. Sincere friends have come to me with an armful of books of poetry saying: "But Anaïs, I don't know anything about poetry, and they have given me these to review." Another friend was made art critic for a fashionable magazine. He had no training in art but at least was honest enough to recognize this and proceeded to educate himself. We possess genuine writers in America but very few genuine, objective critics—very few indeed who follow Henry James's counsel: "The critic's task is to compare a work with its own concrete standard of truth."

My personal experience led me to uncover a great deal of prejudice, of cliques, of dictatorship, of commercial autocracy. A particular resistance to innovation, experiment, and adventurousness. And far more destructive than all of these, I found that arrogance of ignorance which made a reviewer, with a supreme confidence in his personal reaction, mock, deride, and annihilate whatever he did not understand.

All through my life, whenever I encountered something I did not understand, I questioned first my own limitation. When I first read Giraudoux, I felt he was verbose, tiresome. When I first read Proust, I felt the rhythm was too slow. But I never blamed them or turned away. I knew the deficency was in me. I tried again, and again, until I initiated myself to the extraordinary delights they can yield. I learned from them.

I wish reviewers who had never heard of surrealism, psychoanalysis, French literature, or international literature, had behaved in the same way. My advice to young writers is to disregard critics until one is mature enough to distinguish what is objective and what is subjective.

We have never realized that proper evaluation is one of the primary sources of education. The critic should be the intermediary, the interpreter. His personal likes and dislikes are of no value to anyone.

One critic, reviewing an old Japanese classic dealing with a prostitute in the fourteenth century, felt that, to begin with, she should not have become a prostitute! Another one admitted one book of fiction was far better written than another, but as the other dealt with a subject more pertinent to the latest political events in the newspapers, it should be given the place of honor.

Scientists are less exposed to this confusion of values because a minimum of professional knowledge is required to write about science.

The initial negligence is increased a thousandfold by the vicious system of chain reviews. Small newspapers unable to afford a reviewer of their own buy the reviews of syndicates, often shorten and quote them out of context, perpetuating careless statements.

If these newspapers and magazines really believe that the less tutored, trained, initiated will give a more *honest* opinion, they are in error. The outcome is merely a distortion, and a confusion of values.

Part of the reason for the importing of foreign writers (sometimes less interesting than our own) is that they arrive from France or other countries already properly analyzed, classified, and interpreted. The art of criticism is very highly developed in France. Books from France are skillfully evaluated with a constant interest in the innovators. When we do present a new novel to the American public, it is usually met with a barrage of hostilities until unanimously accepted by the number of its sales.

The young writer believes there is a *critic,* as there is a *God,* who will tell him if he is a great writer, who will decorate, bless, or damn him. But there is no such *absolute critic.* The wish for one is the expression of a need. We imagine someone else can tell us whether we are on the right path creatively. This would take a superhuman being. Critics have moods, frustrations, prejudices, limitations, blind spots. The first thing a young writer should ask himself when faced by a criticism is: "*Who* is this critic? What is the history of his adherences and partisanship? What political, racial, religious group does he belong to?"

No mature writer wants praise but accuracy of interpretation. To judge a new French novel, a surrealist novel, a fantasy, an impressionistic happening novel by the same standards applied to the classic nineteenth-century novel is certainly obtuse.

The concept of the infallible critic is childish. A critic has bad moods, subjective problems, neuroses, and a need to rationalize his personal likes or dislikes.

There is an even more serious problem which the young writer should clarify for himself from the beginning. There is a sharp distinction between commercial writing and literature. The publishers and the reviewers confuse the issues. Books go down the same chute, unclassified, and receive more or less the same wholesale evaluation. This confusion in handling and reviewing is both painful and sterile. We have writers equal in originality to the new French novelists, but we have no proper evaluations of them because we are, as a culture, intent on leveling rather than encouraging individual and original innovations. What we forget is that, just as the art film nourishes and renews the commercial film, experimental writing nourishes and renews the conventional novel and keeps it from going stale.

CHAPTER FOUR

Genesis

TRAUMATIC GENESIS: At nine years of age a medical diagnosis that I would never walk again turned me to writing as a pastime. The diagnosis was wrong. But I had settled on a means of expression and activity.

Artistic genesis: I chose writing. At eleven the diary was written to persuade my absent father to return, and the stories were written to entertain my brothers. The duality between fiction and diary writing seemed for a long time to be an insoluble conflict, but with maturity one learns the interaction between contraries.

In my own mind taking notes from reality and recording daily life faithfully seemed the opposite of inventing adventure stories. In talks with Henry Miller later on, he considered them not only as opposite activities but destructive and negating each other.

I did set them up in opposition, but I continued to work on both of them. The diary, being spontaneous and improvised, seemed far more pleasurable. The task of constructing fiction, more difficult.

What I believed was that, in making continuous portraits of people around me, I was making notes for fictionalized characters later on. It was not quite so simple.

Although the construction of fiction seemed on the surface to be a comparatively contrived act, an artificial process, yet it was not entirely so.

As I had learned from the diary writing to accept instant inspiration, I unconsciously applied this principle to fiction writing. While I was writing *Ladders to Fire*, I knew I wanted to bring all the characters together in some form of symbolic game. I admired the work of Martha Graham deeply. I found it full of meaning, rich in symbolism, and her way of expressing emotional dramas moved me far more than Greek tragedies. I found her way of dramatizing Medea far more beautiful than the Greek drama. I was so inspired by one of her dances that I went home and wrote the party scenes at the end of *Ladders to Fire*. To handle the characters which I had documented in the diary, I turned to symbolization for my fiction. I wanted to portray not the banal, usual party but the one I always described as the most unattended party in literature. I was describing not how people were at a party but how, when obsessed by other preoccupations, they were present on the surface but absent emotionally, psychologically *not* there. By symbolism I made the party transparent so you could see the inner drama as you might trace a fracture under an X ray. Symbolization is one process of rendering surface invisible in order to trace the emotional drama.

Human genesis: A character in the novel is always someone I have known and recorded in the diary. But the art of fiction makes composites, expands, extends, alters such a character. In the diary where I follow the development, growth, and ultimate climax, the life of a character develops more slowly in time. When I start a novel, I do not know yet what such and such a character has become. In the diary it takes ten, twenty, thirty years to follow the life of Henry Miller. In fiction time is accelerated. So a new concept of time takes over, and it becomes a different story.

But for the writer every daily experience feeds his work. When I became acquainted with the whole range of colors from my painter friends, I used color for the characters; when I became acquainted with spices, I used them to describe certain vividly flavored characters or relationships. In *Children of the Albatross* I wrote: "The strong spices of human relationship which bore a relation to black pepper, paprika, soy bean sauce, ketchup and red pepper." The realistic detail serves as an equivalent to describe a mood, person, situation. There is always a mixture of the natural and the symbolic to achieve psychological reality. I combine them constantly.

Today I describe this process as allowing the spontaneous image to come to the surface, trusting it, tracking down its symbolic significance.

When I was writing *Children of the Albatross*, I interrupted my work to take a walk. I walked through a snowstorm. When I returned, instead of continuing to work on the novel as I had intended, I felt like describing the snowstorm, the feeling of the mounds of snow, the silence, the glitter. I was annoyed at my own lack of concentration. But I obeyed the impulse. I wrote and wrote until by the very process of writing I achieved an image which corresponded more exactly to my description of adolescent "freeze" than a direct statement. I wanted an image of how adolescence feels: the frozen period, timidity, not yet melted by human life, frozen with fear, purity. From *Children of the Albatross* (pp. 33–35):

Walking through the snow, carrying her muff like an obsolete wand no longer possessed with the power to create the personage she needed, she felt herself walking through a desert of snow. Her body muffled in furs, her heart muffled like her steps, and the pain of living muffled as by the deepest rich carpets, while the thread of Ariadne which led everywhere, right and left, like scattered footsteps in the snow, tugged and pulled within her memory and she began to pull this thread (silk for the days of marvel and cotton for the bread of everyday living which was always a little stale) as one pulls upon a spool, and she heard the empty wooden spool knock against the floor of different houses. . . . The thread slipped through her fingers now, with blood on it, and the snow was no longer white. Too much snow on the spool she was unwinding from the tightly wound memories. Unwinding snow as it lay thick and hard around the edges of her adolescence because the desire of men did not find a magical way to enter her being. . . . The snow accumulated every night all around the rim of her young body. Blue and crackling snowbound adolescence. It was a fort of snow (for the snowbound, dream-swallowers of the frozen fairs). An unmeltable fort of timidity.

There is another example of spontaneous genesis in *Ladders to Fire*. I was nearly finished writing the novel when I was interrupted by a persistent memory. It was that of a garden I had seen through a window while listening to a concert. Again I mistook this for an irrelevant interruption and again was obliged to obey the haunting memory and write it down hoping to rid myself of it. So I did write it out fully. I had written the section called *This Hunger* up to the description of an impasse in the relationship between Jay and Lillian. The memory which came to the surface was that of a beautiful garden I saw while listening to a concert at the Rothchilds' house. It was as clear as a painting. The garden was very green; it had just been washed by a fine rain. It was almost as perfect as a Japanese garden. But what made a lasting impression on me was the strange touch of a three-faced mirror placed in the center of the garden. The incongruity of mirrors in a garden was striking, but such a scene only stirs a deep impression when it touches off some primitive recognition of a symbolic drama.

As I wrote on, about the woman pianist (Lillian was a pianist in the novel), about the real garden and its reflection in the mirror, I still wondered why the impression had been deep enough to last for years and why it should have come to the surface of my memory at this particular moment. It was only when I finished writing that I realized I had continued the story of *This Hunger* and completed it by giving the key to the book: the woman pianist playing with too much intensity was trying to divert a natural instinct (the need of a human child) into music. But the transmutation was not being made. The real garden represented nature, relaxed, fulfilled. The mirrors: neurosis, reflection, artifice, illusion. The mirrors in the garden were the perfect symbol of unreality and refraction, a miniature reproduction, in terms of images, of the drama I had been portraying of a conflict between nature and neurosis.

Psychoanalysis also gave me confidence in such free associations.

The creation of a story is a quest for meaning. The objects, the incidents, the characters are always there as they are for the painter, but the catalyst is the relation between the external and the internal drama. The significance of this relationship IS the drama. The meaning is what illumines the facts, coordinates them, incarnates them.

An example of this is the story called *Rag Time* from *Under a Glass Bell*. The diary merely gives a meticulous documentary, an exact description of the rag picker's village outside of Paris.

The city is Paris. The figure of the rag picker was a familiar one as he walked from trash can to trash can, picking objects and placing them in his brown potato sack. I reported faithfully what I saw. I described the village, the shacks, the laying out of objects, sorting them in order to sell them at the Flea Market. Documentary writing ends there. But that is where the poet begins his work, for the poet is by nature a transcendentalist: he sees the symbolic story. The discarded objects suggested a relation to the past, to what we all collect, hoard, or discard, lose, or throw away, according to our emotional relation to them. These objects are invested with emotional values, they are fragments of our lives which we wished either to conserve or to scatter. Fragments also suggested a broken and incomplete vision into our life, the rare glimpses of completion, the difficulties of achieving wholeness. The objects in the rag picker's bag are those we carry through life because of their meaning, or those we discarded in order to move into the future. They not only evoked our entire life, but we ourselves are like the rag picker gathering faces, impressions, images, to sort them, preserve them; we gather fragments and rarely possess a whole vision of our life. The external scene was welded to an emotional landscape, and now the story became one of our dramatic relationship to objects, to fragments. By symbolism we can integrate two worlds, dramatizing man in his relation to time, the past, to objects, and to death.

The story now has two dimensions instead of one.

Once I found myself in an ancient city of Guatemala. Everything around me was romantic, dramatic, picturesque. All the elements necessary to a story. A volcano, Mayan ruins, Mayan costumes, mysteriously silent people. Yet none of these compiled, tabulated, would create a story. They would only produce a travelogue. For three days I wandered through the city knowing I possessed no key to it, no story. Then I heard about a woman who had taken a sunbath on one of the terraces and had been attacked by a vulture. Following this, I observed the vultures, and the strange fact that there were no birds singing, that the extraordinary muteness of the air was what gave Antigua its static quality. The keynote of Antigua was death. Once I saw death as the theme of the city I captured other aspects of this death: the silence of the Indians, the cemetery quality of the ruins, the absence of plants at the foot of the volcano, the thick layers of ashes, and for the first time I saw similar characteristics in the strangers who lived there—a group of Americans who had achieved a static, arrested form of life.

Without the illumination from within I would have achieved nothing but a still life of Antigua. With this key—the psychological reality of a city—one can go as deeply as one wishes, and as far. Did the external semblance of death correspond to an internal one? What was the meaning of the Indians' silence? Their silence was like death, as if the volcanic eruption which had destroyed their beautiful city long ago had truly annihilated all life and buried the living as well. The people who lived there seemed also to have reached an impasse in their lives. They had broken with their past entirely. The theme of death could be developed to infinity, reaching back and forth in time, from the personal to the historical.

Psychoanalysis reversed the process of the conventional novel form. In the conventional novel, people were portrayed as they presented themselves from the outside; the persona was accepted as reality. In contrast an English psychiatrist, Dr. R. D. Laing, says in *Politics of Experience*: [14] "We all live in the hope that authentic meetings between human beings can still occur. Psychotherapy consists in the paring away of all that stands between us, the props, masks, roles, lies, defenses, anxieties, projections and introjections, in short, all the carry-over from the past, transference, and countertransference that we use by habit and collusion, wittingly or unwittingly, as our currency for relationships."

Long before this was written I had felt that this paring away was the role of the novelist, and if novels had seemed to die it was because they dealt, as D. H. Lawrence said, with dead symbols, dead matter expressed in dead language.

The conventional novel depicted character as a unity, already formed, while psychoanalysis studying the unconscious revealed the opposite, that character was fluctuating, relative, mutable, and asymmetrically developed, unevenly matured, with areas of rationality and areas of irrationality. I wanted to reveal not the fatality of character but its mysteries, its blocks, its negative aspects that interfered with fulfillment and relationship. I wanted to show neurosis as the villain, and the negative as the origin of our tragedies. That was why I focused on dreams, indicating where the secret self still existed, on the potential (which lovers can see in each other, and which is falsely called illusion). I became interested in the secret patterns rather than in the obvious ones (environment or history or races). I could see very early what was later to be made common in *Games People Play* and in Dr. Timothy Leary's more subtle analysis that it was these games which became the fatal traps in which we lost our lives, our living, genuine, sincere, authentic selves.

My depicting of these symbolic, abstract games caused a humorous reaction. The critics stated they were not only dreamlike, but that they *were* dreams. Because so much of the usual upholstery and construction was left out, because they were written like happenings, improvisations, they judged the entire work as *unreal*.

This was somewhat like denying the reality of Modigliani's elongated women, Picasso's asymmetrical faces with four sides to them, or Miró's circus.

But I felt reality lay at the bottom of these subterranean worlds. I could see the psychic games taking place beneath appearances. I could read the unconscious motivations as doctors read X rays.

In *Children of the Albatross* (pp. 160–61) two young homosexuals have an apparently unimportant argument:

"Michael," said Donald, "today I would like to go to the zoo and see the new weasel who cried so desperately when she was left alone."

Michael thought: How human of him to feel sympathy for the weasel crying in solitude in his cage. And Donald's sympathy for the weasel encouraged him to say tenderly: "Would you cry like that if you were left alone?"

"Not at all," said Donald, "I wouldn't mind at all. I like to be alone. Anyhow, what I like best in the zoo is not the weasel, it's the rhinoceros with his wonderful tough hide."

Michael felt inexplicably angry that Donald should like the rhinoceros and not the weasel. That he should admire the toughness of the rhinoceros skin as if he were betraying him, expressing the wish that Michael should be less vulnerable.

In the same book (p. 85) there is a scene between Djuna, the mature woman, and Paul the adolescent:

On the table there was a huge vase filled with tulips. She moved towards them, seeking something to touch, to pour her joy into, out of the exaltation she felt. Every part of her body that had been opened by his hands yearned to open the whole world in harmony with her mood.

She looked at the tulips so hermetically closed like secret poems, like the secrets of the flesh. Her hands took each tulip, the ordinary tulip of every day living and she slowly opened them, petal by petal, opened them tenderly.

They were changed from plain to exotic flowers, from closed secrets to open flowering.

Then she heard Paul say: "Don't do that!"

There was great anxiety in his voice. He repeated: "Don't do that!"

She felt a great stab of anxiety. Why was he so disturbed?

She looked at the flowers. She looked at Paul's face lying on the pillow, clouded with anxiety, and she was struck with fear. Too soon. She had opened him to love too soon. He was not ready.

I would suggest to young writers the study of all of William Goyen's books, for a poetry born of the earth and which welds the physical world to the emotional world. In his writing the two are perfectly synchronized, flesh and emotion, dream and human experience. He is not only a writer who has given style to folk speech, elegance to colloquial expressions, but vivified his style with rhythmic, lyrical imagery. His style flows; he can summon an atmosphere and create an entirely magic world deepened by an undercurrent of sorrow. In *House of Breath* he writes: [15]

You were my first river in the country of childhood and when I discovered you, from a hill in a blue, early morning, I saw you whispering along through the woods murmuring history. Think of me then (was what you were singing) when I had never had a boat upon me or any net thrown or seine dipped into me, flowing only with moonlight or sunlight and all my swimming and breathing things within my womb (and such things as Charity never existed); and of my floods which I had (and caused no dikes to be made nor any human alarm, only the terror of creatures who knew the visits, and endured them, of catastrophes and built rushnests again, afterwards, moved eggs in time or their young away), rolling over on to the bottomlands where I lay heavy and large and pressing upon them. And then when it was time, folded back again over upon myself, a shrunken, lighter lover, and fell back to my size and place and ran on again, in repose, to my bay. What I left upon the bottomlands all I could see—I left my sand in bars and wrote my designs and crystal shapes upon them and then bird's feet made their marks with mine and paws of animals theirs and snakes made smooth, crooked, wiped places with their bellies (what man first found these and asked me what they meant?) and what I left on the bottomlands anyone could have; but I fertilized the land with my sperm of fishes' bones and algae and left crawfish and swollen rats and wooden cattle and all my lavish and manifold plankton, my mulch. Everything flows into everything and carries with it and within it all lives of its life and others' life and all is a murmuring and whispering of things changing into each other, breeding and searching and reaching and withdrawing and dying. Whatever crossing is made each over other, by boat or bridge or swimming, is to another side; and whatever drowning is dying and sinking back into a womb, and what salvation or rescue of the perishing in waters or wickedness, dead or alive, is a union, of silence or rejoicing; and to drop down into any of us into depths (in river or self or well or cellar) is to lower into sorrow and truth. But we are purged, to plunge beneath a flood is to lose all guilty stains and to rise is to be purified. And we are to keep turning the wheels we turn, we are wind we are water we are yearning; we are to keep rising and falling, hovering at our own marks, then falling, then rising. (Who can set a mark or measure us? They cannot name my tides or measure me by the marks drawn on a wall; I hover.

ON D. H. LAWRENCE

The specific genesis of each book is a complex story. Although I was living in Paris, the first writer whose influence I felt immediately, whom I took as a model, and wrote my first study about, was D. H. Lawrence. I wrote about him (p. 13): "The world D. H. Lawrence created cannot be entered through the exercise of one faculty alone: there must be a threefold desire of intellect, of imagination, and of physical feeling, because he erected his world on a fusion of concepts, on a philosophy that was against division, on a plea for whole vision: 'to see with the soul and the body.' For the world he takes us into is shadowed, intricate. It is 'ultimately chaos, lit up by visions, or not lit up by visions.' "

He affected me deeply. He was working from an instinctive, intuitive source. He opened fascinating ways of describing relationships. I felt he opened the way for a vision which could be developed and carried even further. He fused conscious and unconscious, emotion and the senses: as one can see in this description in *Twilight in Italy*:

I went into the Church. It was very dark. . . . My senses were roused, they sprang awake in the hot spiced darkness. My skin was expectant, as if it expected some contact, some embrace, as if it were aware of the contiguity of the physical world, the physical contact with the darkness and the heavy suggestive substance of the enclosure. It was a thick, fierce darkness of the senses.

Frederick Hoffman wrote of D. H. Lawrence:

> Lawrence sensed a definite danger that the novel might deaden the
> senses and simply present dead matter persisting in a dead world. But
> if it is handled as a live portrait it is at once the artist's most fluid
> medium and his best opportunity to convey to the world the mean-
> ing of the world, "the changing rainbow of our living relationships."
> How can creative art accomplish this? Life is so fluid that one can
> only hope to capture the living moment, to capture it alive and fresh
> —not the ordinary moment of an ordinary day but the critical mo-
> ment of human relationships. How to capture this oscillation within
> the prison of cold print, without destroying that movement?

At first I was not aware that this is the very thing I had learned
to do unconsciously by way of the diary, by writing spontaneously and improvising, selecting only what interested me and
without censorship or formal control. I thought at first of the
diary as the enemy of fiction; I did realize it was the depository
of the living moments and that because of it I would become
adept at distinguishing dead writing from live writing. The word
"aliveness" appears so often in D. H. Lawrence's work, and I
adopted it as a touchstone.

Defending and explaining D. H. Lawrence then gave me
my own orientation. I was planning my course. As a critic I also
took a stand: "The business of the mind is first and foremost the
pure joy of knowing and comprehending, the pure joy of consciousness."

It is not a bad sign for a young writer to choose a model, for
if this choice is genuine, it indicates an affinity and helps the
young writer to find where he stands. I find young writers today
too eager to disclaim any influences, to pay any homage to those
who helped them set their course, as if ashamed of their literary
parents. I have no desire to claim that as a writer I was born in
a cabbage patch. I owe my formative roots to D. H. Lawrence,
Marcel Proust, Djuna Barnes, and the novels of Jean Giraudoux
and Pierre Jean Jouve. I was influenced by Rimbaud and the
surrealists.

D. H. Lawrence was the most important influence because he sought a language for instinct, emotion, and intuition, the most inarticulate part of ourselves. Also from Lawrence I learned that naked truth is unbearable to most, and that art is our most effective way of overcoming human resistance to truth.

The genesis of *House of Incest* was in the dream. The keeping of dreams was an important part of that exploration of the unconscious. But I discovered dreams in themselves, isolated, were not always interesting. Very few of them had the complete imagery and tension to arouse others' interest. They were fragmented. The surrealists delighted in the image themselves. This was satisfying to the painters and to the film-makers. But to the novelist concerned with human character dramas, they seemed ephemeral and vaporous. They had to be connected with life. It was psychoanalysis which revealed to me the constant interaction of dream and action. It was a phrase of Jung's which inspired me to write *House of Incest*. He said: *"Proceed from the dream outward."* In other words, it was essentially a matter of *precedence*. To capture the drama of the unconscious, one had to start with the key, and the key was the dream. But the novelist's task was to pursue this dream, to unravel its meaning; the goal was to reach the relation of dream to life; the suspense was in finding this which led to a deeper significance of our acts.

Meanwhile a batch of dreams kept for a year served as a take-off for *House of Incest*. They supplied the atmosphere, its climate and texture. At the same time I discovered that the dream had to be expanded, recreated, could not be told literally for then it became as flat and one-dimensional as representational realism. One had to find a language for it, a way of describing atmosphere, the colors and textures in which it moved.

Henry Miller was writing *Into the Night Life* while I was writing *House of Incest*.

The same arguments about the difficulties of rendering dream atmosphere came up later when I talked with underground film-makers. Maya Deren argued that the atmosphere of dreams was exactly similar to reality, that dreams should be reproduced with utmost literalness and simplicity. I maintained that there was no resemblance at all, that the dream was incomplete, abstract, suggestive, atmospheric and could only be rendered by metamorphosis, by magic alchemy of poetic images. This literalness may be the cause today of so many failures in describing the LSD experiences. They need to be handled by a poet, painter, or filmmaker who is capable of metamorphosis and alchemy to convey magic and visions and sensations.

In *Winter of Artifice* I tried to describe the atmosphere of dreams.

The dream taught me not only the delight of sensory images, but the fact, far more vital, that they led directly into this realm of the unconscious which Joyce, Virginia Woolf, and Proust attained in various ways—Joyce by free association with words, play on words, Proust by trusting the free associative process of memory and staying lingeringly in the realm between sleep and waking which resembles the waking dream, Virginia Woolf by accepting the vision of the poet as reality.

House of Incest was, like a poem, visionary symbolic dream sequences which were woven together. At this point I could not separate the authentic dreams from the imaginary takeoffs which developed from them. The dreams were the key. Once you turn this key, psychological reality is as clear as the surface reality, and one follows wherever it leads. It runs parallel to the mechanism of creation. One image or memory triggers improvisations and elaborations which are finally related to life.

To distinguish between a sleeping dream and a waking dream, fantasy and imagination would not be valuable. The important thing is to cultivate, develop, utilize dreams creatively, for they are the nourishment for the imagination as well as the source of revelation. For example, a phrase like "my first vision of earth was water veiled," is not as important to analyze as it is to observe the fact that water unleashed a flood of images. Recurrent dreams of boats, ocean, sea bottoms, Atlantis. The important thing is to find the image which liberates, unleashes one's unconscious responses. This is temperamentally different. Gaston Bachelard, a French philosopher, wrote several books, each one devoted to the study of poetics: *Poetics of Space, Poetics of Fire, Poetics of Water, Poetics of Air*. He observes how each poet usually stresses one of these symbols at the expense of others. He analyzes poetry in this manner. This classification is inspiring, indicating that we have to find our own element. Mine is undeniably Water. Now the ocean is admittedly a universal symbol for the unconscious. In reality I am drawn to the sea and to ships, and I would have become a scuba diver in reality. Physical limitations thwarting that, I have to be contented with diving deep into the psyche. In fantasy I felt people could communicate through vibrations of intuition, through antennae rather than verbally. According to Dr. Otto Rank, some of these fantasies are "return to the womb" fantasies, where there was neither cold nor heat nor pain nor consciousness. I describe such a fantasy in *House of Incest* (p. 17): "Far below the level of storms I slept. There were no currents of thought, only the caress of flow and desire mingling, touching, traveling, withdrawing—the endless bottoms of peace." The legend of the sunken Atlantis appealed to me for two reasons: The Atlanteans were said to be the inventors of music, and to communicate by way of intuition.

In *House of Incest* I placed myself within the dream itself, but guided by Jung's words to "proceed from the dream outward," I describe at the end the desire of the dreamers to find the way out, into life, into daylight. The dream was to be the genesis, the birthplace of our life. The novels were to be the constant description of going into life and back into the dream to seek the self when it lost its way. In a sense, I continued to say: the dream is the key, the source, the birthplace of our most authentic self.

The poet, or the novelist who writes poetically, is what Antonin Artaud called the *voyant*. The seer. He has merely found a way to shut out the appearance of things and concentrate on the invisible, life of spirit and emotion. The psyche. The surrealists closed their eyes and practiced automatic writing. Blind to the world that distracts, in order to see *beyond* and *above* reality. I used the image of the bottom of the sea to concretize the existence of a subconscious life. Under the surface inevitably brings up an image of subterranean oceans. Marguerite Young in her epic novel, *Miss MacIntosh, My Darling*, refers many times to the characters' drowning. They submerge into the life of dream, fantasy. Sleep, dreams have a way of suggesting sinking away, sinking deep away from the realm of surface we live in. I never thought of it as literal drowning but as a sinking into a nocturnal world below the control of consciousness.

The poet and painter and film-maker can take their images from fragments of memories of dreams, segments of dreams, but some *reconstruction*, some weaving, some metamorphosis must take place. The concept of a sunken cathedral inspired Debussy with different sounds than those he heard from the real cathedrals of France. The dream itself is incomplete, and we have to fish it from the deeps and reconstruct its meaning. But all imagination is a dream. Einstein, when asked where his ideas came from, answered: "I play with images."

The poet in a poem does not say: you are now entering the dream world, a fantasy, a symbolic drama. He is not expected to give a clue. When you read a poem, you expect a transposition. But the novelist is often asked to give a clue. Kafka, Lautréamont, and the surrealists did not give such indications. Because their contention is that they are not separate, that we actually live by superimpositions of conscious and unconscious. Freud proved this scientifically. The artist knew it all the time.

I liked describing at times the bridges and passageways between the two worlds. That was before I really believed that they were fused, and out of fear of blurring the boundaries, a fear I shared with many, I wanted to keep the geography very distinct. Proust did describe many times the in-between states, the passageways between sleep, dream, and waking dream. In *House of Incest* I state: "This Atlantis could be found again only at night, by the route of the dream." That is a conscious statement, as a traveler will make note along his explorations: this is the way I came; then I made a turn to the left, etc. The people who turned to LSD for such experiences recorded these waking moments of consciousness, reported "going in and out" of the dreams, visions, hallucinations. The poet will do this when he seeks to fuse the unconscious with the conscious.

We have feared the writers who do not chart the routes because we have an erroneous idea that to let go of reality is to let go of sanity. That would be like saying that Cousteau, when he went down to the bottom of the sea with oxygen, was losing his life on earth. The need for clues and demarcations comes from anxiety. In many dreams we are fully aware that we are dreaming. The interplay between subconscious and conscious is natural as long as the conscious does not play the role of censor. The fear of being cut off from reality by indulging in the imagination, in reverie or fantasy is neurotic. Every creator and every inventor goes into uncharted realms.

It is the combination of these elements which ends in a symphonic theme. Some images in *House of Incest* are taken from dreams, some from reality (the number of windows in my house in Louveciennes), but they are used in combination to describe subtle states of being. I did know a house which had small windows between the rooms, so the people who lived in it could communicate with each other, but this only achieved meaningfulness as an image when it became an image of Jeanne's communicating with her brothers and not with outsiders. You make physical images stand for meaning, for an invisible drama. Later on, in *Seduction of the Minotaur*, I used the scientific image of the distance between planets, moon, and earth to represent the distance between human beings trying to relate to each other, to communicate with each other.

In *House of Incest* I treated the theme of exchange of personalities, as Bergman did later in the film *Persona*. Sabina and the writer of the poem are in constant danger of identifying with each other and *becoming the other*. In Bergman's film the actress who suddenly refused to talk and the nurse who desperately sought to break her silence by talking to her, entrusting her with her life, looked like each other, became confused identities.

People have associated the principles of psychoanalysis with neurosis, illness. But it was while studying the illness of the heart that we became aware of the function of the normal heart. The principles, the method, the technique of psychoanalysis can be adapted to the novel not merely to describe neurosis but unneurotic characters. It is based on the assumption that the truth about character is relative, fluctuating, that the concept of unity, consistency, or finality is dead. This was easy for me to accept because I had my diary in which I traced the character of people for a long time and recorded changes, recorded a different aspect for each relationship. The diary taught me that there were no neat ends to novels, no neat denouement, no neat synthesis. That in life character changed with experience and continued to grow, expand, and modify itself. There was no finality but death. The conventional novel created artificial ends, climaxes. So becoming aware of this, I began an endless novel, a novel in which the climaxes consisted of discoveries in awareness, each step in awareness becoming a stage in the growth like the layers in trees.

I was trying to carry the characters along a long span of time, as long as the diary span; but dealing with the subconscious, I naturally arrived at the psychoanalytical concept that the subconscious is timeless. The past, present, and future are constantly interacting. The description of a childhood in chronological order is boring. The description of the dynamic moment at which this childhood acts upon the present, either destructively or creatively, is what Lawrence would have described as heightened moments of living. These are the moments of drama.

I always begin with a *real* character, with someone I know well. This gives me the human reality, certain roots in reality. After that I begin the pursuit of the persona behind the façade, assuming that all of us do present to the world (and the novelist) a prepared, arranged, controlled image. A human being is a person but also a symbol, a representation of other human beings. Spending less time on the familiar details, the job, the house, the habits, the car, the opening and closing of doors, the upholstery given in most novels, emphasizes certain traits. It is not an abstraction. It is an intense focus on the psychological substructure. Watching for *other* signs than what Sabina wore, or said, or worked at, I found different revelatory details: her rhythm, her colors, her obsessional words, idiosyncracies. *Other clues.* Assuming that perhaps her apartment, her clothes, her speech were not necessarily significant, might have been accidental and not selective.

The genesis of *Children of the Albatross* was again based on a real character, a young man of seventeen who became for me a representation of adolescent fear. He was inarticulate. I used the wordless language of the ballet to be able to render his timidities, his swift exits, his evasions, his pirouettes. The ballet served as an image of adolescent timorousness, light-footedness, disappearances. Paul had tremendous fears, of life, love, art, everything. It made him oscillate, be ambivalent, elusive. Starting from the ballet, I followed many images which seemed to express adolescence, or at least Paul's. The luminosity of youth, the phosphorescence one sees in children and young people, suggested the albatross. I had been reading about the albatross in a scientific journal. The sailors hesitated to kill them and only did so when utterly starving. The albatross followed ships. The legend of their metaphysical quality may have sprung from the fact that the sailors, after killing them, found their entrails phosphorescent. Phosphorescence and flight. All this grew into equivalents for Paul, means of describing a most elusive state of mind. I had observed that children seemed to lose this luminousness. In Paul it was quite striking. He had a glow and a tendency to take flight in the face of life, of emotion, and of his own dreams.

Another inspiration taken from science was information about birds. "Birds live their lives with an intensity as extreme as their

brilliant colors and their vivid songs. The reserve air tanks pro-
vide fuel for the bird's intensive life and at the same time add
to its buoyancy in flight." This I used for the theme of adolescence.

A scientific image can trigger off metaphors, as well as dreams.
Part of the novelist's richness comes from how much he as-
similates, observes, registers from all the sources. A new word,
a new bit of information—all is nourishment. Anything I see,
hear. Science could enrich our symbolism but requires technical
knowledge and is partly inaccessible to the layman. Science is
full of concrete images which could serve to represent an abstract psychological truth. For example, when film-makers talk
of superimposition of images, everyone understands. One film
exposed over another. Double exposure. When I speak of this
happening constantly in our unconscious, it sounds abstract and
mysterious (we may fall in love with a face simply because it
bears some resemblance to another face we once did love). I
like images from science because they are very concrete. I have
often spoken of the mathematics of emotion. For example, the
fragmentation of the personality (which always existed but which
we have become more aware of in an analytic culture) can be
analogous to the fission of energy. Proust's fragmentation might
have been compared to the microscope, the effect of intense examination of an act causing this magnification of events.

It was a misunderstanding to stress the dreamlike quality of the
novels. What I meant to stress was the interrelation between
dream and life, between dream and action.

Deena Metzger understood this better than Edmund Wilson.
In writing about *Collages,* she said: [16]

There are some who believe that the work of Anaïs Nin is dreamlike, that her subjects and images are from the dream life. They have
repeated themselves until they have created a myth. They say this
because they are afraid of her language. She is too sensual for them
and she tells too many truths. Like a character in her book they
would like to gather together "all the linen of the house stained with
marks of love, dreams, nightmares, tears and kisses and quarrels, the

mists that rise from bodies touching, the fogs of breathing, the dried tears, and take it to the laundromat. . . ." They wash her work in make-believe, in dreams. But if her stories are not real, then nothing is. In their reality is their meaning and their strength. For although *Collages* is a novel about people with dreams they are people who are connected to the world through a thousand sensual links and whose dreams are made manifest by a multiplicity of acts and gestures. *Collages* is premised on the observation that there is a symbolic relationship between a person's inner life and his gestures. The secret thoughts and dreams of the characters spill out through their fingers and define them. The secret lives are dramatized. The barriers between the outer and inner selves have fallen away.

I always wanted to write a free book, a book as light and as humorous as the paintings of Paul Klee, Joan Miró, the collages of Jean Varda.

The ponderous, premeditated designs of novels always oppressed me. Most novels always tried to include everything, like crowded thrift shops.

FELLINI'S 8 ½

For years I collected sketches of characters. I noticed that in life (in the diary) they moved in a more fragmentary way than characters move in novels. They appeared in my life, disappeared, traveled, and all I knew of them were these quick, vivid appearances. But such a book, treating the mobility of characters, did not catalyze in my mind until I saw Fellini's film *8 ½*. The story of the film is that of a director surrounded by producers, writers, actors in search of a role. Friends, associates, wife and mistresses, all are waiting for him to film a story with a plot, a beginning, a middle, and an end, and a role for each of them.

The director hides behind dark glasses, and is busy eluding their questions, their conventional expectations. We are taken not only into what goes on around him but also what goes on in his mind and in his private life. He has love affairs, difficulties with his wife, actors waylay him and tell him their life stories in an effort to make themselves interesting to him. There are parties going on, rehearsals. But the real story, the real humor and drama lie in the telling of this situation, the impatience of the producer, the behavior of the actors eager to display their talent, the hack writer saying: "But you have no plot."

The director throws away their scripts. He lets things happen. He loves, dreams, remembers his childhood, has love affairs, has love fantasies, scenes with his wife. We see the various relationships and the richness of his memories and of his thoughts which do not fit into the film he is supposed to be making. But *we* see them, casually, accidentally, spontaneously; we see spontaneous life opening instead of a cliché plot. A brilliant theme comes to life and a complete story, not the one in the film but the story of the director's life. The confusion and the paradoxical relation between what is going on in his mind and memory, and what is going on around him creates high comedy, and on a deeper level, an insight which the standard plot would never have given us. Before our eyes the director reveals his unconscious story to which others are blind, thinking he is impotent and uncreative.

Fellini himself said: [17]

When I was a kid in Rimini, I used to go to the movies as much as I could. My heroes were Tom Mix, George O'Brien, Wallace Beery and others. What fascinated me was that I thought these actors made the film stories by themselves, as they went along, deciding how they were going to make the movie, depending on what they felt like doing. Only later did I discover there was such a thing as a director, but I've never been able to get over the desire to make films in the way I thought Tom Mix had: *without knowing at the beginning* how they would come out exactly and having all the fun I could in the meantime. A script is a give away. It's like putting all your cards on the table at the beginning of a game. It would not only make it impossible to cheat in such a game, it wouldn't be a game at all! And in a sense film-making for me is a game, but an extremely serious one, a game in which I take all the risks.

When a film makes such a strong impression on you, it means it has an internal resonance, it means an important part of your mind is tuning in to the theme of the film. I was carried away by the free, imaginative game with characters, its casual, highly comical improvisations, its freedom. Characters appeared sometimes for one minute, had their say, and yet were not forgotten. The message was: let things happen, trust chance, spontaneity, improvisation, and the pattern and meaning will emerge at the end. The man who had nothing to say (in the conventional sense), who could not pull together his actors with a plot, was giving us, unconsciously, an unusual story of his life and of himself as a director.

The process of creativity is this daring escape from conventional patterns, not because they are conventional but because they are dead, used up.

In writing *Collages* I allowed myself to live out a mood and see what it would construct. Once the mood is accepted, the mood makes the selection, the mood will give fragments a unity, the mood will be the catalyzer. And so this book, which should have been a novel or another book of short stories, became something else, a collage.

The mood of a book is like the personality of a human being. It draws to itself what belongs to it. As soon as my mood was set, the pieces began to fall into place.

It is a fact that the unconscious always selects the images which will exteriorize, concretize its vision of the world. Leave it free and it will bring you all the images you need.

Collages began with an image which had haunted me. A friend, Renate, had told me about her trip to Vienna where she was born, and of her childhood relationships to statues. She told me stories of her childhood, her relationship to her father, her first love.

I begin the novel with:

Vienna was the city of statues. They were as numerous as the people who walked the streets. They stood on the top of the highest towers, lay down on stone tombs, sat on horseback, kneeled, prayed, fought animals and wars, danced, drank wine and read books made of stone. They adorned cornices like the figureheads of old ships. They stood in the heart of fountains glistening with water as if they had just been born. They sat under the trees in the parks summer and winter. Some wore costumes of other periods, and some no

clothes at all. Men, women, children, kings, dwarfs, gargoyles, uni-
corns, lions, clowns, heroes, wise men, prophets, angels, saints, and
soldiers preserved for Vienna a vision of eternity.

As a child Renate could see them from her bedroom window. At
night, when the white muslin curtains fluttered out like ballooning
wedding dresses, she heard them whispering like figures which had
been petrified by a spell during the day and came alive only at night.
Their silence by day taught her to read their frozen lips as one reads
the messages of deaf mutes. On rainy days their granite eye sockets
shed tears mixed with soot.

Renate would never allow anyone to tell her the history of the
statues, or to identify them. This would have situated them in the
past. She was convinced that people did not die, they became statues.
They were people under a spell and if she were watchful enough
they would tell her who they were and how they lived now.

If I had been asked then what was going to follow the description of the statues, I could not have answered. I was fascinated by the image of these many statues and of the child
Renate inventing stories about them and dialoguing with them.
It may have been that this image expressed the feeling I often had
that people appear to us as a one-dimensional statue until we go
deeper into their life history. People *are* like mute statues under
a spell of *appearance*, and static, until we let them whisper their
secrets. And this only happens at night. That is, when we are
able to dream, imagine, and explore the unconscious. We see
the external self. Because *Collages* took its images from painting
and sculpture, I liked the idea that sculpture and painting could
become animated, speaking, confessing, and then in daylight returning to their previous forms as statues or paintings. They
spoke only to the artist. To me it meant dramatizing our relation
to art, one feeding the other, the interrelation between human
beings and the artist's conception of them. In daylight (consciousness) we catch them all only in one attitude, one form. At
night we discover their lives.

I made Renate the hub of *Collages* because her personality is
mobile and receptive. She turns her whole attentiveness toward
the people who enter her life. She is a turnstile, a turntable, seek-

ing the meaning of inanimate and animate objects equally. She is also the one who relates to everyone. She focuses on them while they are there. When they vanish again we have already perceived as much of them as others might perceive in a lifetime.

They are magnetized by her presence. She brings them to life (statues become people). Renate, being the painter, exemplifies the way in which the world we carry within us can be projected into art and speak through art. The statues, once cast, speak their history. Renate's sense of connection and relationship extends to animals. *Collages*, p. 39:

"When she was a child she felt that she had been born in the world to rescue all the animals. She was concerned with the bondage and slavery of animals, the donkey on the treadmills in Egypt, the cattle traveling in trains, chickens tied together by the legs, rabbits being shot in the forest, dogs on leashes, kittens left starving on the sidewalks. She made several attempts to rescue them. . . . It was only when she reached the age of fourteen that she realized the hopelessness of her task. Cruelty extended too far. . . . So she began to paint the friendship of women and animals."

Reading the lips of statues prepared her to understand an inarticulate young man. Loving animals made her a painter of animals equal to Rousseau. Art always came to the rescue as the alchemy which enriched life.

In my other novels I studied interrelationships of all kinds. In *Collages* I concentrated on dreamers who had a strong core of fantasy, who lived out this fantasy and did not crash (the common notion is that all dreamers are bound to crash). These dreamers had the power to make their dreams concrete. I also showed the power of these fantasies to generate what the poet Gérard de Nerval called a "second life." The power of these dreams kept them afloat. It also kept them, at times, from communicating with others. Sometimes, as in the case of Nina, the fantasy is so intricate that it isolates her from contact with other human beings. She dreams alone. But Renate, who could read the lips of statues, can interpret her dream and reach her. What Nina says could be interpreted as one interprets a poem:

"My name is Nina Gitana de la Primavera. But these are my winter names. I change with the seasons. When the Spring comes I no longer need to be Primavera. I leave that to the season. I am waiting for Manfred, but he is not coming. 'Who is Manfred?' Man-Fred is the man I am going to love. He may not yet be born. I have often loved men who are not yet born."

Nina goes to a play and takes a brown paper bag with her. "During the play there was a scene at a dining table. The actors sat around talking and eating. At this point Nina opened her brown paper bag, took out a sandwich and a pickle and began to eat in unison with the actors. She whispered to Renate: 'The audience should not just watch actors eat. They should eat with them. They will feel less lonely.'"

INTERPRETATION OF SYMBOLIC ACTS

People who do not translate their symbolic acts for others, who live out the unconscious *as the unconscious lives* it, in symbolic form, are unable to communicate their meaning to others, unless they know the language of symbolism. The poet, the artist, the writer (like Renate) who understand what Nina means (we should be identified with the actors, we should be *with it*, we should show somehow that we are part of the play and players) should be able to interpret the language of dreamers, symbolic acts, as we interpret poems or the plays of Ionesco and Beckett. Usually such Walter Mitty fantasies are not acted out. When they are, we call it madness simply because they have not been controlled and translated by the rational mind. Renate can translate her own symbolic acts. She can rationalize them. She can utilize them for painting. We could expand our consciousness, our experience if we learned this language which the psychologists learned to interpret. For every human being contains some fantasy revealed in his dreams, which he does not always confide. In *Collages* I portray the Negro girl who dreams of living the life of Josephine Baker and marrying a French count, the French chef who is lonely because people do not know how to talk poetically about his works of art, his soufflé and his crepe suzette. I describe Count Laundromat running his washing machine while remembering his parents' dusty castle, marrying a pseudo queen, queen of Rheingold Beer. One story concerns a woman who seeks to marry a man resembling T. E. Lawrence.

Such fantasies are common but usually kept secret. Varda the painter creates his own mythical world with his scissors and cloth. His daughter can only share its joyousness and spirit with the help of drugs.

Collages expresses the truth that each person possesses a rich interior world which we are unable to share because we do not take the trouble to explore it. The writer who should be our guide fails when he sees each person only from the outside *as a statue.*

As I put all these people together, they had a chemical effect on each other. At first I did not know what to do with them, as Fellini did not know what to do with his actors. All I had was a series of dreamers, each one in his own cell, in each cell a jewel. I played with their relationships to each other, as one does with a kaleidoscope. I told the story *as they told it.* I offered no translation. I let them appear, disappear. The theme developed by accretion. I placed the separate fragments as Varda places his materials for a collage. I described a woman novelist, Judith Sands, who had withdrawn from life because she felt she had written about people who did not exist. When someone comes to see her who insists that he is one of her "characters," she opens the door (p. 114–15):

"Dear Judith Sands, I know you do not like strangers but . . . I am no stranger because in a sense you gave birth to me. I feel you once described a man who was ME before I knew who I was, and it was because I recognized him that I was able to be myself. You will recognize me when you see me. Remember this, it is good for a writer to meet with the incarnation of a character he has invented. It gives him an affirmation, a substantial proof of his intuitions, divinations."

The separate characters, separate fragments, separate fantasies, which seemed at first accidentally thrown together, begin to form a pattern. At the end of the book all the characters watch a machine that destroys itself. The artist, Tinguely, may have been expressing a wish that machines should commit suicide, but I interpret the spectacle of a crowd solemnly watching a pile of junkyard stuff committing suicide as a satire of the artist more interested in dramatizing destruction than creation. The climate of the day is negative.

"I thought only dreamers destroyed themselves."

The dreamers can create.

The book *Collages* is written.

In Deena Metzger's words: [18]

The book ends with the collision of two artists. One is Tinguely, the creator of the Machine That Destroys Itself—the suicide machine. He is the 20th Century artist who has become so preoccupied with death and destruction, with ashcans and junkyards that he contradicts himself by perpetuating them in art. He establishes his machine at the museum and initiates its devastation. For a moment it seems the suicide is about to fail. He kicks it towards destruction. This action is observed by Judith Sands. It wrenches her from a self-imposed solitude. The havoc generates her own creativity. She is compelled to allow her own creation to re-enter the world. She reads from her manuscript: "Vienna was the city of statues." In art is reflected our conflicts, and the capacity of our imagination to influence reality.

The genesis of a book can be a complex of elements. In the case of *Ladders to Fire* it was a fascination with certain characters I had portrayed faithfully in *The Diary* but whom I wanted to place in different experiences, different situations, weave into composites, expand or prolong or transform to serve another pattern. Faithfulness to life I sometimes found limiting. In life I could not see the complete development of a character's destiny. In fiction I could use imagination. At the time I began *Ladders to Fire*, I felt ready for a longer work, a more developed interrelation between the characters and between the cities of Paris and New York. Keeping to the habit of writing only of heightened moments, of what interested me, and practicing a kind of impressionism, I ran into some difficulties which were pointed out by the critics. I made what is called today in the film world "jump cutting." I was impatient with transitions and with construction. My defense was always that there are such unexplained transitions in Proust. In one volume the hero arrives at the conclusion that he never loved Odette, that she was not his "type," and in the next volume several years later he is married to her. This defense did not impress my critics or would-be publishers. They expected the perfect chronology and design of the conventional novel. They did not realize that what I sought was something like life, living, and that to keep this freshness I had to keep the pattern of life itself which was capricious, interrupted, sometimes incomplete. And the heightened moments, in Lawrence's own words, the moments of crisis in human relationship, were more important. The rest could be easily deduced. I was working very much in a way which paralleled the sparse stage setting of the modern theater.

I did not realize at the time that the novel would be continuous, that the habit of following characters for years in the diary would influence my novels, and that I would want to develop them through long periods and many incidents. All I knew was that I began with real persons and they changed and became transformed by imagination along the way.

The first part of *Ladders to Fire* was titled *This Hunger* and is clear enough. The second part was named *Bread and the Wafer* to indicate physical and metaphysical fulfillment of the hunger. I was interested at the time in clarifying what prevented people from living, from loving, from immersion in experience. I was more and more seduced by what took place behind the scene. I worked on themes, and like a musical theme, carried it as far as I could until it was completely expressed. I improvised. I trusted my unconscious. The design came from the free association, a psychological chain forming itself in a way which the intellect is unable to construct or to reach. Reversing the belief in action, I proved that presence, action, were not necessarily real. The party dramatized this concept. Everyone was there, but this was realism and not reality. For they were absent by their preoccupations and obsessions and lack of contact with each other. From *Ladders to Fire* (p. 146):

Deserts of mistrust. The houses are no longer hearths, they hang like mobiles turning to the changing breeze while they love each other like ice skaters on the top layers of their invented selves, blinded with the dust of attic memories, within the windowless houses of their fears. In each studio there is a human being dressed in the full regalia of his myth fearing to expose a vulnerable opening, spreading not his charms but his defenses, plotting to disrobe, somewhere along the night—his body without the aperture of the heart or his heart with a door closed to his body. Thus keeping one compartment for refuge, one uninvaded cell.

This section ends with: ". . . her dream of a party that she could never attend."

A study in interferences. What would be called today the nonparty or the antiparty. A recognition that loss of contact was, in this case, a greater reality than assuming a party brought everyone together.

The design of the party I have already stated was inspired by the *mise-en-scène* of Martha Graham.

Sometimes the genesis of a novel is suggested by portraits in the diary which cumulatively begin to represent a certain drama or conflict. The study of two real characters in the diary began to appear as a conflict between destructiveness and creativity, between positive and negative. Once I begin to see the real drama, the psychological one, I begin to fictionalize. I use a few real elements, and the imagination and prediction of what such characters can become ultimately guide the rest of the novel. (Naturally, in the diary, which takes hundreds of pages to cover only a few years, no such development or climax is reached.) For fiction, there is the heightening coloration of description, lyrical flights, symbolization which allow one to go further afield than with a portrait.

For the novel *The Four-Chambered Heart* I used the setting of the houseboat which was familiar to me. One of the themes of psychoanalysis had always appealed to me: the concept that we participate in our destructive experiences, that we are by our very temperaments and unconscious drives often allied with our tormentors, our jailers (figuratively speaking), our tyrants. The concept that Rango could very well be in accord (unconsciously) with his wife's particular form of tyranny (hypochondria) never occurred in the diary, but it occurred to me first as a new concept which certainly could be applied to them in a fictionalized way. The psychological reality is that when we feel unequal or unwilling to confront a challenging experience, we take refuge in what the other demands of us. Rango, unable to face the discipline demanded of political commitments, used the illness of his wife as an alibi. Thus he was, unconsciously, at one with her aims, which were to keep him through dependency and need. I had also studied the psychological, subtle paradox that the irrational person often acquired greater power over another than the rational one, because the irrational mind cannot be detected or influenced or defeated when it is acting out an irrational need of our own that we do not wish to confront. It has what you might describe as a subliminal influence. It was like an undetected malady which affected the couple.

Zora has more power in *The Four-Chambered Heart* because her motivations are the same as Rango's. She is protecting Rango from confronting his failure, whereas Djuna is inciting him to test his strength. As a victimized, devoted husband, he could still admire himself. As a political influence, he knew (unconsciously) he could not achieve anything. I had often seen couples in which the emotional person dominated the so-called logical or rational person because the logical person did not understand the irrational behavior and therefore could not grapple with it. Zora was a symbol of the power of negative force. There is a symbolic waking dream scene at the end of the book. Djuna contemplates sinking the houseboat because there is no liberation in sight from Zora's tyranny. Djuna would have to continue to sink with them into blind, irrational destructiveness (as they lived out their unconscious, it was dark and uncreative). Djuna decides not to sink (drown in the dark unconscious). She suddenly understands the *game*. She is saved by awareness.

I also wanted to dramatize the way history and realities of the world could destroy relationships which did not flower into a powerful wholeness. In this case, history is destructive to the personal relationship because it exposes the weakness of Rango, the egoism of Zora, the utopian unrealistic romanticism of Djuna. I dramatized the plight of a man who fails in his personal world and turns to an impersonal cause, where his weakness will once more confront him. It was a study of a romantic revolutionist.

The genesis is never single or simple. It is a combination of elements. The genesis of *A Spy in the House of Love* was more complex. The interpretations of Don Juan always seemed oversimplified to me until I read Dr. Otto Rank's book *Don Juan*. I always felt there were more complex motivations behind sensual restlessness. A story from real life concretized the design. It was the story of a friend who believed her father employed detectives to watch her life in New York among the artists. When her father became seriously ill and near death, she questioned him. He was entirely innocent. Then she realized that she had constantly imagined this, and that whenever anyone looked at her in the subway or in a bar or a restaurant she had fantasied it was a detective. Why? The emotional detective story of this psychological drama began with the question why.

I had also speculated on the divided self, whether it was possible to live out each different part of the self simultaneously. The story called *Pellegrina* in Isak Dinesen's *Seven Gothic Tales* ended in tragedy. I felt there could be another end. As in all divided selves, Sabina lives in relationships which are partly imagined. Both the unreality of them and of her whole life, besides a feeling of dispersion and fragmentation, made her wish for someone who could follow the erratic course of her acts, synthesize her, even if it meant doing so within the context of guilt and judgment. As in all neurosis, the vision of others is partial, and to express this I took inspiration from the film *La ronde* in which there was a carrousel, a merry-go-round feeling. The men moved around Sabina, were highlighted during the encounter, and vanished (as would happen in life). This was completely misunderstood by the critics. They felt personally insulted that the men were not done as fully as the woman, not realizing that I had meant to take the reader inside of the mind and feelings of Sabina, with the limitations imposed by her own vision, obsessions, and fantasies, so that the reader would know how a Sabina felt.

And so once again I had characters drawn from real life in the diary, a theme explored by psychoanalysis, a new way of looking at certain impulses, and a form inspired by a film and a real story.

LIE DETECTOR

The eye of the detective, the lie detector, was not only a projection of Sabina's inner guilt, but also the eye of the world upon her acts, from which the guilt stems. She did not look upon herself with her own vision, but through the eyes of others, and this was also the secret of her disintegration. I do not believe such disintegration need always lead to the madness of Blanche DuBois. It can cause a shock of awareness, lead to a new vision into one's behavior.

The curious handicap I had during the writing of this novel, a state which is well known to writers, was that by placing my awareness *within* Sabina, by placing the camera inside of Sabina (as Bergman did in the eyes of the characters themselves in *Persona*), I became so engrossed in the reality of Sabina that I lost my way. I stopped midway. Like an actor who takes too seriously a role he plays and becomes for the moment possessed by it, I felt the dispersion of Sabina. The writer can enter the world of the subconscious at his own peril, but as artist he must remain in control. That is the difference between the paintings of the insane and of the artists: not only the talent, training, and gift are different, but the art itself is a form of control. Control, not suppression. The insane seek merely to decompress from too rigid a mold, and they explode. That is not the motivation of the artist. He is there to experience and describe experience. During the writing of *Spy*, I became anxious about describing dispersion.

R. D. Laing has something pertinent to say about the artist and the schizoid dream of inner honesty, freedom, omnipotence. He clearly defines the difference which has troubled artists and critics of art in *The Divided Self*: [19]

"It can be readily understood why the schizoid individual so abhors action. The act is simple, determinate, universal. But his self wishes to be complex, indeterminate, and unique. He, his 'self' is endless possibility, capacity, intention. *The act is always a product of a false self*. The act or the deed is never his true reality . . . no footprints or fingerprints of the 'self' shall have been left. The self, as long as it is uncommitted to the objective element, is free to dream and imagine anything."

Sabina's difficulties only develop when she begins to act out her wishes, fantasies, and dreams. Sabina is a close study of the divided self seeking to maintain its own world in a vacuum. Testing it in relation to others is disastrous. She is faced with her impotence to love.

Several writers have entered the world of the divided self with skill and clarity: Herman Hesse in *Steppenwolf*, Max Frisch in *I'm Not Stiller*, Anna Kavan in *Asylum Pieces*. I did not take Sabina over the border. That is too obvious and simple a solution, like killing off the hero, suicide, madness. Melodrama is a cliché. An easy "climax." A way not to penetrate into other layers of liberation. Sabina is clarified by Djuna, by confronting her fantasies. She is not schizoid because she is able to *feel*, to weep; she ostensibly can move to other realms.

The complexity of describing a multiple personality who is not an artist (for someone has said genius is plurality) had finally defeated me.

I was faced with other problems. If the principles of psychoanalysis were the sound basis on which I erected my psychological dramas, and if it was the psychological reality I was pursuing,

I still had not solved the dilemma of presenting the figure of the psychoanalyst who plays such a preponderant role in our culture. In the novel I felt he could not be directly introduced, could not explain the tragedy from the aisles like the Greek chorus. He had to be absorbed by the novelist. We have not had enough time to absorb these new aspects of human behavior, and for the moment I could only poetize as a lie detector, or, as in *Winter of Artifice*, as *The Voice*. The analyst should become a part of the novelist's own consciousness, for that is the major contribution of our time to old themes and old situations and old dramas: a new understanding of them. The analyst is the interpreter, the mirror of our reality. He is in our culture the wise man and the guru. He is the seer who reads our dreams. But he cannot be on stage. He cannot be there visible and twice as large like the Japanese manipulator of puppets. In *Seduction of the Minotaur* I finally succeeded in absorbing the interpretations, the knowledge, the vision of the analyst within the novelist. The theme is psychoanalytical: the search for the origin of the unhappiness in a new country and the problem of being faced with the repetition of patterns and recognizing their inescapable influence unless dissolved by awareness. Lillian makes both journeys, into the past as well as into the present, and becomes aware of their interrelation.

By now it has become clear that the diary was the notebook I depended on for characters and themes. But *Seduction of the Minotaur* was the first book I wrote without any dependence on the diary. It may have been that by constantly struggling with the problem of fusing conscious and unconscious, I had finally arrived at a natural balance. The theme of the book itself is balance, balance between outer and inner, between past and present, between psychological reality and nature, symbolized in Lillian's finally sailing on a lagoon and exorcising the recurrent dream of a boat pushing painfully through waterless countries. At one moment she feels the welding, the fusion taking place.

The speculation on the meaning of this recurrent dream gave

the novel its starting point. Several trips to Mexico inspired the landscape, the climate, and mood of the setting. The cliché outcome of so many adventure books in which men uprooted themselves, fell in love with an exotic place, and could not achieve their inner paradise (see Gauguin in Tahiti, and almost all the stories about white men who settled in Polynesian Islands) was challenged again by the psychoanalytical concept that fatality was interior, an inner-directed pattern, and had nothing to do with a change of country. Lillian proceeds on a dynamic double journey. She begins with a troubled inner life and seeks peace from the outer joyousness of Mexico.

The outside (nature) cannot give us what we do not possess within.

Symbolic images were drawn from many sources, Mexican legends as well as the story of how the Egyptians buried their pharaohs with two barks, one to sail after death to the moon and one to sail to the sun. This image was most appropriate for the story of *Seduction of the Minotaur*. If we did not make the journey on two levels, external and internal, we would not reach wholeness or happiness. What the Egyptians meant by such symbolic twin ships I was not able to find out, but the image suited my psychological theme, my conviction.

Lillian is only partly real.

She was essentially a woman rushing into acts which did not satisfy or assuage the needs of her inner self. The atmosphere of Mexico was in itself *conducive* to a slower rhythm, time for reflection, and the people seemed to live in greater harmony with nature and with themselves.

The dialogue between the Doctor and Lillian is not a psychoanalytic dialogue. He is a man of great humanity and wisdom. He observes her dislocation. He is killed. It was the first time I accepted a physical death. It was frequent, natural, and consistent with life in Mexico. It also forced Lillian out of her evasions.

CHAPTER FIVE

Genesis of the Diary

THE WRITING of a diary has both its negative and its positive aspects. The genesis of mine began with the desire to keep a channel of communication with a lost father. It was intended for him and continued as the travel log of a child in a new country, as a record of family life, of books, of observations of people.

There was a complex genesis. I was shy of speaking, I was full of feelings and ideas I could not express to anyone. It was a measure of growth, at times a log of discipline (today I passed up the dessert, I finished knitting my shawl, I was silent for twelve hours—ways through Spartanism to sainthood I took from Thomas à Kempis' *The Imitation of Christ*, intended to build a strong character!). During its course it became various things, a confidant, a place where I could write improvisations, portray people, make notes for stories. As a gardener of a backyard in New York, I wanted to see flowers *grow*. I would remove the earth to watch the mystery of their growth. Roots. Significant, if you wish. I was not content with the surface, the final product.

School did not give me answers to what interested me. It did not encourage my interest in the English language. So I left it. And read and taught myself.

The negative aspect was that I became so fascinated with the diary itself that I avoided the formal works, novels, or stories. I had tried them. As a child I wrote many adventure stories *à la*

Jules Verne. I filled a complete magazine each month for my brothers. At twenty I wrote a bad novel. At twenty-one bad short stories. At twenty-five another bad novel. The diary remained. I did not know how to utilize the richness of the diary material. I must unknowingly have been an automatic writer, an improviser, a future surrealist. I preferred the freedom of the diary. To write always about what interested me, not what I should be writing. To be open and not self-conscious. To say everything. The secrecy of the diary was a great incentive to honesty. In life (and in the novels) I had a painful awareness of the sensitiveness of other human beings, and like the Japanese, I did not like to offend, to hurt others' feelings, shame them, embarrass them (a concept later confirmed by psychoanalysis which uncovers such scars). So I saved the face of my friends by pursuing my scientific examination of them, of life, and myself only in the diary. I was not lonely in life. The diary was not my only confidant. But I tended to let others confess, talk, assert themselves. I found it difficult to argue, to differ, to attack, to assert. So I observed and listened and poured it all into the diary.

It took little time. It was written at night, rapidly and without erasures. Gradually it became a writer's notebook. For I wrote my book on Lawrence and began to struggle with formal writing.

I carried the diary around in buses, waiting rooms, doctor's offices, cafes, everywhere. At sixteen I went without lunch to write in it because I was modeling fifteen hours a day.

The diary was written very fast, as I lived. No hesitations. In New York, working as a lay analyst, I wrote it between patients. It contained stories I never developed, characters I never wrote about. It became a personage in its own right. I apologized when I had no time for it!

The false persona I had created for the enjoyment of my friends, the gaiety, the buoyant, the receptive, the healing person, always on call, always ready with sympathy, had to have its other existence somewhere. In the diary I could reestablish the balance. Here I could be depressed, angry, despairing, discouraged. *I could let out my demons.* I had a recurrent dream I never could explain. I was walking through the streets of a city. I heard the fire engines. I rushed to the fire. The diaries were burning. I thought it was mere anxiety about losing them. But once, in discussing with an analyst the conflict between the persona, the ideal self I thought people needed, wanted, expected, and my real, far-from-ideal self, we talked about our universal demons: jealousy, envy, anger. The analyst asked me: "And where did you put your demons, since you did not allow them to be destructive or to act *in life*?"

I went home, and that night I had my recurrent dream: the diaries were burning. This was the answer. I had locked up my demons in the diaries where they could do no harm. And if the diaries burned, I would be left only with this persona, smiling, ever available, ever devoted.

I associated honesty with the loss of love. The only women I had known who were honest, belligerent, assertive, undisguised had lost love. I was not going to risk that.

Then there was the *fear of the world*. I had seen destructive relationships, destructive gossip, destructive journalism, destructive critics, destructive wars. I felt the world to be a rather dangerous place. I did not feel ready to confront this. I needed a shelter for my work. The diary was a fine one. A shelter from misunderstanding, from satire, from attack, judgment.

These are elements which might well be common to all young writers. I have often seen them write a poem, a story, rush to send it to magazines, receive a rejection slip, and give up writing. By considering the diary a secret, a pleasure, a casual work, such as writing a letter to a friend, I bypassed all the inhibiting factors. I have also seen young writers destroyed at the beginning of their careers by a scathing criticism of their work by a teacher, a friend, a parent. The young are vulnerable.

To reflect major personalities it is necessary to have a proper mirror. In my effort to perfect myself as an instrument, a sensitive instrument with a wide range, I had to nurture this mirror.

At first diary and fiction conflicted. I was asked to choose, to abandon one in favor of the other. Dr. Rank as analyst and Henry Miller as fiction writer and friend wanted me to surrender it, so I might become a novelist. At the same time they enjoyed my portraits of them.

Today they no longer conflict. As with the conflict between dream and action, they ended by nurturing each other. *The Diary* was no "narcissus pool," as myopic Leon Edel declared in the *Saturday Review*.[20] He failed to see the many people reflected in it, the numerous full-length and minor characters.

D. H. Lawrence's accurate statement that our biggest problem in fiction was how to *transport the living essence of a character into the novel without its dying in the process* was solved by the diary. The *living* essence had to be captured in the now, in the living moment. Transporting it into fiction, fictionalizing it in a way that would not kill it presented a continuous problem, like that of a heart transplant. In the diary no such death ever took place. The living moment was caught. The character was caught while living, with all his ambivalences, contradictions, paradoxes.

The close, the intimate, the immediate exposed one truth. Distance, invention, composition might give another. The second is rearranged by memory and altered by the novelist to suit his theme. I wanted one record of unfalsified, unfictionalized truth. The second I never trusted to give me what I most valued, an intimate contact with human beings.

Here I was, back to the watching of the flower's roots, watching its growth.

A diary is valuable to a writer; I am certain of that. The negative aspect is merely one of range. If it is limited, trivial, narrow in its range, it is valueless. If it grows in depth and range, it can be indispensable to the writer.

It fed the computer-novelist living food. Which does not mean that all my fiction is autobiographical, nor does it mean as some believe, that I am all the women in the novels (it would be pleasant in one life to be so many women!). It simply means that the psychological reality of each character had been taken first from a living heart. Whether or not the transplant was successful, I leave to the critics. It is a pity that to achieve an evaluation, the novels have to undergo dissection.

I advise diary writing to young writers as a discipline. Writing every day as one practices the piano every day keeps one nimble, and then when the great moments of inspiration come, one is in good form, supple and smooth. The writers who do not exercise, and sit and wait for the great moment of the geyser, often find their writing fingers rusty by the time it erupts, if it ever does!

It is also amazing to see how much more vital, colorful, and free one is when one does not write for a judge, the world, or a critic.

For the critics who are so preoccupied with the evil of writing for or about one's self, I have a carton of letters from readers, all saying: "You are writing *my* diary, *my* life."

Another aspect of notebook and diary writing is that it records a pilgrim's progress of the artist at work. I worked out my problems as a woman writer, as a writer of poetic fiction, within the diary. I never remember appealing for help in these matters. I did have discussions with Henry Miller and Lawrence Durrell, but they undermined my confidence, usually, and the diary helped me recover my equanimity and integrity. I was young and surrounded by mature, educated writers, and could easily have been swamped, overwhelmed by them and influenced to imitate them.

Diary writing as the art of self-defense is also worth consideration.

No sooner has a novelist written a body of work than the biographers set to work unraveling all the fiction writer's composites, such as Painter did with Proust's work. It is a task of dissection, and of no greater use than unraveling a sweater. You have a ball of wool again, no sweater, no magic novel. I thought at least the diary would keep such activity accurate, for the novelist is at the mercy of inaccuracies. Very often at the mercy of snipers.

Keeping a notebook also taught me that to achieve perfection while attaining naturalness it is important to write a great deal, to write fluently rather than revise over and over again. Such revisions may lead to monotony and to reworking *dead material.* Some revisions have a withering effect. Continuing to write until ease and fluency and accuracy are reached is more fecund. In too much rewriting there is danger of performing an *autopsy.*

A notebook or diary keeps one at ease with writing. It is informal. It is a discipline, like sketching for the painter.

The diary, dealing always with the *immediate present,* the warm, the near, being written at white heat, developed a love of the living moment, of the emotional reaction to experience which revealed that powers of re-creation lie in the senses rather than in memory or critical, intellectual observation. Most of us, when beginning to write, adopt a pose, create a persona as a defense from the world. Henry Miller covered his sensitivity with an outward toughness of style.

Deena Metzger wrote: [21] "Rarely is the artist capable of going both ways, on two journeys, into the self and into the world. But the diary is of just such nature. It is a combination of the romantic night and the classical day. It is subjective and it is objective. It navigates between the real and the imagined, as Anaïs Nin navigates between them."

When we speak of fiction, we speak of its designing a larger figure by portraying it in a well-rounded way, in a complete way, until it becomes symbolic or representative of an idea, of what is happening in history, in the world.

How this happened in the diary, with its day-to-day sketch of people not yet famous, not yet figures, not yet representative of their time, I think, was due to their being interesting in the first place, original, talented people; second, to my recognition of their potential as well as their actual gifts; third, my portrait of the surrounding atmosphere, so that they became, in fact as well as in the diary, representative figures. I was not aware while writing that my father would be representative. To be representative of anything you have merely to be positively and expansively something or someone definite.

In editing the diary, I disregard this factor of whether or not they became famous. Some minor characters are as interesting as famous ones. Gonzalo to me was a vivid version of a type very prevalent in Europe at that time, caught between his political beliefs and his inability to act, to sacrifice himself, to discipline himself. Max Frisch in *The Firebugs* portrayed Biedermann as the same character.

What concerned me and drove me into fiction was that in the diary I could only describe characters who were in some way related to me, whom I could see. But I was not able to cover their life outside of me, to see all around them. I became aware of this limitation. At one point I lost track of Antonin Artaud. This happens in life. Then suddenly, years later, someone supplied the missing fragment. But *only the diarist is willing to wait for this fragment to be supplied.* When I wrote the story of Artaud, I had to reconstruct the missing half of his life.

Given time, the diary can do this too. I am now completing the portraits of Dr. Rank, of Artaud. When I went to Paris in 1950, I sought out the characters in *Under a Glass Bell* and searched for the end of their story.

The personal vision may be deeper or limited. It can be expanded. It can be intense, intimate, and well-rounded. With time. The novel telescoping time demands an acceleration of development. That is the first artificial acceleration which does not parallel life.

For those who object to a diary's being a self-portrait, I suggest that the diarist must be present in his own diary as a barometer, indicator, receptor, thermometer, and echo-sounder, as a compass, commentator, footnoter, reporter, documentarist.

His presence is indispensable.

The paradoxical command "do not write about yourself" (let the journalists do it) is combined with an insatiable, ferocious, ruthless curiosity about people's lives, a savage code of journalistic aggression. The concept that the life of a public figure belongs to the public. We never stop to analyze the nature of this curiosity, whether it has anything to do with history, knowledge, experience, or is merely prurient, and on a par with small-town gossip. As a diarist I drew my own boundary lines indicating that a respect for the life of a human being is more important than satisfying the curiosity of invaders, violators of human rights.

I do not practice a ruthless invasion. I take delight in the creative possibilities of the intimate portrait, but it has to be with the collaboration of the sitter.

When you repudiate the disguises of the novel to achieve closer reality, you bear a responsibility for the humanity of this portrait. To enter a home to kill with the pen is as criminal as entering with a gun.

If our age is noted for alienation, part of this is due to the callousness with which people treat each other. We cannot trust newsmen and reporters to deal humanly with the truth. Respect for the vulnerability of human beings as well as a desire to know all the facts and not to judge are necessary parts of a diarist's vision, because no truth will come from a callous vision or from the humiliation of another human being.

If the diarist has no humanity, no psychological insight, no ethics, the portrait will lack these dimensions, too. It will read like vivisection. Many portraits have been acts of hatred or revenge, others are so shallow that the characters pass like shadows with names pinned to their lapels. Some resemble the voodoo hexing ceremonies during which a revengeful native sticks pins in a doll as a substitute for the original.

I remind myself that as a diarist I can create a prejudiced view of my model.

I once introduced someone's letter thus: "His war letter from a safe place was a monument of egotism." This statement was prejudicial to the defendant. I crossed it out and quoted the letter itself, allowing others to form their own opinion.

Many manifestations of the personality bloom *only* in the presence of love or friendship.

I gave myself my first lesson in editing when I was eleven. After a quarrel with my brothers, I made the following entry: "This was written in anger."

We learn more about others from relationships than from

objective observation, and a cold scrutiny may well freeze its object.

The diarist is a camera. You, the reader, have the right to know the brand, range, quality, and quirks of this camera. For the diary's truth is ultimately an alchemy of portrayer and portrayed. People relate to a presence. Many manifestations of the personality, repulsive or seductive, are the fault of the portraitist.

People only unmask themselves in the privacy of love or friendship. But such revelations impose *noblesse oblige*. One has to treat them with care and tenderness. A human being who reveals himself should be treated with the same care we accord a new type of fish, a new type of plant. He is unique and we may never see another like him. We must protect him from injury if we are to share his life. Only a long-lasting friendship will give a portrait in depth.

SELF-IMAGE SHOCKING

Everyone has an image of himself which conflicts with the image held by others. People have been shocked to hear their voices on tape; it is never the voice they imagined they had. They have been shocked to see their faces for the first time on film. How much more shocked they are by other's portraits.

The portrait has its evil aspects. It may be an overidealized portrait made by someone in love with his subject, it may be a caricature by someone who hates his subject, it may be a portrait of the subconscious self rather than the persona offered to the world, and the last is the most destructive to the one unaware of this other self.

It was from Georges Simenon that I learned that a portrait is least damaging when all the facts are given without intent to damage. Simenon would study almost scientifically the most complex and perverse character formation leading to its downfall or crime, destruction or self-destruction. He went so deep, and *without judging*, in quest of the truth, that one forgot to judge in the process. Almost always, by knowing all the facts, one ceased to condemn.

It is possible to tell the truth without committing character assassination if one's motive is not to condemn but to understand, not to ridicule or disparage, but to reveal motivations, cause and effect. The desire to be faithful must be stronger than the desire to expose only faults, and if faults are exposed, then both sides of them must be exposed simultaneously, the negative and positive which lie at the bottom of every act.

As a diarist I drew my own boundary lines indicating that respect for the life of a human being is more important than the satisfaction of a sensation seeker, a *voyeur*.

What such transgressions create are alienation, self-defensive methods, and a growing dehumanization. If we continue in this malpractice, we will not have any more human beings to expose, only monsters.

I am not claiming that as an editor (even with the constant coeditorship of Gunther Stuhlmann) I have avoided all the pitfalls. I may have offended certain susceptibilities because one cannot always know what they are, but the real measure of what my method of editing combined with Gunther Stuhlmann's objectivity has achieved is that human beings still trust me with their secrets. And for a diarist or novelist, that is the highest of all achievements.

The destructive aspect of truth is neutralized by a deep probing into motivation which makes one understand a character, and what is understood is not condemned. Psychoanalysis was my invaluable teacher in the study of motivation and interpretation. Understanding creates compassion, sympathy, and empathy.

I was faithful to motivation. But I did not retouch or idealize either. The more we offend, insult, humiliate human beings, the more we cut all lines of communication with humanity, and we ourselves become this golem monster we try to expose in others.

In editing, I sought to make the portraits very full, in depth as well as in range, allowing everyone to speak for himself by way of letters and conversations. In the end, all the elements are there and balance is achieved, which is an approximation of justice. If a man is big enough, he can support a few frailties.

When I dramatized Dr. Allendy's limitations as a psycho-analyst, I also made it clear that this limitation was only in relation to me, as an artist. I included his own revelations about his personal difficulties balanced by a description of his positive achievements, his pioneer work in French courts (he was the first one to introduce psychoanalysis as a factor in the trial of a criminal), his role in the exploration of new ideas. I had hoped to make others feel the valuable human being and the origin of his limitation. I succeeded except for one reader who wrote me that I should have been angry and vindictive toward Dr. Allendy for his inadequacy. One reader missed the balance I call humanism.

A personality only emerges truthfully when all aspects are included. It was toward this balance that Gunther Stuhlmann and I worked.

The solution to the dangers of truth lies in making a portrait so full and rich that all sides are heard, all aspects considered.

The writer is not limited to painting one aspect of the personality as a photographer is. He is able to include all of them. The sum is achieved by completeness. A selection of the major traits takes the place of a petty accumulation of anecdotes which resemble snapshots taken by an unprofessional photographer.

Truth remains relative, but a knowledge of motivation humanizes it. A listing of anecdotes does not add up to a faithful portrait, but familiarity with the inner man gives the key to his acts, which is more important. To study a person in depth is more important than to catalogue his actions. If one is deaf to the vulnerability of a human being, it also means one has no ear for the more subtle recording of his sensitive wave lengths. Giving all the facts, all the incidents, all the anecdotes, rather than a meaningful selection of them in order of their importance and accompanied by clarification, very often leads to a shrunken portrait. If a full psychological portrait is given and if it is accurate enough, one can infer the rest, fill in, read between the lines, as with close friends or a member of one's family. To seize upon the basic, essential lines of a character is more important than details. Nothing essential to a portrait was left out of the diary.

We learn more about others from relationships than from objective scrutiny. Callousness in a writer creates the equivalent of cataracts in the eyes. It not only clouds or deforms his vision but may end in total blindness. Callousness is not operable. It breeds callousness.

We fear to become victims of dehumanization by industrialization and mechanization, but that is not where the danger lies. The danger lies in everyone's *private dehumanization* which becomes contagious, universal, and can end in crime.

The very process of the diary resembles that of a painter making a series of sketches in preparation for a final portrait. This portrait is only achieved by a cumulative effect because a diary never ends. As the diarist does not know the future, he reaches no conclusion, no synthesis, which is an artificial product of the intellect. The diary is true to *becoming* and *continuum*.

I could not make conclusions which even the death of a character does not make. The portrait of Dr. Rank did not end with his death. His values as a psychologist are only being recognized and evaluated now, and I am making new discoveries about him, revising my opinions because of new information.

I have not changed anything in the diary, only omitted what was unimportant, trivial, or repetitious. Repetitions are inevitable in a diary, but they have to be eliminated.

It is true the writer's concern with the accuracy or completeness of a description did intrude upon the diarist at times. In the childhood diary I was concerned with my description of my arrival in New York. Had I done justice to it? I told it twice. This may have been because, with time, I recognized the portentousness of this voyage which was to change the course of my entire life.

As I worked outside of the diary, the concerns of a craftsman did appear. I did not erase or revise, but I occasionally rewrote a description worth retelling. I may say that it was my experience as a novelist which enabled me to edit *The Diary* at all, to be able to select what was essential to a portrait or even to select one description rather than another.

Here the conflict lies in the usefulness of the diary as biographical source, as against the desire of the publisher and the reader to "get on with the story."

CHAPTER SIX

Diary Versus Fiction

ONE THING is very clear—that both diary and fiction tended towards the same goal: intimacy with people, with experience, with life itself. One, in the diary, was achieved by daily writing, daily recording, and continuous interest in the development of people around me and in my own growth. Secrecy seemed to be a condition for spontaneity in my case. The personal interest seemed to be a necessary condition to intimacy. An early intuition that *everyone* had areas of subjective or personal or emotional reactions was confirmed by study of psychology. The more I went into the revelations of psychology, the more I realized that spontaneous writing in the present came closer to the truth than impressions remembered because memory rearranged its collection anew each day with changes in the personality. Stories were altered and fictionalized with time. As the teller changed, so did the versions of the past.

The necessity for fiction was probably born of the problem of taboo on certain revelations. It was not only a need of the imagination but an answer to the limitations placed on portrayal of others.

Not only conventions dictated the secrecy of journals, but personal censorship. Fiction was liberating in that sense. But when it became fixed in a mold, it withered. Until a new form revivified it. The total death of the novel was always being announced, when what should have been observed was the death of certain forms of the novel. People cling to dead forms.

Otto Rank once said that man was more of an artist than woman because he gave freedom to his imagination. Henry Miller was never concerned with the *faithfulness* of his descriptions. He was not concerned with resemblance at all. He invented a world of his own, personages of his own, including himself.

At one time I was very concerned with my faithfulness to the truth. I thought it might be due to uprootings in childhood, loss of country and roots and father, and that I was trying to create relationships based on a true understanding of the other person, in the diary as well as in life and in the novels, too. A world of genuine authentic relationships. Now I can see that what I sought was psychological reality and that this reality has a logic, a pattern, a consistency of its own which cannot be invented. Narrative, or a Joycean symphony, can be invented. Not the subtle plots created by the unconscious. They are marvels of a kind of logic never known before which cannot be imitated or substituted, for every link is essential, every detail. Later I will show how difficult this was to achieve in fiction.

So, the first incentive is to understand not to invent.

This was really the antinovel, antifiction which the French explored recently.

I am still speaking of the time when I separated the two activities as antagonistic and could not see the interrelation between them. Faithful to the notebok and to the human beings I loved, portraying them truthfully, I was wary of invention, and I blamed Henry Miller's inventions for his not understanding people around him. I separated insight from narrative picaresque storytelling. When Henry Miller told a caricatural story about Moricand in *Devil in Paradise*, I felt: this is not Moricand. I only wish he would not call him by his family name. It was *another* story he told. These two drives had to come to terms one day, or I had to choose between them. There is a great deal of conflict and questioning about this in the first two diaries. Finally, I made no choice, I lived out both, and ultimately (thanks to psychoanalysis) they nourished each other and coexisted.

To maintain faith in my vision of people, to be able to say I do understand Moricand, see Moricand, I had to make sure that my vision was clear of all the elements which R. D. Laing enumerated as obstacles to clear insight. In other words, one has to know which areas in one's self are not to be trusted. Acknowledgment of irrational areas.

The diary served a useful purpose in exploring, defining, and then containing these unreliable areas in order to achieve some true objectivity. The idea of total objectivity is erroneous.

The diary, then, was where I checked my realities and illusions, made my experiments, noted progress or its opposite. It was the laboratory! I could venture into the novel with a sense of psychological authenticity and fictionalize only externals, situations, places. Composites, which can do much to enrich, correspond to condensation in the poem and to abstraction in painting.

The necessity for fiction, in my case, also helped to symbolize and add dimensions. The portrait of Henry Miller in the diary is a portrait of Henry Miller, but a composite may become something more than one artist, writer, painter, more than one person —a unit. A composite is no longer the original. It is something else.

How much is lost by retranslating such composites and redistributing each trait where it belongs is exemplified in the biography of Proust by George D. Painter. By replacing all the "types" into the classified box they sprang from, Painter destroyed a magical component.

Only an uncreative person would spend ten years on such reclassification of the alchemist's elements out of which Proust made a world of infinite depth. Why did we read it? Because the personality of Proust himself inspired us with love and a desire for intimacy. We recognized the greatness of the novels, but we were in love with Proust, as well as with his novels, but I do not think it is love of the novelist which drives critics to play sleuth to the personal lives and personal genesis of their art. It is merely the exercise of the art of sleuthing, and as this con-

tinues to be a favored sport among the academicians, it might be
well for the novelists to make their own confessions for the sake
of greater accuracy.

Thus fictionalizing had two motives: one, protection of the
personalities; the other symbolization, the creation of the myth.
We have no richer example of mythmaking, of enlarging, developing, magnifying, in our time than Marguerite Young's
Miss MacIntosh, My Darling. Folk characters, ordinary and familiar, become expanded by her talent for poetry, metaphysics,
surrealism, and achieve universality, become symphonic. It is
the heights and the depths of her measurements, the infinite of
her word arches and bridges which make of them containers of
the dimensions not calculable to science but to the poet.

If at first diary and fiction did not coexist harmoniously, it
was because I could not see their mutual influence upon each
other (as we cannot see the influences which two countries at
war, like America and Japan, exert upon each other). I was writing better in the notebooks because I was writing outside, in the
formal work, and I was writing more authentically in the novels
because I sustained the informal, improvised living contact with
my relationships, cities, the present.

In the diary I documented a visit to the ragpickers. In the
story I showed how it became more than that.

In the diary the preoccupation with the art of expression began
more and more to work in harmony with the fiction. It is in the
diary I observe that dreams in themselves are boring but dreams
related to life are dynamic. It is in the diary that I am first
baffled by the intricate way Moricand tells his stories (as I was
later by the free-form way Varda told his stories) and make a
conscious effort to find a simile for it, a sequence of images which
would resemble his talk. In both cases they practiced in talk the
free association of the surrealists. It was difficult to capture
images and ideas which did not hang together in the usual way
but were born spontaneously one from the other.

I used the symbol of the Ferris wheel to indicate how Moricand kept people at a distance from the core of the wheel, took

them for a voyage and deposited them as far from intimate knowledge of him as they were at the beginning. In the story I refined and expanded upon this.

This intricate interplay could have been disastrous to one form or another. They survived because the same duality existed between my formal art and my love of direct, human contact.

I was always writing fiction as well as the diary. At ten I wrote adventure stories. Completely invented. Unrelated to the reality of my life.

This might be studied as the way the artist finds to walk a tightrope between the two sides of his duality (a duality experienced in some form or other by almost everyone).

The difference between symbolic truth (expressing the inner life, the subconscious) and the here-and-now verifiable truth continued to trouble me. But they continued to run in parallel lines. The diary, creating a vaster tapestry, a web, exposing constantly the relation between the past and the present, weaving meticulously the invisible interaction, noting the repetition of themes, developed the sense of continuum of the personality instead of *conclusions* or *resolutions* which were invalidated by any recognition of the relativity of truth. This tale without beginning or end which encloses all things, and relates all things was a strong antidote to the incoherence and disintegration of modern man. I could follow the real patterns and gain insights obscured in most of the fragmentary or superficial novels with their artificial climaxes and resolutions.

An immediate, emotional reaction to experience reveals that the power to *re-create* lies in the sensibilities rather *than intellectual memory or observation*. This personal reaction I found to be the core of individuality, or originality and personality. A deep personal relation to all things reaches far beyond the personal into the general.

The diary also teaches that it is in the moments of emotional crisis that human beings reveal themselves most accurately. I learned to choose these heightened moments in fiction because they are the moments of revelation. It is the moment when the real self rises to the surface, shatters its false roles, erupts, and assumes reality and identity. The fiery moments of passionate experience are the moments of wholeness and totality of the personality. By this emphasis on the fiery moments, the explosions, I reached a greater reality of feeling and the senses. The preoccupation of the novelist: how to capture the living moments, was answered by the diary. You write while they are *alive*. You do not preserve them in alcohol until the moment you are ready to write about them. I discovered through the diary several basic elements essential to the vitality of writing. Of these the most important are naturalness and spontaneity. These, in turn, sprang from my freedom of selection. Because I was not forced to write about something, I could write about anything which interested me genuinely, what I felt most strongly about at the moment. This enthusiasm produced a vividness which often withered in the formal work. Improvisation, free association of images and ideas, obedience to mood, impulses, brought forth countless riches. The diary, dealing only with the immediate, the warm, the near, being written at white heat, developed a love of the living moment.

There are negative forces which oppress the novelist, which do not affect diary writing. One learns resistance and defiance of them. One of the negative forces is the taboo imposed on certain themes, another is the artificial chronological sequence, a third is the untrained reviewer. Such forces do not oppress research in science. In literature they are preestablished. I am not speaking of the fourth which is commercialism.

Free of all these oppressions, diary writing maintains impetus and the exhilaration born of freedom.

I was discovering the dual aspect of truth: one stemming from the immediate and personal, and one which could be achieved later with an *objectivity not born of detachment* but of the recognition of one's subjectivity and the sifting of it to keep the vital elements intact. The personal involvement is the origin of the life-giving emotion.

Another lesson I learned from diary writing was the actual

continuity of the act of writing, not waiting for inspiration, favorable climate, astrologic constellations, the mood, but the discipline of sitting at the typewriter to write so many hours a day. Then when the magnificent moment comes, the ripened moment, the writing itself is nimble, already tuned, warmed.

Why did I not remain merely a diarist? Because there was a world beyond the personal which could be handled through the art form, through fiction.

Why did I not stay within *House of Incest* and write only prose poems, dreamed material, such as *Les chants de Maldoror?*

Because my drive was stated by Jung: *proceed from the dream outward.* I took this as relating dream and life, internal and external worlds, the secrets and persona of the self. Appearance and reality, illusion and reality.

Without the diary, the prose poem, and fiction I could not have achieved the *relation* between them. It is the *relation* which interested me, the *connection*, the *bridges*, the *interaction*, the *dynamics of relation* among human beings as well as among the ways of expression human beings use.

LIMITATIONS OF FICTION

The limitation of the novel sent me back to the diary. For example, when I finished the novel *Winter of Artifice,* I did not feel that I had finished with the relationship of father and daughter, because in the diary I had an example of a continuum which did not come to an end but which changed. Perhaps a novelist is through with a character when he is finished with his novel. I was not. The continuity of relationship and its alterations, as in Proust, made me feel there was always another truth around the corner, there would always be another revelation, another discovery about my father. The concept that this theme was completed would never even have occurred to me, because I could see its continuation in the endless diary. The diary made me aware of organic and perpetual motion, perpetual change in character. When you write a novel or a short story, you are arresting motion for a period of that story, a span of time. There is something static about that. Proust seemed to me the only writer who had flow and infinite continuum. Other novels did not revolve enough. Even in Durrell's *Alexandria Quartet* the promise that we would look at each character from a totally different point of view, and which was achieved externally by a kaleidoscopic view, a changing focus, nevertheless did not succeed in depth. When Durrell tried to give that by creating journals and notebooks, they did not seem to be revelations or to belong to the different characters but to be written by the novelist. The diary cannot be imitated. And so in many cases, reading novels, I had the feeling of still life rather than a perpetual motion.

I enjoyed writing the diary more than I did the novels because it was unplanned, spontaneous. And even if I did not plan the fiction, and tried to be free of a structure or design except the one which would emerge organically from a selection of material, I was not as free.

I may be free in my first version of a novel, but the editing is a discipline, it is an art. Even if it consists mostly of cutting, taking out what had not "happened" (for I did not believe very much in rewriting). For me the act of rewriting was tampering with the freshness and aliveness. I preferred to cut. There is an element of conscious editing after the spontaneous writing. There is an element of selection, passing judgment. It takes a great deal of the pleasure out of it. The pleasure seems to lie in freedom of choice.

Part of the pleasure comes from not being aware of having to construct something that won't fall apart. In the novels, I am aware of being a craftsman. Not in the diary.

The spontaneous writing in the novel has to achieve, ultimately, a form; its theme and mood create a form. You are not sure if the pieces will fit together, if it will form a design (I am talking about an organic form born of the contents, not an imposed plot or structure). There is a tension. Sabina caused me a great deal of trouble because I wanted to describe fragmentation without the disintegration which usually accompanies it. Each fragment had a life of its own. They had to be held together by some tension other than the unity we are familiar with. I was depicting fissions of the atoms of personality, but I did not want to fabricate a bomb. I was in danger of that every moment in the book. If she had no center to hold on to, she could be destroyed as Blanche DuBois was by those who did not understand her fantasy. In Marguerite Duras' *The Ravishing of Lol Stein*, in describing Lol's schizoid state, she caused it to happen to such a degree that Lol was no longer understandable. All communication was broken.

Madness to me, in a novel, was like murder. It was an easy and not quite honorable solution! For it was no solution. It was a curtain. A drama to me was the conflict between sanity and insanity, conflict and serenity, the individual and society, tensions, but the beauty consisted in the *endurance* of the effort to integrate, to reach another rung of awareness. I felt the novel had to take the adventurer all the way in his journey, to the top of the mountain, or the undiscovered river in the jungle, and somehow the substitution of an end cheated one of a complete spectacle, complete experience. I killed my heroes and heroines off when I was fourteen. I thought it was because I did not know then what else to do.

I do not know how the concept grew that objectivity could only come from one's absence, that erasing one's self, not being in the room, would give a description far closer to objective truth. For I believe the opposite. Deena Metzger felt she was seeing Henry Miller in *The Diary* through *my* eyes, but I maintain that the only way to become truly intimate with a person's character is to view him precisely in relation to others. A thousand objective facts would not reveal as much as watching Miller at a heightened moment of personal relationship, in relation to someone, at a moment of crisis. I remember a playwright's saying he would have preferred me absent in the *Mouse* story. That was an absurd statement, for the story was of the Mouse in relation to someone to whom she finally confessed, opened herself, who was caught in sharing her drama. Without me in the story, the Mouse would remain mute and secretive, undecipherable and unknown. There has to be a presence, a register, a recorder, an eye, an ear, a presence which arouses revelation. I do not believe in reportage. I believe in the capacity of certain people to obtain information, secrets, and confessions.

The active conflict between diary and novel gradually ceased. By 1966 it was the experience of the novelist which helped me to edit the diary. It was the fiction writer who knew when the tempo lagged, when details were trivial, when a description was a repetition. I changed nothing essential, I only cut the extraneous material, the overload.

The final lesson a writer learns is that everything can nourish the writer. The dictionary, a new word, a voyage, an encounter, a talk in the street, a book, a phrase heard. He is a computer set to receive and utilize all things. An exhibit of painting, a concert, a voice, a letter, a play, a landscape, a skyscape, a telephone conversation, a nap, a dream, a sleepless night, a storm, an animal's greeting, an aquarium, a photograph, a newspaper story.

I am a fervent believer in the enriching influence of one art upon another, a believer in cross-pollination between the arts, which is now expressing itself in the integration of the arts, in the use of lights, sounds, happenings, theater, sculpture on the stage (such as Noguchi's sets for Martha Graham).

Bergson said there are two kinds of clarities. "The perception of the artist, of the intuitive mind will always seem obscure to those who prefer clear Cartesian perception."

He spoke of "the fringe of nebulosity which surrounds the luminous core of intelligence, affirming by its presence that part of our existence so clearly perceived by our intelligence is not the essential or the most profound part. This penumbra is what must be penetrated if we would seek reality. An orientation inward implies an enlargement of our mental horizon." He denied that "reality could be attained by the intelligence, by conscious thought."

CHAPTER SEVEN

The Novel of the Future

IN THE PRESENT chaotic state of affairs in the literary world as well as the everyday world, it is a relief to talk about the future. I like to think about the future because there is room for hope there, and the possibility of a new synthesis.

But before we create a future, we will have to rid ourselves of the pollution of humanity by hate. In today's fiction I see far too much caricature and parody. Caricature is a form of hatred. When there is too much of it, it kills the appetite for life and destroys the value of fiction. The *cult of ugliness* is distinct from the acceptance that there is ugliness, just as taking pleasure in cruelty is distinct from the acceptance that there is cruelty in the world. But an obsession with ugliness lies ultimately in the writer's vision of the world, and when the writer loses his perspective and balance, he adds to the ugliness. The only type who perpetually acts out his revolts, his angers, and his revenges against society is the criminal type; and I consider some of today's writers do the same.

We are now in an intermediate period. There has been a chasm between poetry and prose in which writing lost its magical power, a chasm between art and science, and a chasm between the conscious and the unconscious. These will one day be fused.

There are frequent obituaries of the novel because (like the bad novelists) it is easier to kill off one's character than to diagnose him and solve his destructive impulses. So we kill off the novel because we do not like to say that it reflects the "sick society" and that it reflects our divided selves rather than our integrations. Compartments usually create undernourishment. Life is the relation between people and objects. We placed the subconscious writers on one shelf (Joyce, Kafka, Virginia Woolf, Proust) and the naturalistic ones, the realistic photographers, the copiers of nature on another. To our dismay, the writers who dwelt in the unconscious came to resemble more and more contemporary painters, contemporary stage sets, contemporary theater which long ago ceased to copy nature. The writers who had explored the realms which in painting were acceptable as cubism, impressionism, abstraction, surrealism, or hard edge were the untouchables. They were "subjective," "personal," "esoteric," on the periphery of "mainsprings of American literature."

Yet when they reached us already decorated, classified, critically measured, from France, we read the new novel. We had our new novel at home but utterly neglected Marguerite Young, Maude Hutchins, John Hawkes, Anna Kavan, Marianne Hauser, Jerzy Kosinski, the early Truman Capote, the early Kerouac, Nathanael West, Djuna Barnes, William Goyen.

French literature had carried psychological analysis to the highest degree because its concern with the virtuosities of language (frowned upon by the puritanical influence) made such explorations possible. No virtuosity can equal the dazzling feats of language of Jean Giraudoux, of Proust, Blaise Cendrars, or Henri Michaux.

The sharp division between the realistic and surrealistic novel did not take place in France. *Château d'Argol*, a purely surrealistic work, appeared at the same time as Sartre's *Nausea*. One perhaps an antidote for the other. Surrealism as a cure for nausea.

It is the fusion of such opposites which may be the contribution of our contemporary writers. The writers who are aware that we live in a multidimensional world, and that using symbols for mathematics is no different from using symbols to describe an unconscious which stubbornly persists in expressing itself in this way.

Associating symbolism with romanticism and discarding it was an error which psychoanalysis promptly corrected. Symbolism is here to stay. Because of science, the painter accepted abstraction. Because of the familiarity with the psychic X-ray images of our feelings, the poet accepted abstraction, symbolism. Getting inside man's mind without being able to reach the surface (action) was equally sterile. Such a claustrophobia was created by Kafka, who saw only the nightmare of man's anonymous cities and collective life. Staying on the surface is monotonous and sterile, too. I feel America is entering a marvelous period of imagination and expansion of consciousness by way of poetic prose.

The poem became a vignette and inappropriate for an epic America. Writers like Marguerite Young used poetic prose without the complexities and multilanguages of Joyce. Her work is completely subterranean, an epic dedicated to the theme of reality and illusion. She took figures from American folk life, stock characters—the prize fighter, the country doctor, the old maid, the lawyer, the banker, the nurse, the suffragette, the bone-breaker—and plunged them into the revivifying waters of the unconscious, and they emerged as myth figures, in an ocean of waking dreams, visions, reveries, monologues, so that we could *see into the depths* of the full richness of man's mind. The book has an oceanic form, parallel to its contents (we cannot measure the depth of the ocean at some points nor the depths of the unconscious). The tragicomic elements are native, natural, and far-reaching. She has roots in the simplest reality, in the earth, but a power of levitation accorded to very few poets. She uses everything and transforms it into a symbolic drama, investing it with meaning. People drown in their unconscious. The alcoholic old country doctor may or may not have fallen into the river with his carriage and horse one stormy night, but he is plunged into his infinite unconscious and drowned in images, memories, personal and collective, personal and universal.

The novel still lags behind theater, film, and painting, behind modern dance and modern architecture.

But a novel as profound as *Miss MacIntosh, My Darling*, a novel which contains the fantasy of Giraudoux's *The Madwoman of Chaillot*, the comic moments of Charlie Chaplin, the whimsical wisdom of *Alice in Wonderland*, the voyages to the antipodes of Joyce, meets with the resistance many critics and readers have to a voyage in depth, to a multidimensional concept of character and expression.

The most powerful of literary movements, which I call "resistantialism," consists of those who are afraid of going inside, who have a fear of intimacy or contact with human beings. They feel such proximity will cloud their insight or involve their feelings. They defend themselves against feeling with irony and clowning.

It is the absence of involvement which caused so much isolation, and lack of contact with others and with life. D. H. Lawrence insisted that we should have first of all the passionate experience, and then analysis. The fear of subjective experience indicates lack of confidence in the self. You do not lose yourself in a subjective novel. Experience can only be effective, valuable in proportion to the extent and depth of our involvement.

In poetic prose a demand is made upon our senses and imagination. The magic use of words is intended as an invitation to participate. If one prefers objectivity one should read history, psychology, philosophy, science. Fiction has a different purpose. The function of the novel is to give you an emotional experience. To put you in direct contact with lives you may not otherwise have a chance to live. The writing is intended to sweep you along like a ritual. A living relationship to all things animates writing with life and warmth. A personal relationship to all things gives life.

Good science fiction shows you the world of tomorrow based

on scientific probabilities. Good exploratory writing shows you the man of tomorrow, the man you might be, based on psychological probabilities. There is no way to become familiar with this new world within ourselves except by a fearless exploration of it. We are suffering from lack of contact. It is a generalized feeling which is often explained by the presence of the bomb. But danger should actually sharpen and heighten our capacity to live and feel, not numb or reduce it.

The new novel could rectify failures, ugliness. It could point the way to all the *potentialities* of life, of mediums, of art. The fact that life and its realities may weigh heavily on us is not necessarily a reason for becoming heavy. A lightness of attitude, a pleasure in creation help a man to escape his prison of duties and burdens and ultimately to change conditions themselves. Much has been said about the cure of neurosis, but neurosis is simply a negative state of being. The creative writer is the one who teaches expansion and liberation of the human mind.

Imagination teaches that there is always a way out. In the Japanese film, *Woman of the Dunes*, the scientist, studying the life of an insect, becomes trapped by the needs of a village group and escapes madness through a scientific interest in solving the villager's problem.

Even language is necessary to this expansion. When Blaise Cendrars, a marvelous writer much admired by Henry Miller and essentially a man of action and adventure, suffered from his own virtuosity of language, he became a writer only the initiates could read. He was sad to discover in Henry Miller the man of action and adventure who could use the language of the man in the street. But Miller did not remain enclosed in his local, colloquial language. He proceeded to enrich it. When he did this by way of surrealistic flights of language in counterpoint to the plainness and earthiness of daily language, critics like Maxwell Geismar, a natural enemy of all poetry, lamented un-American departures from naturalism.

The language of the man in the street is limited. All life tends to crystallize into a mold. People accept constricted lives because they find it easier to surrender to such molds. But within these molds man dies. Men who live only by habit and routine die.

THE WRITER AS PROPHET

The writer may be a prophet. When Franz Kafka first described the experience of a man who feels small, lost, and confused in a vast world of impersonal institutions and bureaucracy, his reaction seemed subjective, exaggerated, abnormal. But now that we have caught up with such a world the sensation has become familiar to us. I understood Kafka not when I first read him but when I tried to find an office in the Empire State Building through hallways which looked absolutely identical. Kafka was not ahead of his time. He was sensitive to the possible developments of standardization, its effect on us, its dehumanizing process. We were slow to realize the new kind of anxiety which vast, anonymous, headless organizations would cause a human being. The writer, in the case of Kafka, accepted his sensitized (unanesthetized) reaction to a new situation just emerging. Anyone dealing with bureaucracy, passport departments, tax papers could have developed and expanded his anxiety, his feeling of being caught in a vast machine, into the drama fully done by Kafka. Other writers might dismiss such a mood, such a state of mind carelessly and never enter fully into it. The subjective experience of a writer is not unique. It is something he shares with others. What may be unique is his way of expressing it, because each new experience requires a new form of expression. He has to feel his way, invent new words for a latent, potential, as yet unexpressed emotion. He has to light up with his expression worlds which may never have been lighted before.

By annihilating one sense, such as physical vision, an artist seeks to develop other senses, just as the blind develop other forms of sensitivity, and the mute sign language and other expressions. Writing is subject to the influence of other arts. Robbe-Grillet writes scenarios. His skeletonic novels took their structure from a stringent scenario. In films we accepted abrupt transitions, jump cutting, fadeouts, flashbacks, fluid dream sequences, superimposition of images.

We must continue to make the contents of the unconscious as clear as the contents of the conscious mind.

Poetic prose might be compared to jazz. Jazz does not work unless it swings. The beat must be constantly tugged and pushed across the familiar line of the four-four balance until the real rhythmic message is *felt more than heard*. Classical jazz cannot swing because the composer's notation is too rigid. Duke Ellington said: "We're going to do this thing until your pulse and my pulse are the same!"

I am concentrating on the writers who have attempted this fusion of conscious and unconscious. The novels of Maude Hutchins, witty and intelligent, are subtle blends of reality and unconscious streams of consciousness. Anna Kavan explored the nocturnal worlds of our dreams, fantasies, imagination, and non-reason. Such an exploration takes greater courage and skill in expression. As the events of the world prove the constancy of the nonrational, it becomes absurd to treat such events with rational logic. But people prefer to accept the notion of the absurd rather than to search for the meaning, the symbolic act which is quite clear for whoever is willing to decipher the unconscious. The writer who follows the designs and patterns of the unconscious achieves the same revelation.

Anna Kavan made a significant beginning as a nocturnal writer with *House of Sleep* and achieved this kind of revelation with a classic equal to the work of Kafka titled *Asylum Pieces* in which the nonrational human being caught in a web of unreality still struggles to maintain a dialogue with those who cannot understand him. In later books the waking dreamers give up the struggle and simply tell of their adventures. They live in solitude with their shadows, hallucinations, prophecies.

We admire the deep-sea diver exploring the depth of the ocean. We do not admire enough those who are able to describe their nocturnal experiences, those who demonstrate that the surface does not contain a key to authentic experience, that the truth lies in what we *feel* and not in what we *see*. Familiarity with inner landscapes would in the end illumine the mysteries of the human mind. The scientist can report psychological findings, but the writer *has been there*. His is a firsthand report. And this is not a personal, unique voyage to the antipodes of the mind. The unconscious is a universal ocean in which all of us have roots.

In William Goyen reality, illusion, and the dream are often fused as in poetry. Passages of such poetic harmonies occur in all his books. He is the poet of atmosphere, climate, mood, and subtle exchanges.

In America we have few evaluators but many intuitive, nocturnal writers such as Djuna Barnes, John Hawkes, Isabel Bolton, Nathanael West. We never gave to Djuna Barnes the respect we gave Isak Dinesen, because she was less traditional, more original. Isak Dinesen was a classic writer of traditional sources; Djuna Barnes a poet. We did not give Maude Hutchins the attention we give to Marguerite Duras. Why is this? Are we still unable to form our own judgment of contemporary writers (as France can do) so that we feel more secure in admiring already consecrated writers?

France kept an even balance between its naturalistic writers and its imaginative writers, between its classical writers and its innovators. We did not.

Camus was a French writer who turned to American writers and then, after writing *The Stranger*, said: "American technique is one-dimensional. It leads nowhere."

The slicker, the glossier, the more enameled the surface, the more difficult it is to fuse with the subterranean which is fluid, rhythmic, musical, versatile, mobile, fluctuating, rippling.

We once had a radio program titled: *Music Not for Everyone*. It was not snobbery. It was the recognition that some music requires initiation. We should have books not for everyone, books which reflect experience and not a fear of it, confrontations and not evasions, which bring awareness rather than blindness.

The novelist of the future, like the modern physicist, knows that a new psychological reality can be explored only under new conditions of atmospheric pressure, temperature, and speed, as well as in terms of new time and space dimensions for which the old forms and conventions of the novel are completely inadequate.

We are all like Walter Mitty as described by Thurber, going about our daily lives while living a second, a third, a fourth life simultaneously as heroes of amazing adventures. Some of us may ask: "Why do we not leave this hidden man alone if he is so determined to remain secret?" But the truth is that this hidden man makes his presence felt, even as a stowaway, and when we deny him existence he takes his revenge in strange ways: we become unbearably bored with our masquerades, and unbearably lonely because our relationships are between masked selves and ultimately lack reality and warmth.

We should have been able to detect the symptoms: absence of self led to the death of emotion; death of emotion to dead writing; *and the death of emotion has led inevitably to excess violence which is the major theme of our literature today and a symptom of schizophrenia, violence in order to feel alive because the divided self feels its own death and seeks sensation to affirm its existence.*

We paid a high price for our cult of toughness and our disparagement of sensibility. *Violence in place of emotion.*

We protest against the violence, but we do not read the nonviolent writers. We protest against the absence of contact, but we do not read the writers who deal with relationships and not with nonrelationships or antirelationships.

As for the preoccupation of the social critics that the psychological novel or study of one human being could be of no value to society, there was never in any novel of social consciousness a better description of social evils than those of the subjective writer Marcel Proust. In all proletarian literature there was never a more human description of a servant than his delineation of Françoise. There never was a more beautiful description of nature than those of this shut-in man whose cork-lined room was so ironically treated as a symbol of insulation. Which proves that empathy and sensitivity are more important than documentation and door-to-door statistics.

There is a prejudice against subjective writing, but when a personal writer communicates to us the process by which he realizes himself, by which his consciousness is enlarged and enriched, he hopes that our own awareness will be enlarged, our ignorance of life diminished.

When the so-called realists decided that romantic love was an illusion, they forgot that illusion may be at times an intuition of a potential, and that it is in the vision of a potential that the seed of greatness and creation lies.

When we decided to believe only what was visible, we lost the faculty for apprehending what might be. Out of such a distorted view of *what is* came the monstrosities of pop art. Accepting what is (a complete service station in a museum, Campbell's Soup cartons and billboards in our living rooms) is an act of passivity, an act of resignation, of impotence, lack of invention and transformation, also an inability to discard *what is* and create *what might be*. To accept the billboards, blow them up, and live with them denies all the new avenues of design created by science. A cover of the *Scientific American* is now the refuge of aesthetics and beautiful abstractions. The artist has surrendered. The madman who went about tearing down the billboards for their ugliness was closer to being a hero than the pop artist. He might have become the hero-artist if he had redesigned them.

Passivity and inertia are the opposite of creation. The active, fecundating role of the novelist has been forgotten. He is not there to depict man as he is but also as he might be. He is there to give an example of the freedom of choice, freedom to transcend his destiny and his surroundings, master his limitations and restrictions. Today's novelist, like the pop artist, has forgotten (if he ever knew) how to transform, transpose, inspire. The poet and the folk singer remain the ones who can do this. Poetry was the alchemy which taught us to convert raw materials into gold.

Without poetry which makes its appeal to the senses we cannot retain a living relationship to all things.

When we describe inarticulateness, we perpetuate inarticulateness. When we stress ugliness, we perpetuate ugliness. Many of our novels are caricatures of life which will perpetuate revulsion and revolution, hatred and alienation.

There is a form of writing which is like the art of music. It can affect us through the senses directly without first appealing to the intellect, without going through an analytical or conscious process. In this, it acts more like our life experiences, which enter the body directly before we are able to dissect them.

Some critics have tantrums in the face of a mystery. Mystery is simply a dim corner of an unexplored world, and any day we may stumble on its meaning. The end of *Nightwood* was a mystery to me for twenty years. Until I met a woman painter who said to me: "Whenever I am with very conventional people I feel like *barking*!"

The intellect has a dehydrating effect on experience. Analysis by itself has a reductive effect. That is why I sought in my novels to have passionate experience and interpretation in a dynamic relationship, done while living, simultaneously almost. But for this we would need to read the novel as a poem, for its rhythm, its images, its sensory effect.

Three children in a drawing class happened upon a definition of attitudes a writer can select from. Each one was asked to paint a tree. The first one painted a faithful copy of a tree, a natural everyday tree. The second one looked at it and said: "Yours is the kind of tree I see every day and I'm tired of it. Mine is a tree the way I would like it to be." She showed a drawing of an abstract tree, barely indicated, as if swept by the wind into tumultuous wavering lines. The third one painted a fanciful tree with fanciful leaves and fruit and said: "Mine is a tree from a country we never saw."

The writers I have concentrated my attention on are those who use the entire scale of musical notations and use language to its fullest. In fact, those who have invented scales and sounds of their own.

John Hawkes was introduced by *New Directions* in the forties as our first surrealist writer.

In 1948 Albert Guérard analyzed *The Cannibal* meticulously. And then commented: [22]

> . . . This interesting story is left very much in the dark, however; is obscured by brilliant detail, by a submersion in many different minds and their obsessions, by a total vision of horror . . . and by a very distinct reluctance . . . to tell a story directly. As in Faulkner and Conrad, we have the effect of a solitary flashlight playing back and forth over a dark and cluttered room; the images may be sharp ones, but a casual reference to some major happening may be clarified only fifty or a hundred pages later. . . .
>
> Of the true solid ingredients of surrealism—illogic, horror, macabre humor—*The Cannibal* has a full share. . . .
>
> How far Hawkes will go . . . must depend on . . . how richly he exploits his ability to achieve truth through distortion; . . . As Kafka achieved a truth about his society through perhaps unintentional claustrophobic images and impressions . . . so Hawkes . . . has achieved some truth about his [pp. xi, xiii, xv, xvi].

In 1962 Albert Guérard added a new preface to the same book: [23]

> *The Cannibal* itself no longer seems as willful or eccentric as it did in 1948, nor as difficult to read. This is partly in accord with the law that the highly original artist must create the taste that will eventually applaud him. Time, time and powerful reiteration, at last triumph over ridicule. *The Cannibal* prepares us to read *The Lime Twig;* but, even more obviously, *The Lime Twig* and the others prepare us to reread *The Cannibal.* Beyond this, *The Cannibal* doubtless profits from the drift of the novel generally, away from flat reporting and delusive clarities. Readers are no longer as distrustful as they were in 1948 of imaginative distortion and poetic invention.

When Mr. Guérard speaks of difficult writers such as Kafka, Djuna Barnes, and Faulkner, he makes a remarkable footnote: "I understand that Mr. Hawkes had all but finished *The Cannibal* before reading Kafka, Faulkner, and Djuna Barnes. His earlier reading of modern experimental literature was largely confined to poetry."

Leslie Fiedler introduces John Hawkes's latest book, *The Lime Twig:* [24]

He is a lonely eccentric, . . . the least read novelist of substantial merit in the United States. . . . Hawkes may be an unpopular writer, but he is not an esoteric one; for the places he defines are the places in which we all live between sleeping and waking, and the pleasures he affords are the pleasures of returning to those places between waking and sleeping.

. . . he has pursued through certain lunar landscapes . . . his vision of horror and baffled passion.

Counterfeits of insanity (automatic writing, the scrawls of the drunk and doped) are finally boring; . . . compositions of the actually insane are . . . terrible and depressing. Hawkes gives us neither of these surrenders to unreason but rather reason's last desperate attempt to know what unreason is; and in such knowledge there are possibilities not only for poetry and power but for pleasure as well [pp. viii, ix, xiv].

Mr. Guérard misinterprets surrealism and confuses it with the Gothic horror stories. He dismisses Djuna Barnes as effete. Perhaps in this case Mr. Guérard prefers in John Hawkes that he makes "terror rather than love the center of his work." All the women I mention in this book dealt with the anguish of love instead of destruction, and that may also be why I faced the firing squad alone when *Ladders to Fire* first appeared. The erratic course of love is evidently effete, precious, esoteric, and strange.

It is an interesting commentary on the lack of appreciation of *literary* writing that the public love of violence and cruelty never included the surrealistic tales of John Hawkes. I have no personal love of his work because I dislike sadism and violence totally, in every form, but I am paying tribute to his writing, to the quality of his style, and if, like Mailer, he makes "terror rather than love the center of his work," his nightmares are far more subtle and intelligent and terrifying than Mailer's *American Dream.*

It does occur to me now that the reason I had to write my own defenses, and was not supported by the critics who introduced Djuna Barnes and John Hawkes, lies in the irony of Mr. Guérard's own words: he dismisses Djuna Barnes as effete, but accepts the grotesque in John Hawkes's nightmares, an interesting paradox. Djuna Barnes's *Nightwood* and Marguerite Young's *Miss MacIntosh, My Darling* are both powerful extensions of the poem, and there is nothing effete about *Nightwood* unless Mr. Guérard so defines feminine writing. Djuna Barnes dealt with the anguish of love instead of the horrors of destruction and sadism. Possibly because I also dealt with love and not with cruelty, I was labeled effete, precious, esoteric, and strange. And so what William Goyen wittily called "the motorcycle-leather pseudomasculinity" is carefully nurtured by certain male critics, and the perversions of sadism in John Hawkes' work are admired while the studies of love and its erratic course as in *Nightwood* and *Miss MacIntosh, My Darling* are still not fully and justly evaluated.

I hope the younger generation will take note of this unbalance. The world of the critic is predominantly masculine. It is a one-party world.

Maude Hutchins is another writer of style and originality. She makes minute studies of relationships. We need such close-ups of human nature denied us in our crowded lives and crowded books. She is one of our few erotic writers, and by erotic I mean something quite different from sexual. We have many direct anatomical sexual writers. Very few erotic. By erotic I mean the totality of sexual experience, its atmosphere, mood, sensual flavors, mystery, vibrations, the state of ecstasy into which it may plunge us, the full range of the senses and emotions which accompany, surround it, and which the explicit flat clinical descriptions destroy. She deals with unusual relationships, adolescents who discover their bodies, the hypocrisy of adults. A *Diary of Love* is as subtle an exploration of the senses as Colette's books. She has wit and intelligence. Her last published short stories are highly surrealistic.

She makes use of subtle physical images to describe sensual feelings, experiences, relationships. She can say startling things with elegance, and they carry further.

Critics love to describe this as the small, personal world of woman, when psychologists know that this is the soil and roots of our larger involvements. Not all large and crowded canvases have depth of insight. Like Colette, Maude Hutchins concentrates on the family, on a few characters, but vividly and deeply. She is adept at descriptions of nature and animals.

The cult of direct description which has given our literature a false masculinity has made critics unaware of feminine writers. There are many states and sensations which defy barracks language and which are done masterfully by women writers. Maude Hutchins has gone further in sensuous experience than most of our "motorcycle" type writers. She has described intricate and fascinating states of body and mind. She does this by a combination of skill, boldness, wit, and a childlike liveliness and directness. There is not one bland or meaningless line. She has sharp senses, sharp definitions of emotions, a total response to experience heightened by imagination and fantasy. Some of her parents resemble the parents of Cocteau's *Les parents terrible*. It is the adolescents in her book who carry the burden of clairvoyance. They see, they know. It is not a battle between innocence and evil but between awareness and hypocrisy. Her adults are hypocritical. The novels are a quest for truth, and this truth is usually uttered by those at the beginning of their lives. Her work is unique, rich, animated by a sprightly intelligence and verve. It is yet to be evaluated and appreciated.

In her *Diary of Love* [25] the personal emphasis gives physical power.

This morning I helped with the produce. I picked raspberries, or rather I pulled raspberries. It is Indian Summer and a foggy, warm mist soothes the left over garden tempting it to grow a little longer but not providing the energy, the challenge of cooler, or even hotter, flightier weather. The raspberries come off easily, they are so ripe, so willing but without ardor. I lift a handful to my mouth, tilt up my chin, and too lazy to chew, too languorous and affectionate to demolish or bite, I press them to the roof of my mouth with my tongue and the juice, the same temperature, I guess, as the inside of my mouth, I do not feel any more than I do the raspberries themselves; of equal thrust, I suppose, equal density, nonresistant, therefore; they do not seem to be there. It is like the smell of perfume in my mouth. I want more of this but not too fast, a little variety: I pull ten more, lovely and plum colored, away from the small penis-like excrescence of each and the naked immodesty of the little scene settles in my brain. Already, thinking ahead about something else, I carry out my sensuous plan of a moment ago, losing a little of the pleasure. I trundle the ten in my tongue, curving it up at the edges, and then I slowly raise the lovely load to the vault, the red vault, and crush them softly, all of us the same color, the same, even the fog is pink . . . it is a kind of sweet disintegration, a lack of tension; no bones [pp. 3–4].

Henry Miller in *Black Spring* has a whole chapter called *Into the Night Life* which is one of the most surrealistic in all his work. "*My mind searches vainly for some remembrance which is older than any remembrance.*" It uses physical images, familiar images, to reconstruct some nocturnal journey. "At the Brooklyn Bridge I stand as usual waiting for the trolley to swing around . . ." and proceeds in an autointoxication of words and images, play on words and incongruous correlation of images, a drunken journey through grotesque fantasies. "A Coney Island of the Mind." "It is neither night nor day."

It had begun as a parody of *House of Incest* and ended as an experiment of his own, fusing dreams and inventions. My objection at the time was that it was too real, because images in dreams are not so concrete, they are incandescent, luminous, transparent. I felt then it lacked the mystery of the dream, its half-born, half-finished images. But today I realize that each one of us, according to his temperament and his style, will carry with him into nocturnal worlds of imagination his own physical elements, and that Henry Miller was closer to Hieronymus Bosch, closer to Dali than Breton. To write about dreams he turned the world upside down and scrambled images, but it was the contents of the physical world he reshuffled, it was not a metaphysical experience, that is a physical image suffused with light, an X ray of our psychic reconstructions.

Jerzy Kosinski in *The Painted Bird* treats of the violence and cruelty inherent in human beings. He does not describe it with a perverse interest, or an infatuation with sadism as Truman Capote does in *In Cold Blood*. It is organic sadism, inseparable from a period in history, a moment of persecution and its effect on a child of seven. Part of its power is that it is a genuine moment of history, authentic, tragic, reported by a poet, in a style of great beauty and originality which appeals to the intelligence. Once again as in *The Cannibal*, or as in Genêt, the artistic expression gives depth to the experience.

> Lekh . . . would choose the strongest bird, tie it to his wrist, and . . . paint its wing, head and breast in rainbow hues until it became more dappled and vivid than a bouquet of wild flowers. . . . Then we would go into the thick of the forest. There Lekh took out the painted bird and ordered me to hold it in my hand and squeeze it lightly. The bird would begin to twitter and attract a flock of the same species which would fly nervously over our heads. Our prisoner, hearing them, strained toward them, warbling more loudly, its little heart, locked in its freshly painted breast, beating violently. When a sufficient number of birds gathered above our heads, Lekh would give me a sign to release the prisoner. It would soar, happy and free, a spot of rainbow against the backdrop of clouds, and then plunge into the waiting brown flock. For an instant the birds were confounded. The painted bird circled from one end of the flock to the other, vainly trying to convince its kin that it was one of them. But, dazzled by its brilliant colors, they flew around it unconvinced. The painted bird would be forced farther and farther away as it zealously tried to enter the ranks of the flock. We saw soon afterwards how one bird after another would peel off in a fierce attack. Shortly the many-hued shape lost its place in the sky and dropped to the ground. . . . When we finally found the painted birds they were usually dead.[26]

The painted bird is a symbol of what is taking place throughout the book. The persecution of one human species by another, but more often the persecution within the same species of the one who seems not to belong.

All of William Goyen's books contain extensions of the poem

and a perfect integration of poetry and prose, conscious and un-conscious. He enriches his prose with the rhythms and atmos-phere of poetry.

In a story from the collection of short stories *Faces of Blood Kindred* there is an example [27] of the magic atmosphere he creates.

As he sat on his bed, close to where the dream happened, he thought how that day of the dead horse had been filled with the sense of enormous objects falling, like buildings into streets, bridges into rivers and statues into plazas, until the little memory of the day moth had ended it with the sense of fragile flights and glimmer of small risings and flutterings. For he had walked, a fugitive, out of his room of giant disorder, of violence, as though Cain had lived there, where the weight of his secret life was heavy as fallen stone and nothing, nothing would rise out of it or would raise it again; though he knew the fragility of his violence and the delicacy of his ferocity. But he saw, now in his room, that a balance was struggling, that a shape from the outside, in the world, and inside, in a dream, was at work. There is a link, he knew again now, between the happenings of the daily world and the dreaming mind that holds its hidden images. It was as though life were unfolding on either side of a partition, a wall.

Now he held the dream as close as another body in his bed; and now there was a joining, as in love. We cannot believe, he thought, how all things work together towards some ultimate clear meaning, we cannot believe. Human life is at once a conspiracy to prove us of small or no end, and a conspiracy of incidents and images to lead us to a beginning again.

Unlike Truman Capote, William Goyen matured without be-traying his sensitivity, he became stronger without surrendering the qualities which made him both human and subtle, able to handle overtones in relationships without destroying them in the process. The balanced, harmonious maturity of sensitiveness is a rare quality in our culture, for it usually does not have the endurance to survive.

All his books have a haunting, a lasting effect. *The House of Breath, In a Farther Country, Ghost and Flesh* are all of an extra-ordinarily even, sustained quality. He has his own, distinctive tonalities and fluid grace.

THE WORK OF MARGUERITE YOUNG

Everything I have said about writing, every attitude, theory, technique, suggestions and indications, can be learned from the richest source of all, the work of Marguerite Young. Her work represents the nourishment which every young writer needs. It is endlessly fecund and fecundating, it develops free association, inner monologues, and *psychological reality* to the highest degree. It is a constant feast of images, both profound and comical.

William Goyen has summed up [28] the essence of *Miss MacIntosh, My Darling* better than anyone.

A mammoth epic, a massive fable, a picaresque journey, a Faustian quest and a work of stunning magnitude and beauty. . . . Miss MacIntosh, an old, drowned woman, is "reality" to Vera Cartwheel, whose tidal monologue relates her search for that reality. Broken-nosed, bald-headed Miss MacIntosh was a "plainly sensible woman" who spoke in proverbs and axioms to her young charge. She was nursemaid to the voyager narrator, whose mother languishes in grandiose dreams under opium in a baroque New England seaside house among imaginary guests and companions whom she "dreams." Miss MacIntosh is unadorned, bare-breasted fact; the uncovered pate of reality; illusion stripped of its wig, its false bosom. She comes from the real ground of the Midwest, from What Cheer, Iowa. Vera Cartwheel's very environment is illusion, delusion, fantasy. She struggles against "dreaming" people; but when she turns from what is illusion she encounters only illusion again. "What shall we do when fleeing from illusion we are confronted by illusion? When falling from illusion, we fall into illusion?" cries out Vera Cartwheel as she voyages through a kind of drowned world, seeking her darling, truth. For when Miss MacIntosh walks into the sea one day, leaving her aspects and articles upon the shore—her wig, her false breast, her old mackintosh, her black umbrella—Vera Cartwheel begins a search for her drowned reality which was, in ironic effect, illusion. This is the theme and ground of this sweeping, swelling and inexhaustibly breeding fiction, which pulls behind it, on and on, page after page, loads and burdens of images proliferating images; precise cataloguing; inventories and enumerations of facts, plants, hats, heraldries, geographies, birds, rivers, cities ancient and modern, kings and dynasties and archeologies. It breaks into conceits, images, metaphors, preciosities, bizarreries. Concrete character detail elaborates into huge metaphors, into musicalizations, rhapsodies, repetitively rolling and resounding and doubling back upon themselves in an oceanic tumult. The book's mysterious readability is effected through enchantment and hypnosis. . . . The fluent, seminal passages, grounded on these four beings and their basic significance, are so procreative and so fertile that they spurt forth in some of the richest, most expressive, most original and exhaustively revealing passages of prose that this reader has experienced in a long time. . . . Rarely does American fiction break out into fullness of song, into the force and vigor of increase, of organic embellishment. Rather it has shrunk, or dieted itself, into smaller, safer cries and statements, well-formed and studied representations of human experience. . . . In *Miss MacIntosh, My Darling* we have come upon a strong, deep loudness, a full-throated outcry, a literature of expanse and daring that makes most of our notable male writers look like a motorcycle gang trying to prove a kind of literary masculinity. . . . For *Miss MacIntosh, My Darling*, soaring into the universal, has rooted itself in the American reality.

Marguerite Young began as a poet and expanded the poem into prose—*Miss MacIntosh, My Darling*. It can be compared to a symphony. It deals with obsessions, which are played upon, expanded, developed, as they occur in our destiny, occur and recur as they do in life which is full of recurrences, tides, and cycles. It can be compared to the ocean, the favored symbol of the unconscious. It takes place, is born, expands, and lives in the subconscious. It is an oceanic book, with tidal monologues.

The recurrent theme is this submerging into the unconscious and coming up again with phrases which sum up the fusion of illusion and reality, its convergences, and then submerging again for more explorations. The image of "drowning" is one of the key images. Night brings diffusion, and day brings great clarity and definition. The search is for distinguishing between illusion and reality, and the philosophic outcome is that they cannot be separated. Symbolically, both the realistic and the illusory characters disappear at the moment one is about to define them.

Marguerite Young demonstrates the validity of dreams, their power, the deceptions of appearances, confusion of identities, multiplicity of selves that cluster within the integral theme.

"Perhaps all things were illusion—this crying, this crumpling, this falling away, this vanishing, this revelation of depth . . ."

The metaphysical concept that our life has meaning is deeper than that reached by the materialist that the world is absurd and meaningless (Camus). The sense of emptiness came from accepting only what we see and not what lies beyond appearances. What we see is altered by what we feel. The change of mood is like the change of lighting on a stage. In *Miss MacIntosh, My Darling* the quest for reality in a world of illusion is a metaphysical quest which ends in the acceptance that they are undistinguishable because they lie in our unconscious, ultimately, and we see the world through its prisms.

In Paris, before the war, André Breton's *Nadja* was the symbol of the woman who obeyed her unconscious totally and spoke in the language of the nonrational so clear to the poet. There are two kinds of people who attain complete freedom from the conventional world patterns: the poet, who is able to see what is behind the masks, and the madman. Even philosophers regarded the mad as people who wanted to escape ordinary life. In ancient lore the mad were touched with inspiration, were often prophetic or oracular. In a more scientific era we know that those who shut off contact with external reality sometimes attain remarkable visions into their unconscious, reach wilder shores of knowledge closed to those who maintain contact only with ordinary life.

Antonin Artaud was the visionary among the surrealists. It was not his madness which gave him such powers, it was that the madness cut him off from family, wife, friends, children, home, profession, work and left him in an abstract world, confronting only his imagination and intuitions. Other poets did not have to go so far. André Breton observes *Nadja*, is not carried away into her fantasies. Other people seek to shut out the loud, insistent, demanding, invasive outer world through drugs, to contemplate the marvels of the psychic world, dreams, fantasies, visions, reveries. The cultivation of dreams, and writing from the unconscious are the remedies I prescribe. In *Miss MacIntosh, My*

Darling every character is, at one time or another, plunged into the revitalizing waters of the unconscious. The mother is the symbol of illusion because she lies in bed smoking opium and monologuing, imagining people visiting her, mingling memories and hallucinations, dreams and waking dreams. She is the obvious dreamer, the one who can be recognized. The others seem to be the nondreamers, but as the book progresses their realities are questioned. The child is fearful of being drawn into the mother's nocturnal voyages, and turns for security to the symbol of a down-to-earth practical nursemaid, Miss MacIntosh, *who is real*. She talks about common sense, she is organized, ordinary, and familiar.

First, we are allowed into the mother's opium dream:

My mother was oblivious to the realities of flesh and blood. . . . My mother trusted no one, nor was she ever to be surprised, it seemed, by unusual transformations or transports, shifting of form, by anything that might ever transpire, by anything protean, for the opium dreams surrounding her had provided no pillars of strength, no rose which did not eventually fade, no voice which did not fail. She presumed always that things were not what they seemed, that all forms must change their shapes, that all characters must bear, even to those most familiar with them, an element of cold surprise, even of horror, that her life was this play of illusion, that there should be nothing certain but uncertainty, no pavement more secure than the glassy surface of the evening tide and the far wash of waves. All her days were her nights, and all her nights were her days, and there was an eternal twilight, an obfuscation of faces, a crucial bewilderment.[29]

This is, undeniably, the dreamer. But Marguerite Young proceeds to examine the life of other characters: Cousin Hannah, the suffragette. She spent her life trying to overthrow man, but when she died, they found forty trunks filled with wedding dresses.

Mr. Spitzer is the surviving member of identical twins. He is constantly confused about his identity, is not sure whether it was his brother who died, or whether he did.

Perhaps he was so victimized by routine itself, that consulting his planetary wrist watch which told the course of the minutes if not of his own steps through light and darkness, he did not notice many of those details which he took for granted, being unable to live by a continual surprise, unable to die by a continual surprise, and gearing himself at all times to the unexpected as if it were expected, as if no surprise could ever assault him who was always surprised and valued his dignity perhaps more than his life. Perhaps he had already taken his last step.[30]

We are now allowed to examine the reality of the nursemaid as seen by the child, Vera Cartwheel:

Everything definite. Everything in there is reality to this child and Miss MacIntosh . . . old fashioned nursemaid . . . the sunlight was her meat, her drink, the source of her strength, that which kept her so robust, so ready for emergency, her clenched hand uplifted, her common sense invulnerable to any sudden attack of foolishness or weakness . . . and she did not believe in things invisible . . . she was brusque and rough and ready . . .[31]

The first crisis in contemplation of reality for the child is that Miss MacIntosh's hair, "brick-red, perfectly in order, almost Tyrian purple in certain lights," turns out to be a wig on a bald head.

In one of the longest nocturnal journeys ever depicted in literature, Vera Cartwheel sends out all of her energies to search for reality. Reality is embodied in her old nurse, who disappears. It is more than a human drama, this contrast between the mother who represents the dreamed life and Miss MacIntosh who represents a homely reality. The child feels she will only be rescued from dreaming by remaining close to Miss MacIntosh, and she cannot accept her disappearance. Miss MacIntosh is said to have walked into the sea, and her eyeglasses were found on the beach. The motif of disappearing, drowning in the unconscious, appears several times in the book. The mystery of her disappearance makes Vera Cartwheel think she has also dreamed Miss MacIntosh. She has to verify her death.

The reality of all the characters is questioned. They have

homespun, homely, earthy roots. There are the Christian hang-man, dedicated to his profession, the country doctor's mono-logues, the house built by Mr. Spitzer to represent his twinship, a house with two stairways, two pianos, two living rooms, two doors. There are images and scenes which would nourish several Fellini films.

In conjunction with its allegorical meaning, it has great hu-manity. The plight of man caught in his metaphysical quest is done with sympathy. We are not taken into one mind only, but into the nocturnal life of ordinary characters: what they imagine, what they are obsessed with, what traumas, what neuroses, what humorous or comic confusions, all of this as important as what they do.

Obsessions in human beings are recurrent, like motifs in a symphony. They are woven into the continuity of a life. They are never resolved. The wide spaces, the oceanic proportions of the book parallel the illimitable unconscious, which is not measur-able, and the timelessness of our metaphysical existence. It is not ended by death.

I believe this book represents the nocturnal America just as *Don Quixote* became the spirit of Spain, and *Ulysses* that of Ireland. For Marguerite Young, herself a native Midwesterner, Americans are the wildest dreamers of all, and also the greatest poets.

The book is a long lesson in the development of images, in the hypnotic and magic qualities of language, the contagion by rhythm, repetition, and in her own words: ". . . the necessity that every wave of fantasy should rise to its fullest height but always return to shore."

One can learn from it how an image can be pursued, de-veloped, expanded until it yields its fullest meaning. She teaches the patient, thorough, courageous pursuit. The image never shreds, dissolves. It solidifies into a truth, a paradox, a new wis-dom, reveals new shores.

The comic element is strong. Even the animals are both real

and unreal. The existence of a moose is questioned, while its call is heard. "Perhaps all things were illusion."

For students of writing, for those who wish to be opened up, I recommend this fountain of images which can, like a divining rod, lead young writers to their own sources and caches of riches.

A writer of exceptional style and subtlety is Marianne Hauser. When people will tire of noise, crassness, and vulgarity, they will hear the truly contemporary complexities of Marianne Hauser's superimpositions. A new generation trained to imagery by the film may appreciate her offbeat characters and skill in portraying the uncommon.

In a story called *The Other Side of the River* from *A Lesson in Music* there is a unique study of a relationship in space: [32]

No windows, however, could guard her against the storm that had swept her across the seven seas. A new issue of the picture magazine would lie at the foot of her swept doorstep each Thursday to drive her on. Through the blue humming ether she sailed into new adventures, exploring what had already been explored and printed for all to see. She pursued the zigzags of Brook's bold footsteps. Her own walk was lighter than a ghost's. Jealously, slyly, she traced her over through the thick of cancerous jungles; and not one crackling sound betrayed her presence. The giant faces of stone gods, man-made mountains, rose from the wilderness. Blooming shrubs and flowers grew like wounds from spiraled stone ears. Screeching jungle birds nested between the wanton, smiling lips of the gods. Old wonders merged with new wonders, street riots with floods, the shorn heads of warriors with the shorn heads of monks, an endless double exposure. She hunted her lover across lands and sea, almost but never quite catching up with his winged shadow, for she was by necessity always a harbor or half a mountain behind. Yet her own shadow covered the vastest regions; she was the more resourceful traveler—in many places at once. As she rocked Danny in her arm the waves of the Yellow Sea were rocking her. The voices of birds and beasts perforated the stillness of her long nights. How far she had traveled! The world was both flat and round. It was an endless ribbon projected into space. It was a spinning ball. On the island of Ceylon the monks had wandered around the setting sun in their orange robes. She had bent over the lepers in the Chinese dust, the dead soldiers, the harvests, dances, famines, explosions, prayers. The mechanical eye of Brook's camera had become her third, her magic eye.

Her books deserve a special study—*Dark Dominion, Prince Ishmael, Choir Invisible*.

I have given examples of the poetic novel which is an extension of the poem.

Labels often alienate a writer from his readers. When Edgar Varèse was given a dinner to celebrate his seventy-fifth birthday, he was introduced as an avant-garde composer. He said: "There is no avant-garde. The artist is always of his time but some people are a little late."

CHAPTER EIGHT

Conclusion

I DO NOT EXPECT my conclusions to be finite or dogmatic. This is the way I feel about the novel of the future. I do not believe in finite absolute statements. I am leaving it to the new writers to explore all the possibilities, to experiment with their own potentialities.

Pop art arose when individual development was weaker than collective ideas, mass ideas. The pop artist does not struggle to transform his environment but accepts to live with it. With no element to distinguish it from imitation except enlargement and repetitions, it represents the complete opposite of what I hope for the novel. Equally uncreative are those who, unable to transform their environment, protest against it by taking up the religions and philosophies of other cultures, their costumes and music. I hope that the American writer will choose neither of these paths, that he will remain a sensitive American, able to find his own contemporary expression in writing. I hope the novelist of the future will not use the electric blender as a musical note, or photomachine portraits of Marilyn Monroe. I hope the new writer will not reproduce billboards and ask us to hang them on our walls.

In the future novels I see a greater liberation of the imagination (which had taken refuge in science fiction, having nowhere else to go). I see in it a freedom from boundaries parallel to that claimed by science, a freedom from time, a freedom from geography. The realist has been too much of a map maker, tracing roads already in existence. We should also have aerial photographers to reveal virgin land. The realists have been eager to reproduce a still, static image rather than a mobile one. They were the ones who could not imagine the world round, or that we could ever fly. It was Leonardo da Vinci, the wild dreamer, who gave us wings.

The pessimism which has colored present writing would not exist if men had not turned their backs on the science of human nature in favor of all the other sciences. It is a curious fact to observe that the human being has almost vanished from science fiction. It is also strange that, just as we were about to discover our power to change destiny, we surfaced to an almost completely external world where the human being is more than ever in danger of annihilation, not from bombs, but from passivity.

The future novel has to learn to deal with the many new dimensions we have opened into the personality of man.

Dr. Otto Rank predicted a new structure of the personality. The writer will be responsible for inventing a form of writing to contain this.

Dr. Rank also said that the artist is primarily an individual who is unable or unwilling to adopt the dominant ideology of his age, whether religious, social, or other, not because it differs ideologically from his own but because it is collective. For out of his conflict with collective ideas is born the tension which makes us renew our ideas and forms.

The writer acts upon his environment by his selection of the material he wishes to highlight. He is, ultimately, responsible for our image of the world, and our relation to others.

Today we know more about ourselves just as we know more about the universe. Just as the scientists discovered that matter could be disintegrated into energy, the psychologists discovered that the personality could be broken down into its multiple components with a corresponding release of energy. The concept that man is simple is no more true today than the nineteenth-century concept that matter was unchangeable. Proust decomposed personality only to apply the concept of relativity to the emotional nature of man.

The poets were the first to perceive that too clear a conscious knowledge, too analytical an understanding may bring us intellectually nearer to reality but may, on the other hand, diminish in us the capacity for the sensation of reality itself, for feeling.

Today we have more to synthesize, and we have begun to take both man and his psyche apart to watch "how the flowers grow." Proust fragmented the personality as though he were examining it under a microscope. Then with psychology we realized the most important part of man, the psyche, was invisible to the naked eye. We found the old synthesis as false as old notions about science. Having dismembered and fragmented man in order to attain a proof of relativity, we had to reassemble him in a new way. We have far more elements to reassemble. We have to include the expansion of the universe and new powers of communication which have progressed much faster than our power of assimilation and synthesis. This demands an even stronger, more flexible individual core than in the past: first, to resist disintegration in the face of outer pressures and apparent chaos; second, to relate all the new knowledge in a different structure; and, finally, to integrate all these new dimensions.

Much has been written about the fragmentation of the novel, but this reaction stems from an outmoded concept of wholeness. Wholeness, in the past, was a semblance of consistency created from a pattern, social and philosophical, to which human beings submitted. This artificial unity of man was dissolved by a new vision into the selves which were masked to achieve a semblance of unity, a new vision into the relativity of truth and character. Man is not a finite, static, crystallized unity. He is fluid, in a constant state of flux, evolution, reaction and action, negative and positive. He is the purest example of relativity. We as novelists have to make a new synthesis, one which includes fluctuations, oscillations, and reactions. It is a matter of reassembling the fragments in a more dynamic living structure.

This split from an *unreal* uniformity of pattern, this fragmentation, has been the theme of modern literature beginning with Proust's microscopic analysis through the dissolutions of Joyce's play on words; but neither of these processes needed to be fatal to the ultimate integration. One might compare this to the fission of the atom. A new dynamism, a new energy might come from such a fission in our psychological selves. The discovery of the collective richness flowing underground below our consciousness need not result in the loss of the total self. What remains to be created is a new synthesis to include all the newly discovered dimensions.

This book is not only an affirmation of what writers working in similar orientation have achieved. It is an exploratory study, giving certain indications resulting from research into future possibilities. For one thing, I envisage an alliance with science which the contemporary writer is not yet ready to enter because he is still baffled by its highly specialized knowledge and language.

Action does not represent the whole character. Nor do fragmentation of analysis and introspection necessarily threaten the unity of man. False or insincere action can lead to disintegration of the personality as effectively as too much subjectivity.

What seemed at first like a disintegration of the personality in Proust was merely the beginning of decomposition of false appearances, of false singleness and unity, of the façade. Even what was once called the static analysis of Proust is better understood as a suspension of outer action in order to concentrate upon the intense activity of an inner drama. Proust's drama appeared static only in contrast to our concept of motion, just as something examined under a microscope may seem at first immobile and then discovered to be intensely active with another kind of life, another form of action at first imperceptible to our crude eyes.

Unity should come from organic growth. It should not be imposed from the outside, or premeditated.

Character is now being submitted to the same kind of forces that split the atom, the same decomposition for the purpose of creating a more dynamic whole. We protested the slower rhythm of the analytical novel but never the time-lapse camera which captured the growth of a plant. We accepted theories of relativity in time, yet we have not understood the literary implications of relativity in truth and personality. We cling to a fixed point of view in the novel while accepting mobility and transmutation in scientific realms. We accepted case histories but banned certain intimate confessions which added to our knowledge of human beings.

It does not matter when and where a new form begins, but it does matter that we should always remain open to innovation. If the old upholstered furniture has been replaced with a new kind of airy and uncluttered room design to keep up with limited space, with the jet plane, quicker living, lighter living, it is also natural that the novel should change with changes of consciousness.

Experiment and research in the novel are just as necessary as they are in art or science. They break old molds which can no longer express new visions.

Depth alone is what gives perspective to the universal. It is not numerical growth or gigantic physical dimensions which give stature to man.

A large perspective is not achieved by a vast expanse of surface. There is perspective in depth. Many American novels achieve a spectacle, a crowded musical comedy, an opera, a "big show" proportion which is stultifying. A film like *Four Days in Naples* is far more effective than *The Longest Day*. We respond to human scale rather than overwhelming masses. To one man as a symbol of many.

Another way of limiting the novel is to insist that it deal only with specific direct themes of social significance. This is akin to the period when the Catholic church limited painting and music by insisting they deal only with religious subjects. Every aspect of human life is related to the total sum of life and therefore ultimately useful to it. We cannot always tell in advance which theme, which individual will prove most valuable or significant. Proust in his time was considered frivolous for writing about aristocrats, yet his novels served to destroy that society more effectively than if he had spent his time writing about the poor. We have forgotten Zola's and Balzac's servants but will never forget Françoise, the servant in Proust's books. All our activities are related, but such relations need not be made directly by the writer himself. It is the task of the historian or the critic to make a synthesis. The novelist cannot portray in one novel the whole history of a period, only a segment of it. Maxwell Geismar was mistaken when he disparaged Tennessee Williams for depicting merely neurotics who were not part of the mainstream of life. Who is in the mainstream of life? Who is to say what is the mainstream? Williams' neurotics were prophetic of so large a segment that Senator Fulbright and many others in 1966 could speak of "our sick society."

Every man's intimate history is a contribution to universal history.

We will take our symbolism from science. A young filmmaker at the University of Southern California interpreted the drama of the computer system applied to human beings in a different way from Kafka's interpretation of the nightmare of anonymity, uniformity, monotony, impersonality. Science offers all kinds of physical, concrete expressions of metaphysical concerns and emotional experiences.

Our language will take on the rhythm and tempo of our life. It will be influenced by films and other arts. It will be less cumbersome, closer to the jet age, changed notions of time, psychic accelerations, less quotidian, more concerned with expanding our consciousness than with our acquisitions, power drives, revenges, rivalries. Perhaps more concerned with pleasure and love.

I think that natural truths will cease to be spat at us like insults, that aesthetics will once more be linked with ethics, and that people will become aware that in casting out aesthetics they also cast out a respect for human life, a respect for creation, a respect for spiritual values. Aesthetics was an expression of man's need to be in love with his world. The cult of ugliness is a regression. It destroys our appetite, our love for our world.

The cult of ugliness so apparent in our novels is another misinterpretation of reality. Because so many of our writers were born in ugly environments, in monstrous poverty and humiliation, they continue to assert that this is the natural environment, reality, and that beauty is artifice. Why should the natural state be ugliness? Natural to whom? We may be born in ugliness, but the natural consequences should be a thirst for its opposite. To mistake ugliness for reality is one of the frauds of the realistic school. A hunger for the unknown and an aspiration toward beauty were inseparable from civilization. In America the word art was distorted to mean artificial.

We are born with the power to alter what we are given at birth.

When the Japanese paint flowers or the sea on a kimono, they mean to establish a link with nature. But they select only what is beautiful in nature to maintain their love of life.

The creative personality never remains fixed on the first world it discovers. It never resigns itself to anything. That is the deepest meaning of rebellion, not the wearing of different clothes, haircuts or adopting other cultures.

Those who stay in their hostile and hated environment are the neurotics who are traumatized and paralyzed, or the criminal who takes his revenge for whatever befalls him or others. The criminal destroys the innocent instead of destroying the world he hates in himself. He destroys because he cannot create.

The cult of ugliness has destructive effects. Cocteau in *La belle et la bête* shows the beauty of laundry drying on a line, like flagpoles on a feast day in Venice. His camera made beauty. The true creative impulse chooses life rather than death, and love rather than hatred. What I find predominant in so many novels today is born of hatred. When the writer loses his power to alchemize (turning the laundry into an image of beauty), he is giving a catalogue of detritus. What follows is the loss of appetite for life, produced by such books as Burroughs' *Naked Lunch*.

The concept that symbolism vanished with romanticism is false. Psychology and the study of dreams established once and for all that it is a part of man's being. A scientist once asked me if we would ever dream in direct language. I can only say it has not happened yet. Even when the surface of our culture seems predominantly conscious, its actions continue to be symbolic.

An angry student who considered symbolism part of a decadent culture refused to shake hands with me because she disagreed with me, so I said to her: "In not wanting to shake hands with me you are still practicing symbolism, aren't you?"

The symbol is rich and effective precisely because it does not limit meaning and allows for its expansion according to varied lights played upon it. It teaches flexibility. Alfred North Whitehead called this "further qualifications which at present remain undiscovered." He gave a simple illustration: "Galileo said that the earth moves and that the sun is fixed; the Inquisition said that the earth is fixed and the sun moved; and Newtonian astronomers, adopting an absolute theory of space, said that both the sun and the earth moved. But now we say that anyone of these statements is equally true, provided that you have fixed your sense of rest and motion in the way required by the statement adopted. At that time the modern concepts of relative motion were in nobody's mind: so that the statements were made in ignorance of the qualifications required for their more perfect truth."

The sexual revolution, by itself and alone, is not going to put an end to loneliness or alienation. We must find intimacy and relationship by a greater understanding of the complexities of human beings.

We have other frigidities to overthrow. Frigidities toward the unfamiliar, the unknown, the unexplored, a prejudice toward experiment and research in the art of writing. To say that introspection is a trap in which only the self is caught is like saying that we must not practice deep-sea diving because we may get trapped in some cave, or get the bends. The self is merely the lens through which we see others and the world, and if this lens is not clear of distortions, we cannot perceive others. Our novels are full of deaf-mutes.

The danger of photographic realism is that it discounts all possibility of change, of transformations, and therefore does not show the way out of situations which trap human beings. The naturalists never teach one the possibility of overcoming the life situation given us. The expectation of a change from the outside becomes as dangerous as the old religious teachings of resignation to the will of God. It creates a passive man. The reporter who reports a story literally, the documentary which merely informs us of an existing situation are far from the poet-novelist concerned with creating new patterns, discarding the old, finding life inacceptable and seeking to transform it, to keep our dynamism alive by breaking down uniformity, regimentation. The poet reveals the differences which can rescue man from automatism.

The active, fecundating role of the novelist has been forgotten. We have the supine tape-recorder novelist who registers everything and illumines nothing. Passivity and inertia are the opposite of creation. Poetry is the alchemy which teaches us to convert ordinary materials into gold. Poetry, which is our relation to the senses, enables us to retain a living relationship to all things. It is the quickest means of transportation to reach dimensions above or beyond the traps set by the so-called realists. It is a way to learn levitation and travel in liberated continents, to travel by moonlight as well as sunlight.

To conclude this book it might be well to let another novelist comment on the problems of the writer today. Daniel Stern, in

The Nation, raises the entire question while studying *The Diaries.*[33]

The main problems of modern art have not changed since the nineteenth century. Realism or some form of anti-realism—this is still the question at the center of the artist's choice of method. From Zola to William Burroughs, how to deal with an experience grown increasingly monstrous and fantastic remains the heart of the matter. . . . In *The Diaries* she has solved some of the most pressing problems of the modern artist. How real must reality be . . . how does one deal with the dark side, the surreal side of living (which is present as much in Homer as it is in Norman Mailer)? What these diaries teach us is: the way to the subterranean caverns of the spirit may be approached by the artistic manipulation of our day-time language. Reality is never as real as we think. Nor is dislocated language necessarily illuminative. We learn that the world of the grotesque and that of the proportionate may meet in the medium of elegant and accessible language. We learn too . . . that an obsession with recording reality need not be at odds with the creation of other worlds. That we need give up neither reality nor fantasy in our lives nor in our art.

Notes

1. Published by the Alicat Bookshop Press, Yonkers, New York, 1946.
2. John Hawkes, *The Cannibal* (New York: New Directions Pub. Corp., 1949), pp. 86, 87–88.
3. Pierre Mabille, *Miroir du merveilleux* (Paris: Sagittaire, 1940).
4. Gaston Bachelard, *Poètique de la rêverie* (Paris: Press Universitaire de France, 1960), p. 81.
5. Wallace Fowlie, *The Age of Surrealism* (Denver-Chicago: The Swallow Press; and New York: William Morrow & Co., Inc., 1950), p. 182.
6. Djuna Barnes, *Nightwood* (New York: New Directions Pub. Corp., 1961, paperback), pp. 80–89.
7. Fowlie, *op. cit.*, p. 16.
8. Marshall McLuhan, *The Medium Is the Massage* (New York: Bantam Books, Inc., paperback, 1967), unpaged.
9. Daniel Stern, *The Suicide Academy* (New York: McGraw-Hill Book Company, 1968), pp. 145–46.
10. Fowlie, *op. cit.*, p. 29.
11. *Ibid.*, p. 17
12. Pierre Brodin, *Présences contemporaines* (Paris: Éditions Debresse, Vol. 2, 1955), p. 223.
13. Margaret Mead, *Redbook Magazine*, January, 1968.
14. R. D. Laing, *Politics of Experience* (New York: Pantheon Books, Inc., 1967), p. 57.
15. William Goyen, *House of Breath* (New York: Random House, Inc., 1950), p. 28.
16. Deena Metzger, review of *Collages*, Los Angeles *Free Press*, November 1964.
17. Interview with Federico Fellini in *Interviews with Film Directors*, edited by Andrew Sarris (Indianapolis, Indiana: The Bobbs-Merrill Co., Inc.).
18. Metzger, *loc. cit.*
19. Laing, *The Divided Self* (London: Pelican Books, 1965), p. 88.

20. Leon Edel, review of *The Diary of Anaïs Nin: Volume Two*, *Saturday Review*, 1967.

21. Metzger, review of *The Diary of Anaïs Nin: Volume Two*, Los Angeles *Free Press*, 1967.

22. Albert Guérard, Preface to Hawkes, *The Cannibal* (New York: New Directions Pub. Corp., 1948).

23. Guérard, Preface to Hawkes, *The Cannibal* (New York: New Directions Pub. Corp., 1962).

24. Leslie Fiedler, Preface to Hawkes, *The Lime Twig* (New York: New Directions Pub. Corp., 1961).

25. Maude Hutchins, *Diary of Love* (New York: New Directions Pub. Corp., 1950), p. 3; (New York. Pyramid Publications, Inc., paperback, 1959), p. 5.

26. Jerzy Kosinski, *The Painted Bird* (New York: Pocket Books, Inc., paperback, 1966), pp. 44–45.

27. Goyen, *Faces of Blood Kindred* (New York: Random House, Inc., 1963), p. 157.

28. Goyen, review of Marguerite Young, *Miss MacIntosh, My Darling*, *The New York Times Book Review*, September 12, 1965.

29. Marguerite Young, *Miss MacIntosh, My Darling* (New York: Charles Scribner's Sons, 1965), p. 11.

30. *Ibid.*, p. 460.

31. *Ibid.*, p. 39.

32. Marianne Hauser, *A Lesson in Music* (Austin, Texas: University of Texas Press, 1964), p. 98.

33. Daniel Stern, review in *The Nation*, March 4, 1968.

Bibliography and Recommended Books

ALLENDY, DR. RENÉ. *La fatalité intérieur*. Paris: Denoel & Steele, 1932.
BACHELARD, GASTON. *Poètique de la rêverie*. Paris: Presse Universitaire de France, 1960.
BALAKIAN, ANNA. *Literary Origins of Surrealism*. New York: King's Crown Press, 1947. New York: New York University Press, paperback, 1966.
BERNE, ERIC *Games People Play*. New York: Grove Press, Inc., 1964.
BRODIN, PIERRE. *Présences contemporaines*. Paris: Éditions Debresse, Volume 2, 1955.
CAVALLO, DIANA. *A Bridge of Leaves*. New York: Atheneum Publishers, 1961.
COOPER, PATRICIA. *In Deep*. New York: The Delacorte Press, 1967.
DESOILLÉ, DR. R. *Le rêve eveillé en psychothérapie.* Paris: Presse Universitaire de France, 1945.
———. *Psychanalyse et rêve eveillé dirigé*. Paris: Imprimerie Comte-Jacquet, 1950.
ELLISON, RALPH. *The Invisible Man*. New York: Random House, Inc., 1952. New York: The New American Library, Inc., paperback.
FERLINGHETTI, LAWRENCE. *Her*. New York: New Directions Pub. Corp., paperback, 1960.
FOWLIE, WALLACE. *The Age of Surrealism*. Denver-Chicago: The Swallow Press; and New York: William Morrow & Co., Inc., 1950.
GOYEN, WILLIAM. *The House of Breath*. New York: Random House, Inc., 1950.
———. *Ghost and Flesh*. New York: Random House, Inc., 1952.
———. *In a Farther Country*. New York: Random House, Inc., 1955.
———. *The Faces of Blood Kindred*. New York: Random House, Inc., 1963.
HAUSER, MARIANNE. *Dark Dominion*. New York: Random House, Inc., 1947.
———. *The Choir Invisible*. New York: McDowell, Obolensky, Inc., 1955.
———. *The Living Shall Praise Thee*. London: Victor Gollancz, 1957.
———. *Prince Ishmael*. New York: Stein & Day Publishers, 1963.

——. *A Lesson in Music.* Austin, Texas: University of Texas Press, 1964.

HAWKES, JOHN. *The Cannibal.* New York: New Directions Pub. Corp., 1949.

——. *The Beetle Leg.* New York: New Directions Pub. Corp., 1953.

——. *The Goose on the Grave* and *The Owl.* New York: New Directions Pub. Corp., 1953.

——. *The Lime Twig.* New York: New Directions Pub. Corp., 1961.

HUTCHINS, MAUDE. *Love Is a Pie.* New York: New Directions Pub. Corp., 1944.

——. *Georgiana.* New York: New Directions Pub. Corp., 1946.

——. *Victorine.* Denver-Chicago: The Swallow Press, 1959. New York: Pyramid Publications, Inc., paperback, 1960.

KAVAN, ANNA. *House of Sleep.* New York: Doubleday & Company, Inc., 1947.

——. *Asylum Pieces.* New York: Doubleday & Company, Inc., 1940.

——. *Eagle's Nest.* London: Peter Owen, 1957.

——. *Bright Green Field.* London: Peter Owen.

——. *Who Are You?* Northwood, Middlesex, England: Scorpion Press, 1963.

——. *Ice.* London: Peter Owen, 1967.

KEROUAC, JACK. *On the Road.* New York: The New American Library, Inc., paperback.

——. *The Subterraneans.* New York: Grove Press, Inc., 1958.

KOSINSKI, JERZY. *The Painted Bird.* Boston: Houghton Mifflin Company, 1965. New York: Pocket Books, Inc., Pocket Cardinal paperback, 1966.

LAING, DR. R. D. *The Divided Self.* London: Pelican Books, 1965.

——. *Politics of Experience.* New York: Pantheon Books, Inc., 1967.

LINDNER, DR. ROBERT. *The Fifty-Minute Hour.* New York: Bantam Books, Inc., paperback.

MABILLE, PIERRE. *Miroir du merveilleux.* Paris: Sagittaire, 1940.

MICHAUX, HENRI. *Miserable Miracle.* Translated by Louise Varèse. San Francisco: City Lights Books, 1963.

MINKOWSKI, EUGEN. *La schizophrénie.* Paris: Payot, 1927.

MOORE, HARRY. *The Intelligent Heart.* New York: Grove Press, Inc., 1962.

STEELE, MAX. *Where She Brushed Her Hair.* New York: Harper & Row, Publishers, 1968.

STERN, DANIEL. *After the War.* New York: G. P. Putnam's Sons, 1967.

——. *The Suicide Academy.* New York: McGraw-Hill Book Company, 1968.

YOUNG, MARGUERITE. *Angel in the Forest.* New York: Charles Scribner's Sons, 1966.

——. *Miss MacIntosh, My Darling.* New York: Charles Scribner's Sons, 1965. New York: The New American Library, Inc., paperback, 1968.

Most of the quotations and references are taken from the hardback editions, but for the students I have listed paperbacks when available.

I have purposely concentrated on American writers but several books by foreign writers recently translated could be added to this list:

CORTÁZAR, JULIO. *End of the Game and Other Stories.* New York: Pantheon Books, Inc., 1967. Also published as *Blow-Up and Other Stories.* New York: Collier Books, paperback, 1968.

FRISCH, MAX. *I'm Not Stiller.* New York: Random House, Inc., Vintage Books, paperback, 1962.

MOREAU, MARCEL J. *The Selves of Quinte.* New York: George Braziller, Inc., 1965.

Index